CO-AUD-270

DISCARD

R.T. JONES MEMORIAL LIBRARY
116 BROWN INDUSTRIAL PKWY.
CANTON, GA 30114

SEQUOYAH REGIONAL LIBRARY

3 8749 0037 3496 5

Death's White City

Also by James Sherburne
In Thorndike Large Print:

DEATH'S CLENCHED FIST

DEATH'S WHITE CITY

A Paddy Moretti Novel

JAMES SHERBURNE

Thorndike Press • Thorndike, Maine

THIS BOOK IS THE PROPERTY OF
SEQUOYAH REGIONAL LIBRARY
CANTON, GEORGIA

Library of Congress Cataloging in Publication Data:

Sherburne, James, 1925-
  Death's white city / James Sherburne.
    p. cm.
  ISBN 0-89621-164-9 (lg. print: alk. paper)
  1. Large type books.   I. Title.
  [PS3569.H399D47 1988]   88-15950
  813'.54—dc19   CIP

Copyright © 1987 by James Sherburne. All rights reserved.

Large Print edition available by arrangement with Nat Sobel Associates, Inc., New York.

All the characters in this book are fictitious, and any resemblance to persons living or dead is purely coincidental.

Cover design by Armen Kojoyian.

To
Jane and Gene Matthis
and
Helen and Jim Luyster

Contents

1

The Lady on the Train

"The White City? Me?" She took a deep breath and arched her back to raise her full bosom. "I've got a few good years yet before they shovel me under in one of *them* places!"

"No, no, you're missing the point entirely!" I eyed the bosom as I explained, "The White City isn't a graveyard. It's a name they have for the Columbian Exposition. On account of the beautiful white buildings, and all."

"It is?" She looked at me askance, with a mixture of suspicion and coquettishness.

"It is, it is! Would a red-blooded man be sitting next to the likes of you and thinking about graveyards? What I meant was, are you going to the Exposition? As a place of employment, I mean. As a dancer, for instance." I lowered my eyes from her bosom to her slender waist and rounded hips. "It occurred to me that you might be about to give that Little Egypt a run for her money."

She smiled, and the rest of her face pinkened

to match the rouge on her cheekbones. "You've got more blarney than a wagonload of Irish tinkers. What did you say your last name was?"

"Moretti." As she grimaced I hastened to add, "But me first one's Paddy. Does that make it all right?"

She considered the question a moment, then nodded. "That makes it all right," she said decisively. She slipped a slim-fingered, bejeweled hand into her glittering black purse and produced a hammered silver flask.

"Have another belt," she said.

We'd had three or four already. Her name was Velma, and she was a handsome woman in her late thirties, which made her about my age. She had a long, oval face with two slanted, black-lashed blue eyes that repeated the same oval shape. Her nose was slightly crooked, her chin firm and dimpled, and the pores on her cheek and jaw were too large, as though from too much powder and paint. The hair that framed her face with ringlets was an attractive but unconvincing red-gold. Her bosom, as I believe I have indicated, was superb.

We were sitting together on a green plush seat in a B & O Pullman car an hour before our arrival time in Chicago. We had been seatmates since leaving New York, but since the car had been made up as a sleeper when we boarded it, and we had gone directly to our berths, hers the lower and mine the upper, we hadn't become acquainted until the following morning. After breakfast, when I had returned to my assigned space, I had found her sitting in it.

At first our conversation was desultory and impersonal, but as we crossed Ohio and entered Indiana, it became more animated. This was due to two developments, one on her part, one on mine. On hers, it was her discovery that I was a sports reporter, employed by a newspaper that concentrated on horse racing. On mine, it was my growing awareness that that she was not only desirable, but also very possibly available.

She leaned toward me, and the scent of her perfume was like a beckoning finger. "You ever hear of a racehorse owner named Vannatta?" she asked, in her low and slightly husky voice.

I leaned toward her, bringing our heads to within three inches of each other. "Paul Vannatta? Sure — he owns Home Free, one of the horses entered in the American Derby. That's what I'm coming to Chicago to cover."

"Is that right?" Her eyes crinkled, and her lips parted in a wide smile. "Ain't it a small world, though." She picked up the purse on the seat beside her. "How'd you like a little drink, handsome?"

Her whiskey was Canadian rye, a deceptively smooth blend. I took a deep drink to cut the insidious taste of coal smoke in my mouth, and passed the flask back to her. She touched the tip of her tongue to the mouth of the flask, as if to savor the taste, then upended it and swallowed two or three ounces with the gusto of a sailor on shore leave. "That's the ticket," she said as she screwed the cap back on and replaced the flask in her purse. "Now let's talk about *you*, hon. What do you know about this horse of Vannatta's?"

After that first drink the conversation went swimmingly, although somewhat at cross-purposes. Every time I tried to steer it toward her, she turned it back to Vannatta and his derby entry. But finally she seemed satisfied that she had exhausted my knowledge on the subject. She sank back into the corner formed by the window and the seat, letting her head fall back against the faded green plush and stretching her smooth, rounded neck. She looked at me from under lowered lids. "Well, to hell with that," she said huskily. "You know what? I'm just crazy about reporters."

By the time I mentioned the White City we had been talking for two hours, and had just about emptied her flask. She told me a tale of

12

a youthful marriage to a French aristocrat, a tragic early widowhood, and the desperate need to provide for two infant children which drove her to a hazardous but ultimately successful career in the theater. I told her a tale about an Irish-Italian kid from Corbo County, Ohio, who was so crazy about horses he ran away from home to follow them from track to track, and finally discovered the only way he could make a living from them was to become an underpaid, brow-beaten racing reporter for a sporting paper. Her tale was, at a conservative guess, ninety percent hokum; mine was, unfortunately, entirely true.

Somehow we began talking about the reasons we were traveling to Chicago, and I suggested that she was on her way to the White City, and that generated the dialogue that opened this narrative.

The drink she offered me turned out to be the last one in her flask, so I rooted out a pint of bourbon from my Gladstone and we started on that. Outside the window Fort Wayne appeared and disappeared. The swaying of the Pullman car and the rhythmic clicking of the wheels on the rails began to exert a soporific effect upon me, and I put my head back and closed my eyes. A moment later her hand closed on my knee.

"Want to know a secret?" she whispered in my ear.

"Hmmmm?" I opened my eyes and rolled them toward her.

"I told you a story. My name's not Velma at all." She seemed as pleased with herself as a mischievous and unrepentant child.

"It's not?"

"Uh-uh. That's my stage name. Want to know my real name?" Her hand moved from my knee to my thigh and gave me a provocative squeeze.

I sat up straighter. "I can't think of anything that would please me more."

"It's Wilma — Wilma Verhulst. I'm a Dutchie. Bet you never would have guessed."

"Not in a million years." I put my hand on top of hers. "There are all sorts of things I can't wait to find out about you. Where are you staying in Chicago?"

She giggled and drew back from me, her fingers moving lingeringly down to my knee. "Hey, not so fast, handsome. You think you're a jockey or something?"

"Couldn't make the weight. Anyway, jockeys aren't always fast, just when they're riding horses. Sometimes not even then. I should know — I've bet on plenty of slow ones." I uncorked my bottle and offered it to her.

"You want another drink?"

"Thanks." Her eyes were mocking as she upended the bottle and took a long swallow. She licked her lips delicately as she handed it back. "I wouldn't know about slow jockeys. The ones I know are fast every which way."

"I suspect we view them through different eyes."

"I should hope so." She batted her eyelashes flirtatiously, and then, as though dropping a mask, turned to gaze out through the sooty window. Her face was suddenly tired as she said, "Jesus — you'd think I would have learned by now."

"Learned?" I repeated.

"It's not as if I haven't had the chance. If anybody's had the chance, I have. But somehow it just don't seem to take." She rubbed her fingers slowly down her cheek and stared at the featureless scenery beyond the glass. "You'd think it would, sooner or later, but it don't."

Sensing that we were on the edge of what might degenerate into a maudlin memoir, I raised the bourbon bottle and pretended to study its label. "Aha," I announced. "It says here that this remarkable beverage will put wings on the heels of even the most sluggardly newspapermen. Shall we conduct a test?"

We finished the whiskey and watched the

15

Indiana farmland unroll under the hot summer sun. I felt suspended in an aura of sleepiness and lechery. We seemed to have talked ourselves out for the time being, and my eyelids sank lower and lower. I thought to myself, *I'll just rest my eyes a few minutes now, so I'll be in better shape when we get to Chicago.* Then I dozed off, and the next thing I heard was the conductor announcing our arrival.

Velma nee Wilma had one large and two small suitcases, which, added to my own battered Gladstone, necessitated a redcap. I found one and told him to meet us at the cabstand outside the station on Dearborn Street. Then I took her arm, helped her down the Pullman steps, and cried with a gaiety that belied my newly acquired headache, "Welcome to the Windy City, macushla."

The station was more crowded than I had ever seen it. Much of the throng consisted of families who had obviously come to see the Exposition — farm families from Pennsylvania and Wisconsin and Missouri, storekeeper families from Maine and Michigan, preacher families and college professor families and factory foreman families, all complete with crying babies, defiant children, scolding mothers, and long-suffering fathers — but a good percentage of it was made up of single people, young men and women in search of employment or adventure or both, and the predators waiting to feed on them: pickpockets, confidence men, whores, shills, steerers, and the sellers of stolen jewelry and perverse novelties. Passing through the great rotunda of the station was like threading one's way through a hundred grubby crimes about to happen.

Our redcap was waiting beside a cab, and our luggage was already loaded. I gave him a dime, helped Velma/Wilma to her seat, and asked, "Where shall I tell him to take us?"

She raised her eyebrows. "Why, the Palmer House. Where else?"

I relayed the information to the driver and sat down beside her, as the cabbie snapped his reins and moved us out into Dearborn Street's swift-moving traffic.

The Palmer House, I reflected, was a trifle rich for my blood, or, more accurately, for my expense account. My editor, Otto Hochmuth, did not encourage his reporters to frequent the more expensive hostelries. But on the other hand, if my companion was going there —

"What a delightful coincidence," I said. "The very place I was planning to stay myself." *I can always check out tomorrow*, I thought.

We clip-clopped north on Dearborn and east on Monroe and drew to a halt beside the great hotel's canopy. I paid the cabbie as the door-man, more splendidly uniformed than a Russian grand duke, supervised the unloading of the luggage and its transportation into the lobby. We followed it toward the desk. I breathed in the aroma of cigars that cost as much apiece as I made for a day's work, and of perfume that went for as much an ounce as prime beef goes for a hundredweight. Velma's fingers squeezed my arm. I glanced at her and saw that her expression verged on the ecstatic. Clearly, I thought, she was no more used to the opulence than I was.

The desk clerk, a pale-faced young man with thinning hair, a toothbrush mustache, and pursed lips, looked at us guardedly. "Yes?" he asked.

Velma drew a breath and elevated her wonderful bosom. "I believe you have a reservation for Mrs. Velma LeSeure."

"Mrs. LeSeure — one moment, please." He flipped through the pages of a ledger, stopped at one page, and ran his finger down a column of names. "Ah, yes — Mrs. LeSeure. That was a single, I believe."

Velma nodded graciously. "That's correct."

"Very good. Delighted to have you with us, Mrs. LeSeure. If you'll just register, please —"

He offered her a pen and turned to me. "Yes, sir?"

"I'd like a single room, please."

"Oh? Do you have a reservation, sir?"

I smiled apologetically. "No, I'm afraid not." Beside me Velma was writing her name on a registration card. I noticed that her handwriting was careful and childish, with round letters and curlicues.

The clerk raised his eyebrows and twisted his lip. "Oh, I'm *very* sorry, sir, but without a reservation, I'm afraid there's nothing we can do for you. With the Exposition and all. You understand." His eyes slid away from me and returned to my companion. "Thank you, Mrs. LeSeure." He struck a small bell on the counter beside him. "Front!" he called.

"Now just a second," I said. He glanced back at me in surprise, as if he had forgotten my presence. I dug one hand into my pocket and found two crumpled bills among a handful of change. A surreptitious glance informed me they were ones. I placed my hand on the counter so that the corners showed between my thumb and forefinger. "It's really very important for me to register here," I said. "If you'll just check your vacancies, I'm sure you can come up with something."

He lowered his head and leaned forward

slowly, until his face was within six inches of my hand, and studied the two wrinkled corners and the numerals printed upon them. After a few moments he shifted his position as if to verify the evidence of his senses. Then he raised his eyes to mine, and said sorrowfully, "I'm afraid that Fortune is destined to pass me by, sir. There are no vacancies."

I felt myself coloring, and stuffed the bills back in my pocket. "Well, if you're sure − I mean if you're *sure* you're sure −," I stumbled.

Velma put her hand on my arm. "No vacancy? Oh, what a shame." The clerk handed Velma's key to a redheaded bellboy and said, "Show Mrs. LeSeure to room 662, boy." The bellboy tucked the key in his hip pocket and began arranging suitcases under his arms. When he picked up my Gladstone I tapped him on the shoulder.

"Not that one," I said. "It doesn't have a reservation."

He gave me a contemptuous look that was barely short of a sneer and dropped my bag on the floor. I was grateful it no longer contained my pint of bourbon. Carrying Velma's luggage, he started toward the elevators.

"Well, Paddy, don't say it ain't been fun," Velma said. "Maybe some day −"

"No, wait a minute. I was thinking we might

share a bird and a bottle this evening. In the nature of a small celebration of our arrival in Chicago, you might say. A modest repast, and a bit of genteel conversation – I'll find myself a room somewhere and be back here by seven o'clock."

She shook her head, smiling. "Not tonight, hon. I got other fishes to fry tonight."

"Then tomorrow? How about tomorrow?" The eagerness in my voice must have reached her. She gave a throaty laugh.

"All right, Paddy. Tomorrow it is. Come about seven, and we'll have us some of that genteel conversation of yours." She squeezed my hand and added, "And maybe some that ain't so genteel." Her blue eyes sparkled at me a moment behind their fringe of black lashes, and then she turned and followed the bellboy, her back straight and her hips swaying.

I watched her until she disappeared, then picked up my Gladstone and headed toward the street entrance. For lack of anything better to do I glanced idly at the faces around me. I was almost to the Monroe Street door when I saw one that stopped me in my tracks.

The man sitting in a leather armchair and smoking a Perfecto-Perfecto looked like a successful banker who was volunteering his services to raise money for widows and orphans, until you looked closely at his eyes. His hair was white, his complexion pink, and his nose was aquiline. His jaw was firm, and the skin under it fitted it smoothly. His linen was snowy, his suit superbly cut, and his shoes had the deep warm glow that only comes with fine leather and regular attention. But his eyes were small, quick, and furtive.

I raised my right arm and touched my eye with my first two fingers, as if brushing away a lash. A moment later he did the same. I sank into the chair next to him, fixed my gaze on a painting of nymphs and satyrs on the wall across the lobby, and said from the corner of my mouth, "You spotting?"

His lips didn't move as he replied almost inaudibly, "Whatcha think? Don't queer it, Paddy."

"I believe the extent of your indebtedness is fifty dollars, not including interest, which I am willing to forego to reach an amicable settlement," I said. I moved my eyes from the nymphs and satyrs to a group of Arabs amusing themselves at an oasis. "Pay me, you *ganef*, and I'll pretend I don't know you."

Skeeter Huff was a short-con artist who often doubled as a spotter for a hotel heister named Ty-Ty Davenport. It was Skeeter's job to spot women with expensive jewelry or men who flashed fat bankrolls when they checked into the hotel, find out their room numbers, and pass the information to his confederate. Since he had to work in lobbies, under the noses of hotel detectives, it was necessary that he appear absolutely respectable, like Caesar's wife. One whiff of suspicion here, and he would be unable to work Chicago's premier hotel for the rest of his life.

He squirmed in his chair and ran his hand over his healthy pink chin. "Have a heart, huh? I ain't got it on me, I swear I don't." He covered his mouth as if stifling a yawn and continued, "Come back tomorrow and I'll follow you out and pay you the whole fifty. Now take a walk."

I craned my neck and surveyed the crowded lobby. "Where do you suppose the house dick is, Skeeter? Within earshot, would you think? Close enough to come if I were to yell at the top of my voice, 'Skeeter Huff is spotting for Ty-Ty Davenport'?"

"Oh, God!" he groaned through immobile lips. "I tell you I ain't got it, Paddy. I'll pay you — I *want* to pay you — but give me till tomorrow. Jesus, if you beef gun, Ty-Ty will kill me!"

I reflected that what he said was probably true, and I didn't see how getting him killed would help to repay my fifty dollars, which

Skeeter owed me as the result of a welshed bet at Saratoga Springs two years before. Although my chances of collecting the money tomorrow were slim, they would be better if Skeeter were still breathing.

"Okay, tomorrow — and you better be here," I said. "Take care of yourself crossing streets, Skeeter." I drew my feet under me, preparing to rise.

Skeeter's small, shifty eyes flicked toward me. "That dame you come in with — them was nice sparklers she had on her fingers." He gave me an un-bank-executive grin. "You got yourself a piece of something, Paddy?"

"Don't you worry, old friend. That's outside your territory. You've got enough to worry about with my fifty dollars. See you tomorrow, Skeeter." I walked briskly across the lobby without a glance back at him.

In anticipation of my forthcoming expenses for the bird and bottle, or bottles, and whatever else proved to be necessary for the wooing of Velma, I walked past the cabstand and caught a southbound streetcar on State Street. Every seat was taken, and the aisle was packed with standees. Before I could find a strap the conductor engaged the moving cable and the car jerked forward so violently that only the press of bodies kept me from sprawling backward. I found myself supported on the ample belly of a man in a seersucker suit and a panama hat.

"Pardon me," I said as I pulled myself erect. "I'm not used to these fast starts."

For answer the man grunted and turned himself sideways to me, which reduced the pressure of our bodies on each other. I located a strap and grasped it firmly. An elbow dug into my back, and somebody sneezed moistly on my neck.

"They certainly crowd the people on these cars, don't they?" I asked the big-bellied man.

"Goddamned right they do!" he cried. "They plan it that way. You know what Yerkes says."

"Yerkes?" The name was vaguely familiar, but I couldn't place it.

"Yerkes," he repeated. He made an encompassing gesture with his hand. "The streetcar mogul, the crook who owns these sardine cans. He says, 'The straphangers pay the dividends,' that's what he says."

I thought about that. I was still thinking about it a few moments later when the car stopped at Van Buren Street and the conductor shouted, "Everybody off!" Immediately the passengers began to climb down from our car and make their way to another, empty car, on the other side of the street.

"What's this?" I asked the big-bellied man.

"Have to change lines," he said impatiently over his shoulder. "Different company south of Van Buren." He waddled rapidly down the aisle. I trotted after him.

"We have to pay again?"

"Of course! I said they were different companies, didn't I?" We dashed between cabs and wagons and gained the safety of the new streetcar, where the conductor accepted our fares. All the seats were taken, so my companion and I wedged ourselves in among the standees. A moment later the car jerked violently forward, and we continued on our journey.

"Well, whoever owns this company seems to agree with your friend Yerkes about straphangers paying the dividends," I said.

He gave me a pitying look. " 'Whoever owns this company,' you say? Why, Yerkes owns this company, you poor mutt. Yerkes owns *all* the companies."

"Then why doesn't he put them together and make one single system for the whole city?"

"Because then he couldn't charge you a new fare every time you rode a dozen blocks, that's why!"

"And the city government lets him get away with that?" I asked in surprise.

His face darkened perceptibly, and a vein began to pulse in his forehead. "The city government," he cried. "The city gov – Oh, just shut up, for God's sake!" He turned away from me, presenting me with a view of his fat red neck for the rest of my trip.

I arrived at Twelfth Street with no additional streetcar transfers. The Tuscany Hotel was three blocks west, at Clark, and I walked there, carrying my bag and considering the Free Enterprise System as practiced in Chicago.

The Tuscany was the hotel my editor, Otto Hochmuth, always recommended to reporters on assignment in Chicago. I don't think it was because he received rebates from the hotel management for all employees of *The Spirit of the Times* who registered there – Hochmuth, whatever his other faults, had never seemed a petty grafter to me – rather, I think the dinginess, the drabness, the dank and dusty dilapidation of the place appealed to his sense of appropriateness; it was just the kind of establishment, he would have reasoned, that people like Paddy Moretti deserved.

I entered the dim lobby and breathed in the smell of mildew and stale tobacco smoke. A half-dozen elderly persons of both sexes sat slumped in their chairs as though they never expected to rise from them. A young man with a morbid skin condition was picking his teeth with a fingernail behind the desk.

"Do you have a single?" I asked.

He nodded, as I knew he would. If there were one empty hotel room in Chicago, it would be at the Tuscany. I sighed and reached for the pen.

"I'm with *The Spirit of the Times*," I said.

"I figured," the clerk said.

I followed a wizened bellman to my room on the third floor and tipped him a dime. When he had closed the door behind him, I stretched out on the bed and closed my eyes. The headache, which had been with me since my arrival in Chicago, was suddenly throbbing painfully.

I think I'll take a nap for a few minutes, I thought. *Then when I wake up, I'll find good old Boz Markey and do the town.*

I didn't wake up until five o'clock the next morning.

2

A Lump in the Throat

Since the White City of the Columbian Exposition was located only a mile from Washington Park racetrack, I would be able to enjoy a few hours of sight-seeing at the one, before reporting for duty at the other. The prospect brightened an otherwise bleak awakening.

At seven o'clock, deciding that no further sleep was possible, I got up and dressed and descended to the lobby, where the clerk on duty, a toothless ancient sporting a greasy celluloid collar and a black leather tie, sold me copies of the *Chicago Tribune, Inter-Ocean,* and *Examiner,* and directed me to a restaurant serving breakfast down the street.

I brought myself up to date on the racing news from Washington Park and the other major tracks in the nation while methodically pushing bites of leaden pancake and greasy sausage down my throat. The *Inter-Ocean*'s racing columnist, Iggy Grodnitz, devoted half a column to the American Derby. Although the race was three days away, he wrote, advance betting had been unusually heavy, with Mustafa, owned by Anton Birkmann, favored at eight to three, and Home Free, owned by Paul Vannatta, a strong second at five to one. The third-place favorite, Glenlivet, trailed in the betting at ten to one. I tore out the column and tucked it into my pocket.

Two cups of coffee did nothing to alleviate the headache that seemed to have taken up permanent residence directly behind my eyeballs.

After breakfast I walked along Twelfth Street to the Illinois Central station to catch a train to the Exposition. Even though trains departed for the Midway Plaisance every fifteen or twenty minutes, the station was jammed with eager fairgoers waiting for their turn to board the cars. I took my place in line, and it was half an hour before I was seated in a coach.

The train roared south along the lakefront, my fellow passengers speculated about the wonders of the fair and gaped at the white sails that dotted the wide blue water, and I closed my eyes and silently cursed my headache. Maybe this excursion was a mistake, I thought — maybe I should have stayed in my room with a bottle of whiskey, dulling the pain and strengthening the inner man.

But my first glimpse of the Exposition put that idea to rest.

Nothing I had read about the Columbian Exposition prepared me for the impact it made when seen for the first time. Writers have referred to it as a fairyland, a land of Cockaigne, a fantasy kingdom by the lake — but that misses the point entirely. The overpowering fact about the fair was that it was *real*; the gleaming white buildings, each larger than a half-dozen football fields laid side by side, were *real*; the enormous statues, the geysering fountains, the great lagoon with its hundred Venetian gondolas, the Ferris wheel that carried more than a thousand riders on each dizzying trip high into the air, the Wooded Isle with its fifty thousand blooming roses — all these wonders and lunacies were *real*, planned and built by real craftsmen, ostensibly representing the real city of Chicago to the nation, and bought and paid for with real money.

It was, in this year of bleak national Depression, perhaps the greatest irrelevancy in America.

It was also, I hasten to add, an experience not to be missed. As I made my way from the Illinois Central platform past the Woman's Building (pausing for a peek at St. Gaudens's scandalous nude statue of Diana), continued

31

along the moving sidewalk to the gigantic Mc-Monnies Fountain, to gawk at the gilded statue of the Republic towering a hundred feet in the air, I knew I would never see another White City in this life.

From the Great Basin I made my way south along the lakeshore, past the Liberal Arts Building and around the end of the lagoon, to the Midway Plaisance. By the time I reached it, I felt I had enjoyed enough Culture, perhaps, and was now entitled to more plebeian entertainment. Specifically, what I had in mind was the Streets of Cairo and its featured performer, Little Egypt.

I passed a German village, a Dahomey village, a Persian harem, an Eskimo igloo, and an Old Viennese coffee house before an intense smell of camel signaled my imminent arrival at the desired concession. Although it was barely 10 A.M., the Streets of Cairo was jammed. Gawking farm boys pressed against portly businessmen, and backsliding Christians tried to make themselves inconspicuous among unashamed sensualists, and all were lined up outside a green-and-yellow canvas tent. I took my place at the end of the line, behind a man in a white linen suit and white shoes. He glanced over his shoulder, smiled, and asked, "Planning on an anatomy lesson this morning, friend?"

"It's never too early to improve the mind," I replied.

"How true, how true. And have you had the pleasure of attending one of these seminars before?" I replied that this would be my first visit, my matriculation, so to speak. "Fortunate fellow," he said warmly. "I've become something of an habitué during the last month, and I must say it's added a new dimension to my education."

He was in his mid-thirties, a handsome man with a high, domed forehead, an upturned mustache, and candid light-blue eyes. He was of middle height, and his body was trim and athletic. His voice was his most striking characteristic; it was deep and melodic, and would have been a great asset on the Chautauqua circuit.

"I'm ready for a new dimension or two myself," I said.

"You've come to the right place, then. Fahreda has depth."

"Fahreda?"

"Fahreda Mahzar. That's Little Egypt's real name." He picked an invisible bit of lint from his lapel. "I've gotten to know her a bit recently."

The man behind me jostled me impatiently, and I realized the line was moving. We passed

into the tent before I had a chance to investigate my new acquaintance's intimacy with the nation's most famous exotic dancer.

Little Egypt was amazing. She was a small woman with a good figure, judging by what you could see of it, concealed as it was in a red, fringed short jacket and baggy black skirt. The only part of it that was bare was her stomach, from three inches above her navel to two inches below. She had a pale face with sloe eyes, long black hair, and full red lips that turned down at the corners. Her expression was solemn as she began to dance.

She started slowly, and her movements were restrained. She raised her arms over her head, straightening one leg and bending the other, her hips swaying in time to the droning Eastern music that accompanied her. Her expression remained unsmiling. Gradually the hip movement increased, she added a forward-and-backward pelvic movement that presented her navel enticingly to her audience and then drew it swiftly away again. I found my eyes were riveted to that tiny shadowed depression. It seemed to be winking at me, beckoning, challenging. The men around me began to breathe heavily.

The tempo of the music increased. Little Egypt seemed to become conscious of the

voluptuous pleasure of her dance. Her solemn expression changed to one of tentative enjoyment as her hips rolled more vigorously. The soft flesh of her belly swelled and flattened, now concave, now convex. One leg appeared through a slit in the baggy black skirt, a black stocking below, a flash of white thigh above. A groan arose from the watchers, as if from a simultaneous lower abdominal pain. The tempo continued to accelerate. The dancer threw back her head, and her expression was transformed — eyes wild, lips a wide red slash across her face, black hair swirling around her shoulders. Suddenly she seemed more than a woman; she was a maenad, a Fury, the incarnation of desire that draws men willingly to their destruction. The music swept on, faster, more insistent. Men began to shout and swear, and one bald-headed businessman would have jumped up on the stage if he hadn't been prevented by a burly roustabout. I caught a glimpse of my acquaintance from the ticket line outside; his eyes were as round as marbles, and the tip of his tongue flicked from one corner of his mouth to the other as if hunting for moisture.

The music accelerated for one final turn of the screw. The dancer's body was all motion: sinuous, twisting, coaxing, thrusting. Her eyes were closed, her mouth wide open, and a film of perspiration gleamed on her cheeks and at her throat, between her breasts. And then, with a crash, it was over. Little Egypt was kneeling on the stage, arms spread in supplication, head hanging and hair spread before her. For a moment the silence was complete, then the tent erupted with cheers and roars of approval. The dancer rose slowly to her feet and regarded us. Her expression was as it had been before the dance — cool, solemn, distant. She bowed her head gravely and left the stage.

Outside the tent the man in the white suit was waiting for me. "Well, did you encounter those new dimensions, my friend?" he asked in his mellifluous voice. "Did you find the seminar a success?"

"Cheap at twice the price," I said sincerely. "It's an experience, all right."

"One that seems to me to require liquid resuscitation. Will you be my guest? They serve a commendable pilsner at the Austrian rathskeller, if it's not too early in the day for you. My name is Holmes, by the way." He put out his hand, which was quite small, with disproportionately long fingers. His handshake was firm.

I introduced myself and assured him that the hour was late enough. "Cold pilsner sounds good to me." I winced as my headache reminded me it was still in residence. "It may even do something for this miserable headache of mine."

"Headache, eh?" Holmes said with interest. "Well, we'll see about that. I may have a prescription that will help you."

"Are you a doctor?" I asked.

"Oh, no, no, although I share many skills with the Hippocratic fraternity. I am a pharmacist, Mr. Moretti. A simple pharmacist, although perhaps with a few more arrows in my quiver than most."

We walked along the midway, past a chamber of horrors, a Pompeian house, and a full-sized replica of the Venus de Milo modeled in chocolate, and arrived at the Austrian rathskeller. The beer was as good as Holmes had promised, and refreshingly cold. We toasted Little Egypt. "Salome herself can hardly have surpassed her in the arts of seduction," he said in his rich, rolling voice.

"It's the Gospel you're speaking," I agreed. "Do you really know her personally?"

"That pleasure is mine, yes. Fahreda and I have enjoyed a number of conversations. She is a woman of considerable native wit and surprising simplicity." He opened his eyes very wide. "I have hopes she may decide to take up residence at my establishment."

"Your establishment?"

He waved one hand. "Oh, nothing sinister, if that's what you're thinking. I own a house across the street from the pharmacy. I can afford to be discriminating – I don't need the money."

"I wouldn't mind being Little Egypt's landlord," I said with a touch of envy.

"The luck of the deal, my friend. Here, drink up, and let's have another."

We sat in the cool quiet of the rathskeller for half an hour. Holmes bought the first and third rounds and I bought the second and fourth. He was an interesting conversationalist, with a varied background. I gathered that he was a college graduate, that he had lived in Texas and California, as well as the East, and that he had tried his hand at a number of trades, including insurance, stocks and bonds, and inventions. "But the bouncing ball has come to rest at last," he said, wiping a rime of foam from his mustache. "Or, to mix the metaphor, the horse has come to pasture. I have my business here in Chicago, my fine house across the way, my friends, my diversions – what else could a man want?"

I agreed. "You're a fortunate man, Mr. Holmes, and I've enjoyed this chat with you.

But duty calls, and I'm afraid I have to lug me beer-besotted body over to Washington Park and begin earning a living."

"Before you go — how's that headache, Mr. Moretti?"

"I'm afraid it's still there, waiting to jump out again."

He nodded. "I thought so." He drew a small twist of paper from his pocket and handed it to me. "Just wash this down with a swallow of beer, and I don't think you'll have to worry about that headache anymore."

I unfolded the packet and emptied the white powder into my palm. "What is it?" I asked.

"One of my own preparations. Don't worry; it's been proven both harmless and effective a thousand times." His deep voice was so reassuring I popped the powder into my mouth and swallowed. It had a faintly bitter taste, which I washed away with a swallow of pilsner.

I offered to pay for the medicine, but he waved off the suggestion. As I pushed my chair back to rise, he asked, "Do you have a satisfactory place to stay, Mr. Moretti?" I said I had a room at a hotel on Twelfth Street. "But isn't that quite a distance from Washington Park? Wouldn't you rather be located where you could walk to work in ten minutes?" I acknowledged that living that close to the track would be a convenience. "My establishment is at the corner of Sixty-third and Wallace, and I'm happy to offer you excellent accommodations at extremely reasonable terms," he said, with the smile of a man who is happiest when he indulges his generosity.

"Well, thank you, Mr. Holmes, that's very kind of you. But my paper has a sort of an arrangement with the hotel where I'm staying, and I think I'd better keep my room there." Also, of course, Twelfth Street was closer to the Palmer House and the bright lights of the levee than Sixty-third, but I didn't mention that.

He shrugged. "Well, if you should change your mind, remember the address – Sixty-third and Wallace." He put out his hand. "Good day, Moretti. It's been very pleasant." We shook hands, and I left him sitting at the table and staring at the pilsner glasses in front of him, a half-smile on his lips.

I walked along the Midway Plaisance until it left the Exposition grounds and entered a workaday Chicago that seemed pedestrian and ugly by comparison. After a block or two I noticed that my headache was gone, and in its place I felt a buoyancy, a feeling of confidence and mild euphoria. *Well, Brother Holmes,* I thought, *I don't know how you are as a landlord, but there's nothing wrong with you as a pharmacist.*

I arrived at the track a few minutes before the first race, and strolled to the paddock to inspect the entrants. My friend Boz Markey, currently the *Tribune*'s racing columnist, was leaning his tall, soft body against the rail and staring morosely at the horses parading around the ring. His normally pink face was putty-gray, and there were dark pouches under his watery blue eyes.

"Good day to you, Boz," I said cheerily, elbowing my way to a place beside him. "It's good seeing you. One glance at your suffering features makes me feel joyous by comparison."

He turned toward me with a start. "What? Who? Oh, it's you, Moretti. Here for the derby, eh? How providential. It has made my day." He raised his hand and wiped it across his brow. I noticed it trembled.

"That I am, Bosley, and looking forward to the festivities with unalloyed enthusiasm. I read your piece in the *Tribune* this morning. Interesting background."

He grinned sourly. "Oh, decided to get your information from a trustworthy source for a change?"

"That I have, Bosley, just like the rest of your legion of faithful readers."

"And now you want me to tell you about the

horses in today's races, so you can sound like you know what you're talking about when you write your dispatch tonight."

" 'Tis the very reason I sought you out."

"Prevailing rates?"

"Prevailing rates," I replied. Prevailing rates for the exchange of information among the fraternity of racing columnists were all the liquor the respondent could drink in half an hour at the saloon of his choice.

"Done," said Boz, and proceeded to identify and comment on all the horses in the paddock. His remarks were knowledgeable, incisive, and amusing.

Boz Markey was, as I said, presently employed by the *Chicago Tribune*, although that fact was almost as mutable as the color of the suit he was wearing on a given day. During the last five years he had worked for every newspaper in Chicago, and would no doubt work for all of them again before he entered that great City Room in the Sky. His job mobility was explained by three things: his excellence in his craft, his appetite for strong waters, and the fact that an independent income paid him enough each month to allow him to continue his dissolute ways even when temporarily unemployed.

When I had filled ten pages in my notebook I

slipped it into my hip pocket. "One thing more," I said. "The early betting for the derby. Why is it so heavy?"

Boz shrugged. "Who knows with horse bettors? Mustafa's a good horse, but eight to three good? I don't know, Moretti. Maybe Anton Birkmann knows something, maybe a lot of other people think *they* know something. Why don't you ask Birkmann?" The bugle for the first race sounded. "Look, the *Tribune* pays me to watch races, not to bribe other reporters to do my work for me. I'll meet you at the betting ring after the last race, and God help you if you aren't there." His narrow-shouldered, broad-bottomed body moved with surprising speed, and in a moment he disappeared in the crowd.

I watched the first three races from the grandstand. In between races I studied my notes and blocked out the beginning of my dispatch to Otto Hochmuth, describing the Washington Park racing scene against the background of the Columbian Exposition. I considered including a reference to Little Egypt, but the recollection of my editor's unalterably dour and bloodless expression was enough to make me drop the idea.

After the third race I pocketed my notebook and strolled toward the boxes. A policeman with a face like the map of County Clare was standing at parade rest beside them. I approached him diffidently.

"Pardon the bother, Officer, but I'm wondering if you might point out Mr. Anton Birkmann to me, since I've a message for the man and have never set eyes upon him at all."

He frowned at me magisterially and answered in a brogue as heavy as the one I had assumed, "Mr. Anton Birkmann? Him that owns Mustafa? Of course I know him. That's his box down there — the fourth one on the left."

I looked in the direction he pointed. "Ahh, that one — the one that's next to Mr. Vannatta's is it?"

"Mr. Vannatta's?" he repeated condescendingly. "Naw, Mr. Vannatta's box is on the front row, down at the end." He frowned with sudden suspicion. "You'll not be saying you have a message for him, too, will you now?"

"No, no, Officer, just Mr. Birkmann is all. And thanks for your trouble." I gave him a deferential smile and walked down the aisle between the boxes. I stopped at the fourth box. It was occupied by three persons: an elderly man with a bald head and burnside whiskers, a second man of about my age, whose silvery hair contrasted with his smooth pink skin and matinee-idol profile; and a woman in her twenties, with auburn hair and a creamy complexion, whose conservative shirtwaist and skirt did little to conceal the robustness of the body within.

"Mr. Birkmann," I said, "Moretti of *The Spirit of the Times*. I wonder if I could have a word with you about Mustafa."

"What? What? Who?" The elderly man peered at me shortsightedly. "Moretti? *Spirit of the Times?* Oh, *that* Moretti. Come in, come in. I guess we can spare a couple of minutes for the working press, eh, Schacter?"

The silvery-haired man looked at me with expressionless eyes. "If you like, Judge," he said.

"Well, I *do* like. I've read this boy's stuff for years. Most entertaining and undependable writer in the business. Glad to meet you, Moretti." He gestured to the other two occupants of the box. "My secretary, Miss Verlac, and my associate, Mr. Schacter." I bowed admiringly to the former and coolly to the latter, and received a brief nod from each. "Now I suppose you want to pump me about the derby, eh? All right, I'll let you in on a little secret." He drew me closer and whispered hoarsely in my ear, "Mustafa's going to win. How's that for a scoop, boy?" He guffawed in delight.

I took out my notebook and poised my pencil over a blank page. "I'll be needing a bit more than that if I'm to escape the wrath of my editor, Mr. Birkmann. For one thing, how do you explain all the betting so long before the race?"

"Because people know which horse is best, that's why! God Almighty, boy, when you see a real crack running against a field of milk-wagon plodders, why wait till post time to put your money down? By that time the ribbon clerks will have figured it out for themselves and the odds will have gone to hell."

I made a note, more to reassure him that his words were receiving careful attention than anything else. "You don't think Home Free represents much of a threat, then?"

He snorted. "Hell, Sparrow's ridden two other horses that beat him, one in Sarasota and the other in Kentucky, and Mustafa's beaten both of *them*. What does that tell you?" Sparrow Simpson was the jockey scheduled to ride Mustafa in the derby. I nodded wisely and made another note.

"How about the third favorite, Glenlivet?"

Birkmann assumed an expression of comic perplexity. "Who did you say? Glenwhatzit? Never heard of him."

We talked another five minutes, while Miss Verlac looked bored and Mr. Schacter regarded me with increased impatience. Finally, after

Birkmann had concluded his derisive evaluation of all the derby entrants, Schacter interrupted.

"Excuse me, Judge, but if Miss Verlac and I are to have the benefit of your advice on the next race, we'll have to have it in the next three or four minutes." He glanced at me and added, with a slight sneer, "*If* you'll excuse us, Mr. Morelli."

Not deigning to correct this careful mispronunciation of my name, I thanked Birkmann, gave Miss Verlac a final approving glance, and left the box. I made my way through the hurrying crowd of last-minute bettors to the last box on the front row. It was unoccupied, but from the presence of a picnic hamper and a pair of field glasses on two of the chairs, I concluded that the occupants would return shortly.

I was correct. Almost immediately a party of four crowded past me and entered the box. Leading the group was a man of forty or so, dressed in a splendidly cut dove-gray suit, gleaming patent leather shoes, and pale-yellow gloves. His movements were abrupt, and his face was frozen in an expression of irritation. Behind him was a woman whose figure and carriage were those of a female somewhere between eighteen and fifty; it was impossible to narrow the range because she was heavily veiled and also wore gloves.

The other two members of the party were men. One was a swarthy southern European – Sicilian, I guessed – with a thin, pointed face and two mismatched eyes, one quick, brown, and glittering, the other milky blue and dead. His companion was a plug-ugly with a battered face, wearing a checked suit too small for his powerful chest and shoulders.

After they were inside the box I followed them. "Mr. Vannatta," I began, "I'm Moretti of *The Spirit of the Times*, and I wonder if you might give me a minute of your time."

The man in the handsome suit turned toward me, his expression of irritation deepening. But before he could speak, a voice boomed from the adjacent box: "Vannatta, you auld fox, who d'ye like this time? If ye say Charlie's Darling, I've got fifty dollars that says you're a liar!"

Standing with his ample belly pressed against the rail that separated the boxes was one of the most colorful men I have ever seen. His suit was a delicate lavender, his vest was checkered dark green and white, and his shirt was dark-brown silk. Above this harmonious combination his ruddy face appeared like that of a Prussian sergeant major, with thick blond hair cut *en brosse* and mustache waxed into two upstanding points. His arms were around the waists of two young women who looked as if they were, as the English say, no better than they should be, and four more of like appearance clustered behind him.

Vannatta glanced away from me and answered, "Hello, Bath. No, I don't like Charlie's Darling, so you better take your money somewhere else. Otherwise you might find we're betting on the same horse, and we'd both hate that."

"That's a fact, now." He made a courtly bow to the veiled woman. "Good day to yez, Mrs. Vannatta." He nodded to the other two men. "Razor. Loogan." The veiled woman inclined her head silently, as did the Sicilian; the plug-ugly didn't respond.

The girl on the big man's right arm wriggled against him and said, "Ooh, I'm hungry, John. When are we going to eat?"

He patted her hip affectionately. "After this race, darlin'. Try not to faint from hunger now." She made a moue as the bugle announced the next race. I watched it from the back of Vannatta's box, making notes. The man in the next box roared for his favorite, and the six women with him formed a soprano obbligato to his booming baritone. In contrast, Vannatta and his party watched the race in silence. When it was over, the big man pulled a marker from his pocket and shredded it into confetti. "So Charlie's Darling did it after all," he shouted. "Well, you saved me fifty dollars, Vannatta. We both lost."

"Did we?" Vannatta asked coolly.

"Well, didn't we?" the big man cried. "You said flat out you didn't like Charlie's Darling. You're not telling me you had a marker on him, are you?"

Vannatta produced a square of paper from his pocket, held it up mockingly for a second, and then handed it to the Sicilian. "Sometimes I hedge my bets, Bath, but I never overhedge them. Would you mind collecting for me, Razor?"

The big man swore. The Sicilian pushed past me and disappeared in the crowd behind the box. I stepped forward and cleared my throat. "Mr. Vannatta, if you have a moment for the press —," I began.

He looked at me in surprise. "You still here?" he asked disagreeably. In the box beside us the big man had evidently succumbed to the entreaties of his hungry companion and was opening a large hamper, while the six *filles de joie* danced around him clapping their hands.

I re-identified myself and began to question Vannatta on his derby entrant, Home Free. He answered my questions curtly, volunteering nothing and obviously begrudging the time spent. At one point I tried to widen the conversation by directing a question to Mrs. Vannatta, but received no answer. The man called Loogan watched me with a bored expression on his ugly face.

Out of the corner of my eye I saw the inhabitants of the next box begin to eat. The women nibbled daintily on their fried chicken, but the big man stuffed thighs and drumsticks into his mouth and pulled out the naked bones, his heavy jaws working like some efficient new eating machine.

The Sicilian returned and handed Vannatta a packet of bills, which the latter thrust into his pocket uncounted. I asked another question, but his patience was clearly exhausted. "Razor, this fellow doesn't seem to know when to leave," he snapped. "How would you like to show him the way out?"

The swarthy man grasped my elbow and squeezed. His thumb pressed down into that depression called, inappropriately, "the funny bone," and I leaped six inches into the air. "Thanks for your time, Mr. Vannatta," I bleated. "I hope you like the story —"

I was interrupted by a shrill scream from the adjoining box, and we all glanced automatically in that direction. The six young women, their faces distorted by fear and revulsion, had drawn away from the big man in the colorful clothes, who had added a further hue to his ensemble. Slumped on his chair, his arms dangling loose at his sides, his formerly ruddy face was now the color of skimmed milk. His mouth hung open under his double-tined mustache, and his eyes, almost popping from his head, stared sightlessly before him. He was not breathing.

"My God, Bath!" Vannatta cried. "What's the matter with you?" He leaped to the railing and slipped under it, into the next box. He seized the big man's shoulder. "Can you hear me, John? John, what's wrong?" The ill man began to slide sideways from his chair, and a moment later he was sprawled on his back, mouth agape, eyes staring blindly up at Vannatta squatting above him. The screams of the six women reached a new crescendo. "Shut up, you bitches," Vannatta snarled. He slapped the milky-blue face below him, first on one cheek, then the other. "Razor, get a doctor, fast!" he called.

Instantly the Sicilian disappeared from the box. It couldn't have been more than fifteen seconds before he reappeared with another man in tow. The new arrival dropped to his knees beside the prostrate man, pulled off his gloves, and drew back one sleeve. "Give me room," he snapped at Vannatta.

As Vannatta stepped back, the newcomer pressed one hand into the open mouth below him, continuing to thrust until a third of his forearm had disappeared. With his other fist he struck the big man sharply in the upper abdomen. "Aha! There it is!" he cried triumphantly, and a moment later withdrew a great gobbet of chicken as big as a hen's egg from the open mouth. He glanced at it and then flung it away. "Great pig. Serve him right to let him strangle on it," he said disgustedly.

Returning from the Valley of the Shadow, the big man began gasping and coughing, and his face changed color like a chameleon's, taking on the hue of medium-rare roast beef. He struggled to a sitting position, felt his throat gingerly, and said, "Faith, Doc, it feels like you got me tonsils while you were at it!"

The doctor, a stocky, middle-aged man with blunt features and an irascible expression, rolled his right sleeve down and drew on his gloves. "Next time you jam food down your gullet, Mr. Alderman, try to do it when I'm not around," he growled. "I came here to watch horses, not to unblock swine." He gave one brief nod intended for everyone crowded into the box, turned on his heel, and walked briskly away.

After that everything rapidly returned to *status quo ante*. The big man enfolded a *petite amie* with each arm, and the remaining four surrounded him, chirping comments on the recent drama. Vannatta rejoined his veiled wife in the next box, and Razor and Loogan turned to me. Before any further action was required of them, I called, " 'All's well that ends well,' eh, Mr. Vannatta? A pleasure talking to you, sir." And with a wave of my hand, I hurried away down the crowded aisle.

I passed Anton Birkmann's box, noticing that the elderly owner was no longer in his seat, and that his two guests, Schacter and Miss Verlac, were deeply engaged in conversation, their foreheads almost touching.

The policeman from whom I had inquired directions was still at his post. He gave me a hard glance as I hurried past. "You there — I'll be having a word with you," he barked.

I halted. "Yes, Officer?"

"You was down by Mr. Vannatta's box — I seen you heading that way. What was it happened? How come Doc Menifee to go tearing off down there?"

"Menifee? Was that the doctor's name?"

"Of course it was! Doc Menifee, the police surgeon. I've seen him a dozen times. So I'm asking you, what was he doing in Mr. Vannatta's box?"

"It wasn't Vannatta's," I answered. "It was the man in the next box. He got a piece of chicken stuck in his throat and almost died. The doctor pulled it out."

"It wouldn't have been a big fellow in funny-colored clothes with a pointy mustache, would it?" the policeman asked eagerly.

"That it would. He had six women with him. I heard Vannatta call him Bath."

The policeman nodded, his thick lips curving into a smile. " 'Twas Bathhouse John Coughlin, for sure. That spalpeen. When he dies, he'll be too busy eatin' to notice. Or if not eatin', then drinkin'. Or if not eatin' or drinkin', then the other." He chuckled and slapped his thigh. "A credit to the auld sod, he is."

After the last race, I met Boz Markey at the betting ring, and he impatiently conducted me to a saloon on Cottage Grove Avenue. It had one of the largest free lunches I've ever seen. Boz helped himself until his food formed a tottering tower on his plate, and then we repaired to a corner table. As I sipped my beer I told him about the excitement in the boxes that afternoon. He was so busy eating and drinking as much as possible, he couldn't spare much time to comment. "Bathhouse John Coughlin

— First Ward alderman, gourmet, and aesthete," he said, spraying me with cracker crumbs. "Also racehorse owner. No entry in the derby, though. Lucky for him Doc Menifee was there."

"Well, the doc's not here now," I said, "so you better watch out how you stuff that pig's foot down your gozzle."

Boz grinned, raising his glass. "The trick is washing it down, Moretti. You can swallow a live porcupine if you wash it down." He drained the glass and handed it to me. "If you would do the honors, old man. As per prevailing rates."

I replaced his glass with a full one and took a modest sip from my own stein. "Well, you're in fine fettle," I grumbled as he gulped down half the contents of his fishbowl. "Three hours ago I doubt you could have looked a beer in the face."

He licked off his white foam mustache. "What are you talking about?"

"You — you looked like the hind end of total demoralization."

"Me? How you talk. A touch of indigestion, a slight unsettling of the humors, due no doubt to an iffy oyster at dinner."

"An oyster? In July?"

He raised his eyebrows in mock astonishment. "You mean you don't spell July with an *R?* No wonder they never let me work the copy desk."

"Anyway, you looked like hell. Congratulations on a marvelous recovery."

"Thank you. It's going to cost you." He drained his fishbowl, then extended his arm. "If you would be so kind, Paddy."

After the requisite half hour of bibulous gluttony, I left Boz and caught a Cottage Grove car northbound. The seats were, of course, all occupied, so I hung from a strap until we reached Thirty-ninth Street, when like obedient sheep we changed to another car. This one took us as far as Twenty-third Street. A third carried us to Twelfth Street, and I left a fourth car at Monroe Street.

It was almost seven o'clock when I reached the Palmer House. Automatically, I headed for the registration desk, then hesitated. I remembered the number of the room the clerk had assigned to Velma nee Wilma; it was number 662. Why shouldn't I bypass the formalities and present myself directly at her door?

There was no reason I shouldn't, I decided.

Five minutes later, my heart beating rapidly and my mouth slightly dry, I rapped on the door of room 662. There was no response, so after ten seconds I rapped again, this time saying softly, "Velma?"

The latch snapped back, the door swung open, and I found myself looking into the face of a man in his late twenties or early thirties. Half of his face was covered with soap, and there were traces of it on the other ear and cheekbone. He held a bone-handled razor in his right hand. He was in his shirtsleeves and stocking feet, and his suspenders hung down around his thighs. "Yeah, what is it?" he asked sharply.

"Why — why, I'm sorry to bother you, but could you tell me where I could find Mrs. Velma LeSeure?" *And what the devil you're doing in her room half naked*, I added mentally.

"Who? Velma LeSeure? Never heard of her." He started to close the door, but I pushed my shoulder against it.

"No, wait a minute. Are you sure you don't know her? This is her room number. I was with her when she checked in yesterday."

"Well, she must have checked out by herself, because she ain't here now. I been here since this morning, pard, and if there was a woman in the room with me I would have known it. I guess you got run out on. Now get your shoulder away from that door."

3

Disappearing Women Aren't News in Chicago

There was nothing to be accomplished by standing in the corridor and arguing with a man holding an open razor. I stepped back and allowed the door to slam in my face. Then I descended to the lobby.

At the registration desk I waited until the pale-faced clerk with the toothbrush mustache was free. When I caught his eye, I asked, "Excuse me, but I wonder if Mrs. LeSeure left any forwarding address when she checked out?"

He wet his finger and smoothed one corner of his mustache. "Mrs. who?"

"Velma LeSeure. She checked into room 662 early last evening, and apparently checked out again sometime before noon today. I thought perhaps she left an address or a message at the desk. My name's Moretti."

"LeSeure — LeSeure," he repeated. His expression was bored, but his eyes were furtive, and one eyelid twitched. He turned away and glanced at the pigeonhole for room 662.

"No sir, no messages," he said.

"Well, could you tell me what time she checked out?"

He hesitated a moment as if weighing options, and then answered unwillingly, "I believe I remember the lady. Mrs. LeSeure. Yes, I'm sure I do. She checked out quite early this morning. It must have been eight-thirty or so."

"I wouldn't have thought she was such an early riser. What about a forwarding address? Did she leave one?"

He shook his head. "She did not."

"Are you sure? Maybe with one of the other clerks?"

His lips pursed as if he had bitten into something sour. "She didn't talk to any of the other clerks. I handled her checkout myself."

"Oh, you did. Well, tell me, was she alone? And did she happen to say anything about where she was planning on going when she left here?"

"No, she didn't. She just paid her bill and left. Now, if you'll excuse me —" He started to move away. I reached across the counter and rested my fingers on his arm.

"Wait. Which bellboy carried her bags out? He might have heard the address she gave the cabbie."

The clerk jerked his arm away. "I don't know

— I didn't see the bellboy!" At the same moment, a much deeper voice just behind me said pleasantly, "We're not having any unpleasantness here, are we, Chester?" I turned to look into a broad, flat face as impassive as a bowl of oatmeal. Colorless eyes under sleepy lids regarded me with mild interest. "May I be of assistance, sir?"

"If you're the house detective, maybe you can. I'm looking for a woman who was registered here yesterday, a Mrs. LeSeure. Apparently she checked out early this morning, without leaving any forwarding address. I'd like to know where she went."

The man's face showed even less interest than before. "And she didn't leave you any message?"

"No, she didn't, Mr. Frankel," the clerk chirped. "I checked her out myself, and she didn't leave anything."

"Then I guess she didn't care to have anybody know where she was going," the detective said. "And that includes you, Mr. — ahh?"

"Moretti, Paddy Moretti, of *The Spirit of the Times*. I'm a reporter," I said spiritedly, hoping in spite of years of evidence to the contrary, that this would impress him.

"Well, Mr. Moretti, I'm afraid you've lost your ladyfriend. Too bad, but it happens to the best of us." His hand slid under my elbow and he drew me away from the desk. "But, if I was a good-looking fellow like you, I wouldn't worry about it."

I leaned back on my heels. "Wait a minute! Let's find the bellboy who carried out her bags. He may have heard where she was going."

Frankel's fingers tightened to a numbing grip. "Come on, Mr. Moretti, let's not get all hot and bothered about this. If the lady had wanted to leave word where she was going, she would have done it, wouldn't she? Face facts. And it ain't like she's the only woman in Chicago. Come on, now."

He walked at my side through the lobby, his hand firmly attached to my elbow.

As we neared the Monroe Street entrance I saw a familiar face. Skeeter Huff was sitting in a high-backed velvet armchair, leafing through a magazine and puffing on a cigar. His handsome face bore an expression of benevolent and incorruptible authority. As his eyes met mine, I touched the corner of my right eye and then flicked my two fingers forward, toward the street entrance. His authoritative expression disappeared, and his eyes darted to left and right as if searching for a way out. I frowned threateningly and touched my index finger to my Adam's apple. He paled, licked his lips, and brushed an imaginary lash from his cheekbone.

At the door Frankel released my arm, which was half numb. "We all have our problems with the ladies, God bless 'em," he said with a companionable smile that didn't reach his eyes. "Take my advice and find yourself a girl to take out to White City. Have yourself a real Chicago good time."

"Thank you. I'll keep your advice in mind." My smile was as artificial as his. "Good day, Mr. Frankel."

I started along the sidewalk toward State Street, and he reentered the hotel lobby. Then I stopped and took up a position with my back against a plate-glass window. Three or four minutes later Skeeter Huff stepped through the door, slapping his rolled-up magazine nervously against his thigh. When he reached me I fell in step beside him.

"That was the house dick you was with in there!" he said accusingly. When I nodded, he cried, "What in hell are you doing dragging the house dick over to eyeball me?"

"I wasn't dragging him, Skeeter. If you noticed, he was dragging me. He bounced me out of the hotel."

"Did he make me, Paddy? God, if he did, Ty-Ty'll kill me."

"Don't worry. He was too busy giving me the boot to think about anything else."

"You're sure? 'Cause if he did, I got to tell Ty-Ty, so he don't get set up to take a fall. And God, you don't know what Ty-Ty's like when he's got to switch his plans!" His voice was drenched with dread; in profile he looked like a Roman senator watching the Huns ride into his villa.

"I'm sure," I said impatiently. "Listen, Skeeter — remember when I saw you in the lobby yesterday?"

"I ain't got the money, Paddy. We ain't made a score yet. You got to give me another day or two."

"Forget the money for now. That's not what I want to talk to you about."

"It ain't?" We turned the corner and headed south on State Street. Skeeter began to regain his composure. His back straightened and his firm, round chin thrust forward. When he spoke again his voice had deepened into an orotund baritone. "Then what may I do for you, old friend?"

"I was with a woman when I came in, remember? She registered at the desk, and a bellboy carried her bags to the elevator. You mentioned her afterward — you said she had some nice sparklers on her fingers."

His eyes widened. "I did?"

"Certainly you did. A big, good-looking woman with kind of reddish-yellow hair and a figure like this." I sculpted an hourglass in the air. "She was wearing a black dress with a neckline down to here, and was carrying a black handbag."

Skeeter frowned judiciously, thrusting out his lower lip and beetling his brows. "Well, maybe I did, now you mention it. Nice-looking piece of goods. What about her?"

"She checked out this morning. Did you happen to notice?"

His composure slipped again. His eyes darted toward me, then away. "Well, I don't know, Paddy. There's a lot of coming and going in the lobby there. What time would it have been?"

"About eight-thirty. There wouldn't have been many people in the lobby then. How about it?" He opened his mouth, but didn't answer. "Goddammit, Skeeter, you either saw her or you didn't. Now which is it?"

"Yeah, all right, I saw her. Like you said. She checked out about eight-thirty." He spoke rapidly and avoided my eyes.

"Did you see the bellboy with her?" I demanded.

He shook his head so rapidly his dewlaps trembled. "I didn't notice no bellboy. I mean, maybe there was one with her, but I just didn't pay no attention." He gave me a sickly grin. "Who's looking at bellboys when there's a dolly like that around? Ain't that the truth, Paddy?"

"She wasn't with a man, was she?"

"Hell, I don't know! Not right next to her, anyway. Maybe there was some john ahead of her or behind her, I don't know." His grin widened. "She walked out on you, huh? Well, don't take it so hard. There's plenty of other fish in the sea."

I didn't speak for a moment. My headache was back; it began to pound in time with the clanging bell of a passing streetcar. *I've got to get some more of that fellow's headache powders*, I thought. I put my hand on Skeeter Huff's shoulder and said quietly, "Are you telling me the truth? You saw her check out, and as far as you could tell she was alone?"

"Like I said, Paddy. Why should I lie to you?" He widened his small eyes ingenuously.

"No reason I can think of." I sighed. "Okay, Skeeter — you get back to the hotel and scout up my fifty dollars; I'll be looking you up again in a day or two. It's been nice talking to you."

Skeeter leaned toward me and patted my arm in a comradely manner. "Me, too, Paddy. And don't take it so hard — we all of us lose out on the dollies once in a while."

66

"Good-bye, Skeeter."

I watched as he pushed away from me in the pedestrian traffic and disappeared from sight. *He's right,* I thought, *we all lose out on the dollies once in a while. Why does it bother me so much?* Jostled by the impatient elbows around me, I moved slowly along the sidewalk. *Maybe because the dollies are fewer and farther between?*

No, Velma liked me — she was looking forward to our "modest repast and genteel conversation" tonight as much as I was. Even if she had to leave town, she would have left me a note. I know she would.

Try to be honest with yourself for once, the antagonist jeered. *You weren't important to her, that's all. She had other fishes to fry. Too bad, Moretti — better luck next year.*

A hurrying pedestrian caromed into me from behind and snarled as he sped by. I mumbled an apology and thought, *Well, what should I do now?*

Have a drink, Paddy, I answered with infallible logic. And then immediately added, *with Boz Markey. Have a drink with Boz Markey.*

The thought lifted my spirits appreciably, and I set out for his Huron Street apartment immediately.

His apartment was on the second floor of a yellow brick three-flat between State and Dearborn. The stairway smelled of cooked cabbage, stale beer, and the moldy rubber mats that were tacked to each step. The doorway at the second landing was decorated with one of Dore's illustrations from Dante's *Inferno*, showing a number of unclothed sinners in a river of molten lava, under which was crudely handprinted the message: ABANDON HOPE, ALL YE WHO ENTER HERE.

I pushed open the door and entered the front room. I opened my mouth to call a greeting, then hesitated as I heard voices raised in argument in the next room.

"Then you absolutely refuse to help," said a woman's voice in crisp anger. "Regardless of the fact that three young women who are personally known to me, three young women who came looking for assistance and trusted me with their problems, have disappeared from the face of the earth —"

"Oh, don't make a speech, sissie," replied a voice I recognized as Boz's. "An audience of one does not a public meeting make. And I told you, it's a blind alley. There's absolutely nothing I can do. As long as that damn raree-show on the midway lasts, there's nothing anybody can do. Would you mind adding a dollop of medicinal spirits to this glass while you're up?"

"Yes, I *would* mind — I would mind very

much. I don't intend to help you rot away whatever vestige of brain you still possess!"

I walked to a frayed sofa and sat down carefully. It was necessary to sit carefully because of the statue that stood behind the sofa. It was a nude male figure, seven feet tall, that Boz and a group of fellow blithe spirits had created one night with plaster of paris over a twisted wire armature. A heroic but anatomically implausible creation, it was noteworthy for its priapic dimensions; its plaster phallus thrust out over the sofa like a lumpy Louisville Slugger, and sofa-sitters were forced to sit down and stand up in a crouch to avoid banging their heads on it.

I sat in the shadow of the monstrous fertility symbol and listened to the conversation in the next room.

Boz Markey's voice resumed: "Very well. If you want to take that attitude." There was the creaking of springs, the sound of bare footsteps on the floor, and the clink of glass and the gurgle of liquid. "Ahhh. Now listen, sissie. Those three girls of yours are a drop in the bucket. Do you have any idea how many women come to Chicago to make their fortune in the big city, and are never heard from again? Hundreds, every year. And this year there are more than ever, because of the Exposition.

They come, they wiggle their cute little derrières down State Street, and phhht! — they're gone with the snows of yesteryear."

"And there's nothing you can do about it?" Her voice was edged with scorn.

"It's not news, Alison! It's just plain not news!"

"Like it's not news when the son of your biggest advertiser commits rape? Or when a socially prominent meat packer makes an out-of-court settlement for selling diseased beef?"

There was silence for the length of a deep swallow, and then Boz said flatly, "That's right, sissie. Just like that."

"Well, it's not good enough. You and Joseph Medill and the other great opinion makers may think you can ignore unpleasant facts and make them go away, but it's not true. But don't you worry, Boz. You just sit there with your nose in a glass. It's none of your business. Somebody else will take up the torch, and somehow the truth will come out, but don't you worry. You — oh, God, I'd be ashamed!"

Her words ended with a sob, and her footsteps pattered across the floor. She appeared in the doorway, a tall, slender woman in her late twenties, with light-brown hair severely tied back, a finely boned face almost, but not quite, long enough to be called horsey, and a wide, full mouth which was now thin-lipped with anger. She stopped dead, staring at me. "And who are you? Somebody waiting to get drunk with my brother?"

Instinctively I rose, banging my head on the anatomical Sword of Damocles, and causing the statue to sway alarmingly. "The name is Paddy Moretti, miss, and I assure you such an intention has never crossed my mind." I touched my head gingerly. "I am here for purely professional reasons."

"I'll just bet," she snapped with flashing eyes.

Boz Markey appeared in the doorway behind her. He was dressed in a yellow silk robe, badly soiled, below which flapped the tails of a striped flannel nightshirt. He was unshaven, which gave his round, childlike face a debauched look. It took him a moment to recognize me, and then he said, "Faith and begorra, it's the Moretti, or I'm an Orangeman. And sober, too, by the look of him."

"And with every intention of remaining that way," I said virtuously, "as I wish you'd explain to this indignant young lady."

"She does go in for generalizations," he answered. "Alison, just because a man works for a newspaper and is an acquaintance of mine is no reason to assume he's a slave of John Barleycorn. Many of my dearest friends are teetotal."

She looked at me coldly, hazel eyes bright under stern brows. "If I've hurt your feelings, I apologize," she snapped. She turned back to face her brother. "And that's your last word? It isn't news, so there's nothing you can do?"

He shrugged his shoulders. "I'm sorry, sissie."

"So be it. I hope you sleep well tonight." She pushed past me without a glance, chin raised and shoulders squared, and slammed her way out the apartment door. Boz and I listened in silence to the clacking of her heels on the stairs, followed by the bang of the street door below. Then Boz gave a sigh.

"Almost enough to make a man go back to bed again," he said disconsolately.

"Don't think of it. I didn't come all the way over here to sit by your bedside and watch you pound your ear."

"All right then, it's almost enough to make a man fix himself a drink."

"That's more like it. While you're at it, fix two."

I crouched down and resumed my seat under the massive member while Boz mixed the drinks. He sat beside me and we clinked glasses. "Confusion to the enemy," he said. The whiskey was rye, very strong and grainy to the taste. "Ahh, that'll keep out the cold."

"I didn't know you had a sister, Boz."

"Oh, yes. For my sins." He regarded the dark liquid in his glass. "Alison's a Believer. Last year she fell into the clutches of Jane Addams, and since then she's had the fate of half the city in her hands – she thinks. She's out at Hull-House seven days a week, and if she isn't there she's in some deadfall in the levee trying to persuade a broken-down chippie to get a respectable job and leave her life of shame. Not that she's moralistic about it," he went on with an ironic grimace. "She's much too advanced a thinker to worry about morality. It's a question of social value. Waiting on tables or running a sewing machine has social value, and prostitution doesn't." He glanced at me. "Did you know that, Paddy?"

"I'm not sure that I did, Boz."

"Neither did I, but she assures me it's true. I suspect she believes in free love, which she thinks means that nobody should ever be allowed to pay for it."

"She does, does she?" I asked with interest.

"I wouldn't be surprised. She's the compleat emancipated bluestocking. God knows what all she believes in."

I took a sip of my drink. "What was that she was saying about some women who are missing?"

He waved one hand in dismissal. "Oh, she says three of the doxies she's been proselytizing have faded from the scene in ways suggestive of foul play. As if that doesn't happen down there every day and twice on Sundays."

"What makes these three so special, then?"

"She says they were in the process of leaving their lives of degradation, moving out of the neighborhood, and applying themselves to more decent if less lucrative professions, that she had arranged for them. She says they were through with the bad old days, so why would Fate choose this time for them to disappear?"

"A reasonable question, surely," I said, holding out my empty glass.

"A foolish question," he answered, filling it up. "A friend of mine in the department says that a dozen women a week come to Chicago and disappear. Since the Exposition started, the figure's gone up to two or sometimes three dozen. Each of them's somebody's darling, and the home folks back in Peoria can't understand what happened, but I can — if she's lucky, the little flower is ensconced at Carrie Watson's; if she's not, she's in a panel house on Goose Island, or working a twenty-four-hour crib on Custom House Place. And who gives a damn, as long as nobody makes trouble?"

"But you're talking about women disappearing *into* whorehouses, Boz. The ones your sister's talking about are women disappearing *out of* whorehouses."

He shook his head impatiently. "That's not the point. The point is, disappearing women aren't news in Chicago."

"Not even twenty or thirty women a week?"

"Not even a hundred a week — not as long as the Exposition is running. You know what news is, Paddy. News is what the papers print. And no paper in this town is going to print anything that suggests the Gem of the Prairie is any less safe than the front pew of a Methodist church at high noon on Sunday."

We considered our glasses in philosophical silence. When it seemed there was nothing more to be learned from mine, I said, "It's odd we should be talking about disappearing women."

"It is? Why is that?"

"Because I've just had one disappear on me, and it bothers the devil out of me."

He filled both our glasses again, which emptied the bottle, and then settled down facing me, with his elbows on his knees and his fists supporting his moon face. "Tell your Uncle Dudley," he ordered.

I told him the whole Velma/Wilma story. He listened in silence, his clever eyes fixed on my face and his lower lip at full pout. When I finished he picked up his glass and eyed its contents thoughtfully. "Assuming the lady was not indulging an understandable desire to escape your attentions" — he raised one hand to silence my protest — "then I have to agree the episode is perplexing. No forwarding address, no recollections of bellhop or gentleman friend, if any — it seems unlikely such a conspicuous charmer as you describe could depart so inconspicuously."

"Can you offer any explanation?"

"No, I cannot. Not at this time, and probably never." He emptied his glass and stood up. "Furthermore, the effort involved in thinking about it has created a thirst which I have not the resources on the premises to assuage. I suggest we continue our discussion at Billy Boyle's." Peeling off his robe, he draped it carefully over the plaster of paris phallus behind the sofa, and then retired to his bedroom to dress.

4

Perils of a Crocodile Bird

Billy Boyle's, at State and Madison, is the premier hangout for Chicago politicians and newspaper reporters. Whether the pols originally came first and the reporters followed them for news, or whether the reporters came first and the pols followed them for publicity, the result was the same — a symbiotic relationship resembling that between the crocodile and the crocodile bird, Boz Markey explained.

"I assume we ink-stained wretches are the crocodile birds," I said uneasily. "I don't suppose the crocodile ever forgets we're inside at the free lunch counter, and clamps down those jaws of his."

"Perish the thought. They need us more than we need them," he assured me.

We made our way across the large, crowded room to a round table in the far corner, beside which was a flight of stairs leading to the second floor. Boz gestured toward the stairs. "Up there is where they go — down here is our stamping ground. That way they have their privacy, and we get our shot at them coming and going."

Since no one was either ascending or descending the stairs at that moment, we found ourselves seats at the round table. Boz's arrival was greeted with assorted groans, witticisms, and insults, which he answered in kind. Then he introduced me to the table at large, and identified his colleagues to me one by one. My neighbor on the left was an affable, middle-aged man with a prankster's smile and sorrowful eyes, whom he introduced as Gene Field, a columnist for the *Chicago Record*. I recognized the name. "Little Boy Blue?" I asked, impressed.

Field rolled up his eyes as if addressing a silent prayer skyward, and Boz said hastily, "Don't be gauche, Paddy. There are some things that gentlemen simply do not mention in public. Field prefers to be remembered, if at all, as the supreme purveyor of unpublished and unpublishable scatalogical verse in the Chicago literary establishment − a role he is excellently equipped by nature to fill." The two men bowed formally to each other. Boz continued, "Perhaps you would offer up an example for our Eastern friend, Gene − something a little more typical than

'Winken, Blinken and Nod,' I hope."

Field furrowed his brow a moment. "Does he know about how we're reversing the Chicago River, so that all our sewage will flow south to the Gulf of Mexico, instead of out into Lake Michigan?"

I said I had read about this amazing engineering project, which had been begun the previous year.

"Very well, then." Field raised one finger and declaimed, "Ode Celebrating the Reversal of the Chicago River":

> "A Chicago lady named Rose
> Had breasts that hung down to her toes;
> While taking a crap
> They fell through her lap,
> And are now in the Gulf, I suppose."

Unperturbed by the chorus of groans that greeted this effort, Field blew kisses around the table and sat down. Boz continued his introductions. Eugene Field wasn't the only recognizable name in the group – Finley Peter Dunne, author of the Mister Dooley columns, sat behind a fishbowl stein of beer and a plate piled high with pickled pigs feet and hard-boiled eggs. I hoped that he would respond to Boz with a characteristic political comment in brogue, but he contented himself with a grin and a wave of the hand.

It was a cheerful group, and the waiters were quick to replace empty glasses with full ones. I switched to beer, and Boz stuck with rye whiskey. The topic of conversation was the rumor of a possible pardon for the three surviving Haymarket anarchists — it had been almost six years since four of the group had been hanged and the fifth had blown most of his head off with dynamite smuggled into his cell. A reporter from the *Daily News,* obviously far along in drink, insisted his spies had informed him that Governor Altgeld intended to issue pardons to Fielden, Neebe, and Schwab, the three survivors, before the month was out. His statement was met with general derision. Finley Peter Dunne said that if Altgeld did such a thing, he would become politically deader than Kelsey's nuts, "which until now have served as the exemplar of total torpidity." Gene Field agreed, as did most of the others.

"I suppose you're right," Boz said, "but, God, I'd like to see it happen. Old Medill would have a litter of kittens on the city room floor. Phil Armour and Gussie Swift would start curing each other's hams — I mean the ones in their pants — and Marshall Field might even be shocked into paying his salesgirls a living wage."

"The ephemeral fumes of fantasy, my friend," Field said sadly. "The rest of the country's in a Depression, and the only reason we're not is because of that white plaster dog-and-pony show on the lake. Do you think any political animal is going to turn loose three convicted murderers on the streets of Chicago to scare away the visiting firemen at a time like this?"

Remembering Boz's comments about disappearing women not being news in Chicago this year, I said diffidently, "Apparently there's nothing in the world important enough to risk rocking the boat for in this town."

Field thought for a moment. "I think that's a fair statement, don't you, Finley?"

Dunne snorted. "If this were Sodom and Gomorrah the papers wouldn't even suggest that travelers refrain from looking back over their shoulders at it."

"It's a question of being positive," Boz said. "That's where the skill lies. Any jackleg scribbler can write a column or two about a mass murderer or an epidemic. But thrilling your readers with a spelling bee or a flower show — ah, that's the stuff that makes a newspaperman swell with pride."

"It's a skill that is sadly lacking among the sensation-mongers of New York, I understand," said Dunne kindly.

"That it is," I answered. "Personally, I blame it on the easy success of James Gordon Bennett in catering to the low appetites of his readers."

As the waiter was serving me a fresh fishbowl, two men in bowler hats approached the stairway. Boz called out, "Mister Alderman! Any new surface line franchises being offered in the next few days?" The larger of the two men regarded us with the face of a professional mourner at a funeral and shook his head. The smaller man frowned in irritation and shot his cuffs importantly. They both disappeared upstairs. I asked Boz who they were.

"The big one is Johnny de Pow — Johnny Powers, actually — Yerkes's man on the city council. He's never missed a wake or a funeral in his life. He's been known to sell the franchise on one city block three times — once for street rights for cable cars, once for air rights for elevated trains, and once for underground rights, for gas and electric lines. Really a genius, in his grubby way."

"Who's the little one?"

"Oh, that's Little Mike Ryan. He's an alderman, too." Boz took a deep drink and smacked his lips appreciatively. "Let me tell you a story about Little Mike. Couple of months ago the boodlers on the council were sitting around discussing a proposal some civic improver had made to gussy up Lincoln Park by putting a half-dozen gondolas in the lagoon. Little Mike was against it. 'Why waste the taxpayer's money buying six of the craytures?' he wanted to know. 'Why not buy a pair of 'em and let Nature take its course?' "

Finley Peter Dunne set his beer stein down with a bang. "So it's come to this, has it?" he cried accusingly. "Doing Irish politician jokes with a brogue, and cutting off the only means of livelihood of a man that's never done you a bit of wrong at all! I'd be ashamed."

Boz bowed his head. "You're absolutely right. I was thoughtless. Next time I'll do it with a Yiddish accent. Little Mike Ryan will sound great talking with a Yiddish accent."

"He couldn't sound worse than with your brogue," Dunne grumbled, addressing himself to a pig's foot.

The evening swam along on a tide of gossip and alcohol, occasionally interrupted by the arrival or departure of an alderman. No news leads developed from these, and I doubted if any would; from the newspaperman's point of view, at least, evenings at Billy Boyle's were social rather than professional events.

I tried to engage Boz in serious conversation, but he waved me aside. "You know, friends, it's a marvelous thing about our colleague Dunne," he said to the table at large. "Since fame has found him out, there is literally no place he can hide from his admirers. On the street, at the theater, even at an *intime* table for two in the most discreet cafe, it is only a matter of time before some starry-eyed devotee bursts upon him, babbling his praises and demanding his autograph."

"Here, here," cried Gene Field, striking his glass with his fork vigorously.

"To give you an idea," Boz continued, "last week our friend, while pursuing a story in the hinterlands, felt the call of Nature. Well, sir, no sooner had he located a nearby one-holer, ensconced himself behind locked doors therein, dropped his trousers, opened his newspaper and read the first four pages, than the predictable occurred; a fist beat a passionate tattoo on the door, and a voice cried excitedly, 'Ain't you Dunne?' With a sigh of resignation, our colleague admitted his identity. 'Then haul your ass out of there,' the bumpkin bellowed. 'I got to take a crap.'"

This terrible joke produced the silence it deserved. After a moment, all the men at the table began speaking to one another in undertones, as at a funeral. I tugged at the crestfallen raconteur's sleeve. "Listen, before you think up another rib-tickler, I want to talk to you."

He turned a sad moonface to me and said, "Oh, all right. Nobody has a sense of humor anyway. What lugubrious topic did you have in mind?"

I lowered my voice. "The disappearing women we talked about. I've been thinking – how'd you like to work on it with me?"

He grimaced. "I told you, Moretti. Disappearing women aren't news in Chicago."

"Do you like people telling you what's news and what isn't? I thought you were a better reporter than that."

He made a rude noise and swallowed some rye whiskey. "If I had any professional pride I wouldn't take that off you." He regarded his glass thoughtfully a moment. "Just for the sake of argument, what were you thinking of?"

"Those three chippies your sister mentioned, the ones who were about to turn over a new leaf. If you could follow up on them, and I could find out what happened to my girlfriend at the Palmer House – well, we might just turn up a story for ourselves."

Boz frowned suspiciously. "You work for a horse-race paper. What do you care about missing *filles de joie*?"

"Because I can smell a story here. And so could you, if you hadn't destroyed your olfac-

85

tory sense with spirituous liquors. And also I have some unfinished business with Velma — at least I think I have. Is that enough?"

Boz pulled on his lower lip. "Old Bridey would know, if anybody would," he said thoughtfully. "If there's anything big going on in the cribs and parlor houses, she's heard about it. Whether she'd talk, that's something else again."

"That's more like it. And who's Bridey, may I ask?"

"Bridey Tumulty. A blind old beldam who thinks she's Queen of the Tenderloin. Holds court in a hellhole near Twelfth Street. She claims to have run the swankiest whorehouse in New York City twenty years ago, until she lost her political cover and had to come West. She's half crazy, but nobody's ever quite sure which half it is."

"You think she'd know about those girls your sister was talking about?"

"If she wouldn't, then I don't have any idea who would." He looked at his empty glass glumly. "Damn you, Moretti, I hate to talk shop when I'm drinking. Just when I've reached an ideal state of vaporous unsubstantiality, the whole shooting match is sicklied o'er with the pale cast of thought, and there I am looking at the dirt under my fingernails. I call it an unfriendly act, Moretti."

"One minute, and you can go back to your boozing with my blessing. Just tell me, have we got a deal? Will you see what you can dig up tomorrow, from the Tumulty woman or whoever else you can think of? And I'll see what I can shake out of the Palmer House. Then tomorrow night we'll put our heads together and see what we've got. Is it a deal, then?"

"Oh, God, I guess so. Will you promise to stop talking about it if I say it is?"

For answer I beckoned the waiter and pointed to our two empty glasses.

By eleven o'clock, the group at the round table had been reduced by attrition to Boz, me, and a financial writer from the *Tribune* named Sweetwater. Field had departed around nine o'clock, Dunne a half hour later, and the other tipplers weaved away at five- and ten-minute intervals thereafter. When I laid money on the table to cover the beer I had drunk, Boz stared at me incredulously. "Whassa matta you?" he demanded. "Siddown. Shank of the evening. Have another drink, go see the girlies. Just you, me, good ol' Sweetwater here. Right, ol' Sweetwater?" Sweetwater, whose head was cradled on his folded arms, answered with a liquid snore. "See?" Boz demanded, "he's raring to go. Whassa matta you?"

I patted him on the shoulder and made my way out to the street.

It was a pleasant evening, so in hopes of exercising away the loginess the beer had left with me, I walked the mile and a half to my hotel. Even though I kept to well-lighted main thoroughfares, I was propositioned at least fifty times. If there were as many Cyprians working indoors as there were working outside, I reflected, then a substantial part of the population of Chicago made its living on its back.

At the hotel, I was gratified to find no telegram waiting in my box. Often on my out-of-town assignments, that was not the case. My editor, Otto Hochmuth, often subjected me to cabled advice and exhortation when I was out of his physical clutches; these *billets-doux*, inspired by the man's jaundiced view of my personal and professional probity, did nothing to improve my spirits.

In my depressing room I removed my collar, tie, and shoes, intending to make myself comfortable before mixing a nightcap from my traveling bottle. Then I remembered that Velma and I had emptied my bottle on the train. With a groan I completed my undressing, donned my nightshirt, and climbed between the worn sheets. Lying in the dark, stuffy room that smelled of dusty carpets,

I felt my head begin to throb.

That fellow Holmes, I thought as I tried to find a cool place on my pillow, *where did he say his shop was? Sixty-third and Wallace? I better stop by there tomorrow for some more of that remarkable medicine of his.*

I tossed and turned for ten minutes before I fell asleep. It seemed only an instant later that I awoke to discover the overhead light glaring into my face, and two men standing beside my bed, looking down at me. The smaller man, the one with the ice pick, was smiling. His companion, a six-footer with shoulders a yard wide, expressionlessly slapped a cut-down baseball bat against the palm of his free hand.

The smaller man leaned over me and touched me on the throat with the point of the ice pick. "Don't say nothing unless you want to whistle out of your Adam's apple, Moretti," he said in a husky whisper.

I drew away, but the point followed. "What —," I began, but the point pressed down, silencing me. I froze, eyes bulging, mouth agape.

"I talk, you listen," the man went on. "I got to deliver a message. You keep your mouth shut and do what you're told, maybe you'll get back to New York alive. You make trouble, you get the pick through the neck. Understand?"

I nodded carefully. But as if he hadn't noticed, he turned his head to the other man. "Maybe he ain't awake yet," he said. "Wake him up, Howie."

The big man moved with surprising speed. He raised the baseball bat and brought it down across my thighs. I reacted to the explosion of pain by jerking backward and pulling my knees up against my chest. The point of the ice pick continued to press into my thyroid cartilage. "He's awake," the man with the club said.

"That's good." The needle point began a slow circle around my Adam's apple. "You listening now? . . ." I stared up at the images that swam before my eyes and nodded again. "Fine, fine. Now you just remember what I'm telling you. You're here to watch the races, so that's what you *do*. Now, here's what you *don't* do." The pressure of the needle point increased. "You don't make a nuisance of yourself looking for ladies who don't want you to find them, understand? It ain't polite. A lady wants you to find her, she would have left a message. But she didn't, so what does that tell you? Get the drift?"

I licked my lips and nodded.

"If I was you, I wouldn't go within two blocks of the Palmer House from now on. If you're looking for a woman, try a whorehouse. Right?"

"Right," I croaked.

"Good. Put your legs down." I slowly straightened out in the bed. When my knees were flat, the smaller man asked his companion, "What do you think, Howie? Has he got the message, or you want to get his attention again?"

"I don't know, John. Whatever you say," the big man said diffidently.

The ice pick man looked thoughtful. "What do *you* say, Moretti? You think you got the message all right? Or you want us to help you concentrate?"

"Got it fine," I whispered.

The pressure on my throat increased for a second and then eased. The smaller man straightened and slipped the ice pick under his belt. "Then I guess we might as well vamoose and let you get your beauty sleep." He stepped back from the bed. "Just you stay quiet in bed for a minute or two. We'd hate to have to come back and shut you up." He gestured to his companion, and they both stepped through the hall door and closed it behind them.

I stayed in bed for two minutes, which was the time it took for my muscles to relax and my heart to stop pounding. Then I got up and checked my neck and thighs for damage; the skin over my Adam's apple was inflamed but, except for three tiny dots, unbroken, and the bruises above my knees were twelve hours away from assuming the full purple-and-ocher brilliance their soreness guaranteed.

Cursing the absence of my traveling bottle, I drank two full glasses of tepid water as I stared at myself in the streaked wall mirror. The face that looked back at me was one I felt no fondness for. *It's a big mouth you have, Moretti,* I told myself, *a big mouth and a lustful nature, and between the two of them they'll be the death of you.*

I drank another glass of water, visited the bathroom down the corridor, and returned to my musty room. I was too keyed up to sleep, and it was much too late to return to Chicago's streets — at 4:00 A.M. I doubted if even the police would venture on Twelfth Street in less than pairs. I dropped into the shabby brown armchair, shifted my position until a projecting spring no longer pressed into my back, and began to run over everything that had occurred since I first spoke to Velma LeSeure in the green plush opulence of the B & O Pullman car.

Our conversation had been lackluster, I remembered, until I had told her that I was a reporter for *The Spirit of the Times.* Her reaction had been to ask me if I knew Paul

Vannatta, the owner of the derby contender, Home Free. When I replied in the affirmative, she had questioned me about him until she had satisfied herself that she knew everything that I did. But she hadn't offered any information in return.

I thought about my brief meeting with Vannatta the next day, in his box at Washington Park. Certainly he had told me nothing of value, but his hostility was understandable — many horse owners disliked *The Spirit of the Times* and its employees, often with good reason. I thought about his two companions, the swarthy southern European called Razor, and his associate with the battered face — not the most confidence-inspiring colleagues for a sporting gentleman, surely. And the colorfully dressed personage in the next box, variously referred to as Alderman, Bath, John, and Coughlin, who had briefly balanced on the brink of eternity with a windpipe full of chicken — apparently he was a betting rival of Vannatta's. Was that significant?

I thought about Vannatta's competitor, the owner of Mustafa, Anton Birkmann. What was it Boz had said? Mustafa was a good horse, but eight to three good? Maybe Anton Birkmann knew something, or maybe a lot of other people thought *they* knew something.

And what could any of that have to do with the presence of two thugs in my hotel room at four o'clock in the morning? It was as unlikely as a connection between them and Little Egypt, or her devoted admirer, the personable H. H. Holmes.

I thought about Boz Markey's sister Alison, and the three women whose disappearances had prevented their entry into the world of the morally employed. Interesting — but as Boz pointed out, something less than page one news in Chicago. I lingered over the recollection of Alison for some time, trying to imagine how her mouth would look when it wasn't thin-lipped with anger.

These and other questions circled through my mind like painted horses on a carousel, until I realized that the sky outside my window was gray and I was sleepy again.

I drank another glass of water, stretched out in bed, and closed my eyes. The last picture in my mind before I fell asleep was of Alison Markey, and her lips were full, red, and smiling.

5

A Depressing Morning

Detective Arbuckle listened to my story almost without interruption. His hazel eyes moved lazily from my face to the items on his desk, to the clock on the wall, to the uniformed policemen who bustled into and out of the big room, and back to my face again. He was slight for a law officer, no more than five feet four, with narrow shoulders, a sunken chest, and small, delicate hands with nicotine-stained fingers. His face was pale and freckled, with a high forehead and projecting ears.

When I finished, he regarded me for a moment with remote neutrality. "The man with the ice pick — you say he called the other one Howie?" I nodded. "And the ice pick man — was he kind of a pretty boy, with long eyelashes and sideburns down to here?" He touched the corner of his jaw. I nodded again. "Little scar running down from the corner of his mouth?" Again I confirmed the detail. "Well, that's that, then," he said, with brisk finality. "Thank you for coming in, Moretti. Good day."

I gaped at him. "Good day?" I repeated blankly.

He frowned. "Was there anything else?"

"Well, yes, I thought there might be! Such as, for instance, what was all that about last night? And who were those two assassins in my room? And why don't they want me asking questions at the Palmer House? What's going on here, anyway?"

Arbuckle produced a bag of Bull Durham tobacco from an inside pocket and began to roll himself a cigarette. He didn't speak until he had lit it and drawn the first mouthful of smoke into his lungs. Then he said, "It's just my own personal opinion, Moretti, but I think that was good advice you got. If I were you, I'd take it to heart. Mind your own business, write your own horse-race stories, and go back to New York where your friends are. Seems very sensible to me." His eyes widened to show white all around the irises, then narrowed immediately, in a kind of physical punctuation. "Who do you like in the American Derby? Mustafa? You think he's as good as the odds say?"

I stared at him a moment before I spoke. "I haven't given it the thought it deserves, Lieutenant, having been distracted by people sticking me in the windpipe with ice picks, and all. God Almighty, man, they told me that disappearing women aren't news in Chicago, but they forgot to mention that murder isn't either."

"Oh? You know about somebody being murdered?"

"The somebody is *me*, the last time the subject came up!"

Arbuckle inhaled deeply, crushed out the stub of his cigarette, and placed both his hands on the edge of his desk. "Moretti," he said quietly, "you don't seem to be a bad fellow, but you don't listen very well. The only thing you've been asked to do is mind your own business. Think about it. People in Chicago are busy. We don't have time to worry about outsiders running around getting in the way and making trouble. If you have time on your hands, go out to the Exposition." He rose from his chair and stood resting his weight on the desk. "Thank you for coming in," he said, making no move to shake hands.

I stood up facing him, my head eight inches above his. "You know who those men in my room were. Who were they?"

He smiled tightly. "Thank you for coming in," he repeated. "Good-bye, Moretti."

I glared at him for a moment in silence, then turned on my heel and left the building.

It was only a little after nine o'clock, and I had three hours before I needed to leave for the track. I began to walk north on Wabash, my thoughts in confusion and my emotions wavering between apprehension and anger. *There's a terrible lot going on that I don't understand,* I thought, *and what I need is a place to sit down and relax and sort things out.* I happened to be passing a saloon called The Bottom Dollar, and it seemed like the most natural thing to turn in between the swinging doors, cross the freshly mopped tile floor to the mahogany bar, and order a stein of beer from the opulently mustached bartender. It was only as I was licking foam from my upper lip after the first cool swallow that I told myself guiltily, *Not yet ten in the morning, and here you are drinking already. It's a dark and desolate road you're traveling, Moretti!* I set the glass on the bar before me as though it were a poisoned chalice.

The bartender eyed me curiously. "Something wrong with the suds, mate?"

"Nothing that's not wrong with all alcoholic beverages. They have no respect for the time of day. You give them your evenings, and they want your afternoons; give them your afternoons, and the next thing you know they're trying to move in on your mornings as well. It's sinister. It can rot a man's fiber."

The bartender wiped a glass on his apron. "You gotta watch it," he said neutrally.

I studied my glass with distaste. "You know what my dear old mother back in Goshen, Ohio, used to say? 'Oh, that a man would take into his mouth that which would steal away his brain.'"

"She said that?"

"She said that. Often."

"Well, I guess she had something there." He stopped polishing the glass and held it up to the light. Satisfied as to its cleanliness, he filled it with whiskey and raised it to his lips. "Here's to the lady's very good health," he announced.

Since only a churl would refuse to drink to his own mother's health, I joined him. This time the beer tasted even cooler and more refreshing than it had before. As propriety dictated, I pointed to his empty glass. "Fill it up again, friend." When he had replenished his supply, I raised my stein. "To *your* dear old mother's very good health," I said. We drank again, and I set down my stein empty.

"Hey, I've got a mother, too," said a husky voice at my elbow. "You don't want to leave her out, do you?"

I glanced at the woman standing beside me. She had hair of an improbable peach color, rouged cheeks and lips, and powder caked in the creases that webbed her face and neck. She put a hand on my arm. "Be a sport, Charlie. Buy me a drink so I can drink a toast to dear old Mom."

Drawing back slightly, I began, "You'll have to forgive me, but it's a bit early in the day —" then stopped as I heard the gurgle of pouring liquid on the other side of the bar. "No, wait —," I cried, but it was too late; two brimming glasses of liquor now sat side by side on the mahogany, and the bartender was filling my stein from the tap.

"You're a gentleman of sentiment, I can see that," he said as he slapped down the beer in front of me. "Here, Gert, and say thanks to the man." He handed her one of the glasses and raised the other. "To Gert's mother. I never had the privilege of knowing her, but if she's like her daughter, she's every inch a lady."

"Goddamn right," Gert said, tossing down her drink.

I swallowed half my beer and intercepted her empty glass before the bartender could refill it. "I bow to no man in maternal respect and admiration," I said, "but let's call a halt to the toasts while we're still able to remember the ladies we're toasting, for heaven's sake."

The bartender twisted one end of his mustache and regarded me with disappointment, as if I had been tested on the scales of sentiment and found wanting. The woman decided to try another approach. "You're right, big boy," she said, squeezing my arm against her bosom. "To hell with them old bags. Let's drink to *us*."

The bartender's face brightened, and he had two fresh glasses on the bar in a twinkling. "A very romantic thought," he said approvingly as he sloshed in whiskey.

I sighed and raised my stein. "I'd be honored if you both would join me in the absolutely last toast I'll be proposing today, due to the fact that a sudden run on the exchequer has left me entirely without funds and stony broke — unless, of course, either of you dear friends wants to take over the funding, in which case I'll be standing with you until the last cat is hung." I bowed to the peach-haired siren. "To us, my sweet."

She threw down her drink and set down the empty glass. "What a mope," she said, tossing her head and moving off down the bar. The bartender licked a final drop of amber spirits from his mustache and announced, "Two dollars and forty cents, mate."

Mother was right, I thought as I dug two bills and a half-dollar from my pocket. "And cheap at twice the price. Please consider the ten cents change as my tribute to a craftsman at the very peak of his abilities. It was instructive meeting you, my friend." The money disappeared into an apron pocket, and the bartender, arms folded, watched me expressionlessly as I crossed the tiled floor and pushed through the swinging door.

Outside, I continued my pedestrian way north. The sun seemed much brighter than it had ten minutes before, and I squinted my eyes against it. The day promised to be very hot, the two beers were not sitting well on my stomach, and I could feel my headache returning. I continued walking along Wabash until I reached the Palmer House.

I paused just inside the entrance and surveyed the great lobby. Frankel, the house detective, was not in evidence. Skeeter Huff, impeccably groomed and wearing a superbly cut suit of lightweight gray flannel, modestly pin-striped, stood beside the cigar counter, accepting a light from the salesgirl. His expression communicated a chivalrous and slightly condescending approval of the young woman's attention perfectly appropriate to the place and time and their respective stations. He didn't see me.

Behind the registration desk was the clerk who had registered Velma and then unaccountably forgotten it. He was busy with a guest and didn't see me either.

Three bellboys stood against the wall near the desk. I approached the oldest, a man of my age with a boy's body and a roué's face. "Are you the captain?" I asked.

He looked up at me with veiled insolence. "That's right. What can I do for you?"

"I'm looking for one of your bellboys. I wonder if you could tell me whether he's on duty today."

"Yeah? Which one? And what do you want him for?"

"He carried out the bags of a friend of mine yesterday morning — a lady. At eight-thirty or thereabouts. I just want to ask him a couple of questions. If he's got the right answers, he can make a couple of dollars."

His eyes narrowed and he pushed out his pursed lips. "Questions like what?"

"Just questions. How about it?"

He shook his head dubiously. "Lot of people checked out yesterday morning. Lot of women. I'd need something to go on."

I found a dollar bill in my pocket and offered it to him. He tucked it away and rocked back on his heels. "Divorce stuff, huh?" he asked, grinning.

I grinned back. "I guess they don't put much over on you," I said with a touch of admiration.

"Not so's you'd notice it," he agreed smugly. "Okay, what about the lady?"

I described Velma LeSeure again, emphasizing her hair, her figure, and her jewelry. At the mention of her rings he snapped his fingers. "Hey. Now I remember. I took her bags out myself. You're right, it was about half-past eight. Some looker, buddy – no wonder you don't want her to get away."

I felt a sudden surge of excitement. "Was she alone, or was somebody with her?"

"All by her lonesome. I remember, 'cause I thought about trying to make a little time. But I didn't, of course. Can't take no chances of getting reported."

"Did she say anything about where she was going?" He shook his head. "Outside, when she got into her cab – I assume she *did* get into a cab –" He nodded. "– did you overhear the address she gave the driver?" He wrinkled his face in concentration for a moment, then shook his head again. "Are you sure? Think now, man. It's important."

He gave me a look of commiseration, but there was a flicker of derision in his eyes. "I'm sorry, mister, after you give me a buck, and all. But there ain't nothing to tell. She must of told the driver where to go after she got inside. I didn't hear nothing. She climbs in, the cab

104

starts off, and I come back into the lobby. That's all there was to it."

Somehow I didn't believe him. I stared into his face for a moment, trying to think of a question that would elicit a particle of information. I couldn't think of one. "And that's all you can tell me? You're sure?" I finished lamely.

"That's right, mister. I'm sure — *real* sure." Now I was positive there was mockery behind his words, and the realization made me angry. I drew myself to my full height and frowned down two feet at him.

"For your sake, I hope you're telling the truth," I snapped. "The police don't like people who lie about mysterious disappearances."

His mouth widened into a grin, displaying a number of gaps between his teeth. "Well, I wouldn't never do nothing the police don't like. Honest to God. Count on it, mister!"

Just then a bell rang behind us and a voice called, "Front." The bell captain's eyes held mine a moment before he said, "I'll take this one," and pushed past me toward the registration desk. The two bellboys who remained standing against the wall regarded me silently, their expressions wary.

"Well, you heard that," I growled at them. "I don't suppose either of you birds want to tell me your boss is a liar? No, I didn't think you would."

Turning away from them, I saw that Skeeter Huff was no longer at the tobacco counter. I located him half concealed behind a newspaper, not far from the Monroe Street entrance. I wove my way toward him, stepping carefully around the intervening feet, and only stumbling, and then intentionally, when I reached his brilliantly gleaming oxfords. He dropped his paper to glare in wordless outrage, first at his smudged shoeshine and then at me. I brushed an imaginary eyelash from my cheek as I sauntered past. A few seconds later I was on the sidewalk in front of the hotel, glancing into shop windows.

I heard footsteps behind me and started to turn. "It's time we got something straight −," I began, and then my words turned to a gasp of pain.

The man behind me was not Skeeter Huff. Skeeter Huff could never have seized my arm with one hand and my belt with the other and lifted me four inches in the air as effortlessly as a boy tossing a ball. The hand on my arm was only to balance me; my full weight was suspended on the crotch of my trousers, which threatened to advance the bifurcation of my legs to a point well up into my abdomen.

"Oh, Christ, would you be cutting a man in two?" I gasped. "Let me down, man, before I split!"

Ty-Ty Davenport studied me like a fisherman debating whether to keep a marginal fish or throw it back into the water. His bushy black eyebrows were knitted in concentration, their wiry fringe almost hiding the asymmetric eyes beneath. His lipless mouth was half open, exposing occasional teeth, and his large nostrils flared hairily.

"Skeeter told you to stay away," he rumbled. "How come you're back here bothering him?"

I waved one hand in a placating gesture. "I'm dying to tell you, if you'll let me down first!"

Skeeter Huff's distinguished head popped around Ty-Ty's great shoulder. "Don't let him get away," he cautioned in a hoarse whisper. "Teach him a lesson. Show him why he shouldn't mess with us."

Oblivious to the curious stares of passersby, Ty-Ty continued to suspend me in the air as he considered his partner's words. "What about it, Moretti, you want I should bounce you a little?" he asked thoughtfully.

"Put me down, man! You're attracting too much attention. Put me down and I'll explain everything!"

He thought about it for another few moments and then slammed me down on my heels.

"All right, let's hear it," he growled.

I gestured toward Skeeter Huff, who was cautiously positioned behind Ty-Ty. "It's your friend the Senator, there. Who would believe such a distinguished citizen, such a Man To Be Reckoned With, would play the deadbeat and welsh on a fifty-dollar bet?" I shook my head regretfully. "And when I brought the matter up, he made no effort to settle his debt like an honorable man. Instead, all he could think about was concealing the facts from you, Ty-Ty. He seemed to think it was more important to keep you from hearing about it than it was to pay me my money." I gave Skeeter a stern and virtuous glare.

Without releasing me, Ty-Ty grasped his colleague by a pin-striped gray flannel arm. "You welshed on a bet to Moretti? Why didn't you tell me that?"

"That's not what he's been yapping about! It's some damned chippie he's looking for! He keeps coming around asking questions and making trouble, and I just didn't want him to mess *us* up, that's all!"

Ty-Ty frowned, and his brief forehead corrugated in thought. "What are you talking about? What chippie? And who's he making trouble for?"

Skeeter and I both started to answer, but Ty-Ty silenced me with a bone-crushing squeeze of the left biceps. Skeeter leaned close to him and began to whisper in his ear. Ty-Ty listened in silence, his mismatched eyes resting broodingly on my face. After fifteen seconds Ty-Ty interrupted by asking, "Who?" Skeeter leaned closer and continued for another ten seconds. Then Ty-Ty nodded and released the pin-striped arm. He said to me, "Forget the woman, Moretti. Skeeter will pay you your fifty bucks, and you won't come back here no more. Not if you want to keep walking around. Pay him, Skeeter."

"The whole fifty?" Skeeter asked in a shocked voice.

"The whole fifty," Ty-Ty repeated inexorably. As Skeeter produced a gleaming snakeskin wallet from his breast pocket and withdrew bills from it, Ty-Ty said to me, "Take it. Now you got no more business here. Good-bye, Moretti."

I stuffed the money in my pocket. "You wouldn't consider giving me that name that Skeeter just whispered in your ear, would you?"

Ty-Ty drew a deep breath, and his body seemed to expand before my eyes. "Good-bye, Moretti," he repeated. "You take good care of yourself now. Real good care. Then you'll get back to New York in one piece. Maybe."

I decided that further attempts at persuasion were unwarranted. I nodded and smiled. "Whatever you say, Ty-Ty. You're a man who knows his own mind, and I for one would never dream of letting any disagreement come between us. Thank you for the fifty, Skeeter, it's a great pleasure doing business with you. A very good day to you both." I gave them a cheery wave and walked briskly away from them down the crowded sidewalk. At the corner I looked back. Since I couldn't see them, I deduced they had returned to the hotel.

It was time for me to go out to Washington Park.

6

How I Formed an Alliance with a Bluestocking

I didn't see Boz Markey either at the paddock or the betting ring, and so concluded that he was at his apartment nursing the aftereffects of his evening's debauchery at Billy Boyle's, or wherever he had subsequently continued his carousing. As a matter of fact I was a bit relieved at his absence; I had bought all the information I needed from him at "prevailing rates," and didn't feel up to a repetition of the bibulous camaraderie he seemed to inspire in me. But on the other hand I wondered what his comments would have been when I described my encounters with the thugs with the ice pick and ball bat, Detective Arbuckle, and Ty-Ty Davenport.

At the betting ring I discovered that the odds on the two favorites in the American Derby, Mustafa and Home Free, were still eight to three and five to one respectively. Glenlivet, who ranked third in the betting, was now quoted at twelve to one.

I wondered again at the short odds on Mustafa. Part of the reason, I decided, must have to do with the reputation of the jockey, Sparrow Simpson. Simpson was known throughout the racing profession as a man to bet on at the track and to avoid at all other times, due to a constant compulsion to win at every activity he engaged in. Owners and trainers said he would kill his horse or himself to win, which was doubtless the reason he had no more mounts than he had — not everybody wants his horse ridden to death in every race; second-place and third-place money can also be attractive.

But Simpson's obsession was even less pleasant in his personal life. There were many stories of scenes in restaurants, saloons, and gambling halls — waiters abused for insufficient deference, drinking companions attacked for an imagined slight, women insulted and even struck for looking with favor on other men — particularly if the other men were of normal size. No, Sparrow Simpson was a person most sensible people avoided, if they were offered a choice in the matter.

What does this tell me about the heavy early betting on the derby? I asked myself. That the consensus believes that Mustafa *can* win, and that, with Simpson up, he *will* win — because it is inconceivable that Simpson could ride a winner in any other manner than to win?

"Of course," I mused aloud, "having a jockey like Sparrow up on Mustafa would make everyone think the race was straight, whether it was or not." *Now what makes me say that, I wonder.*

Between the third and fourth races I saw a face I recognized in the passing crowd. It was the man I had met in Anton Birkmann's box, the carefully handsome Mr. Schacter, his silver hair curling immaculately over his forehead, and his lips barely curved in a smile, expressing polite disdain for the two-dollar bettors around him.

Remembering his cavalier mispronunciation of my name the first time we met, and because I had nothing better to do until the next race, I decided to approach him with the most irritating questions I could devise. He was eight or ten feet ahead of me as we approached the paddock. I walked briskly to catch up, but before I could reach him he turned to the left and continued his way along the paddock rail, paying no attention whatever to the horses parading around the cinder oval.

The crowd thinned out as he approached the far end of the paddock. Suddenly he stopped, and something about the tenseness of his body caused me to turn away from him and inspect the nearest horse with apparent concentration.

From the corner of my eye I saw him turn and study the faces of the people closest to him. When he was satisfied that he was not under observation, he cut diagonally across the walk to the rear of the grandstand and passed around behind it.

I hurried after him. As I rounded the corner of the grandstand I stopped dead in my tracks and pulled back against the side of the building. Schacter was standing with his back to me, talking with two other men. One was the swarthy southern European who had collected Vannatta's bet for him and gone in quest of a doctor for Alderman Coughlin; the other was his associate, the plug-ugly in the checkered suit. Razor and the Loogan, if memory served.

I drew back until my body was concealed by the corner of the grandstand, and watched them as they conversed, or rather as Schacter and Razor conversed, since the Loogan contented himself with chewing a toothpick and staring straight ahead through half-closed eyes. Schacter ran one hand through his silver hair and shook his head, and Razor leaned toward him and poked him in the chest with his forefinger. Razor was grinning maliciously, and as he spoke, his good eye glittered like a polished chip of brown glass.

Schacter shook his head again, this time

turning his profile to me. I pulled back instinctively, and my sudden movement must have registered in the periphery of his vision, for he turned and stared directly in my direction. Nothing of me but one eye and a couple of square inches of cheekbone showed around the corner, but that was enough to cause Schacter to start toward me.

Perhaps my recent experiences had made me jumpy, but I had no desire to conduct an interview behind the grandstand. I headed back into the crowded paddock as fast as I could walk.

I didn't glance over my shoulder until I was back by my seat in the stands, safely surrounded by spectators on all sides.

There was no sign of Schacter, Razor, or the Loogan. I had no idea whether they had identified me or not – and I wondered why I hoped so much they had not.

I watched the next two races from the grandstand and then walked to the clubhouse in hope of either an interview or a drink. My headache, which had been waiting in the wings since morning, now moved to center stage and began performing the prologue of *I Pagliacci*, complete with bass drum. I found no one I wanted to interview, and the drink I bought myself had no effect on the throbbing inside my skull. I closed my eyes and rested my head on my hand for a moment. My mouth tasted like sulfur and burnt ashes. *I don't even think another drink would help me today,* I thought dismally.

The balance of the day's races passed at a leaden gait. I made my notes dutifully, spoke to no one, and at the conclusion of the last race stuffed my notebook in my pocket and joined the crowd leaving the park. But instead of heading east toward the lake, I turned south. At Sixty-third Street I turned right and crossed Grand Boulevard. Two blocks farther, at Indiana, I caught a streetcar that took me west on Sixty-third, past State and Lasalle and Wentworth, to Wallace, where I got off.

H. H. Holmes's pharmacy was two doors from the corner. It occupied the first floor of a small brick two-story, and the sign in the clean plate-glass window read,

QUALITY DRUGS

Prescriptions Filled
Rest assured — we are worthy of your trust

H. H. HOLMES, PROP.

When I pushed the door open a bell tinkled

at the rear of the shop, and a woman seated at a small desk against the side wall glanced up from the account ledger open before her. "Yes?" she asked politely, but with a trace of petulance.

She was a comfortable-looking woman, somewhere around forty, with a snub nose and a pretty mouth, and the beginning of a double chin. Her bosom was the handsomest I'd seen since Velma LeSeure's proud elevation.

"Good afternoon to you, ma'am," I said with an appreciative smile. "I'm looking for Mr. Holmes, and I wonder if you could tell me where I could find him."

"Mr. Holmes? What do you want to see Mr. Holmes about?" Her slightly protuberant eyes narrowed, and she sat up straighter in her chair.

"Why, he was good enough to give me some medicine for a headache the last time I saw him, and it did such a job for me I was hoping he could whip me up another batch." I broadened my smile. "The last time the prescription was on him, but this time I'll be glad to pay the tariff, whatever it is."

"Oh." She looked at me for a moment in silence before she pushed back her chair and rose. "He's in the back. I'll ask him to come out and talk to you."

"Don't bother, Minnie, I'm on my way," cried a mellifluous baritone from the rear of the shop. "I heard the bell when the gentleman entered."

Holmes was in his shirtsleeves, his vest was open, and his cuffs were turned up. As he approached he brushed his hands together, creating a small cloud of white powder. A lock of hair hung over his high forehead. The welcoming smile he gave me contained interest, but no recognition. "You say you want a prescription filled, sir? Delighted to oblige. What prescription would that be?"

"It was something for a headache. Yesterday morning, at the White City. You and I had just paid a visit to —"

"— to one of the unique educational and cultural exhibitions on the midway," Holmes finished quickly, as his blue eyes flicked to the lady behind the desk and then back to me. "Of course I remember. We were discussing some of the philosophical implications of the exhibit, and you complained of a particularly painful headache. Fortunately I had a twist of one of my anodynes with me —" He smiled at the woman self-deprecatingly. "You know how I am, Minnie, always walking around with my pockets stuffed with medicines, like some kind of pharmacological Good Samaritan in search

118

of a sufferer —" His twinkling eyes returned to me. "So, my friend, you found my formulation efficacious. I'm delighted."

"So much so I came ten blocks out of my way to look you up, Mr. Holmes. And as I told the lady here, I'm not asking for any free samples. I'll be glad to pay the full price for a refill."

"Well, the laborer is worthy of his hire, as the Good Book says. I don't expect I'll bankrupt you." He put his hand lightly on my arm. "It will just take me a minute or two. You keep Minnie here company, and I'll be back in a jiffy."

Moving silently in a pair of gray felt slippers, he disappeared behind a tall counter topped by a row of apothecary jars. After a moment I heard the sounds of clinking glass and rustling paper. I cleared my throat.

"Ah — Mrs. Holmes, is it? This is a nice place you have here, Mrs. Holmes."

She shook her head and advanced her lower lip slightly. "Williams," she said.

"I beg your pardon?"

"Williams is my name. Not Holmes — Williams."

I couldn't tell if she was complaining or merely stating a fact. "Oh, sorry. Well, tell me, Miss Williams, what do you think of the Exposition? Being this close to it, I'd guess you get over there all the time."

She sniffed. "Well, you'd be wrong. I've never been there, and I don't expect I ever will be."

"Really? Why is that?"

Her eyes bulged angrily at me, and her bosom swelled as she drew a deep breath. "There are some people that don't need to spend their money looking at hussies wiggle their naked stomachs in public," she said loudly.

"Hussies wiggling their stomachs?" I repeated with a frown. "Why would they want to do that?"

"Because men pay them to, and men are shameless, corrupt animals!" she snapped. "I suppose you've never heard of Little Egypt?"

It seemed to me the rustling behind the apothecary jars had stopped. "Little Egypt?" I repeated. "Why, yes, I believe I've heard her name. Doesn't she perform some kind of historical or traditional dance? Must be fascinating to students of Near Eastern culture."

"Culture? If that's culture, then bawdy houses are museums! It's lewdness, that's what it is! And the men who pay to see it are no better than adulterers!" She narrowed her eyes as a new thought struck her. "You sure you weren't watching her wiggle her stomach the other day?"

"Absolutely not! I'm a stranger to your city, Miss Williams, and it was me first visit to the Exposition, and I was in the Hall of Transportation studying the flying machines when this terrible headache came upon me and practically stretched me moaning on the floor, which it surely would have done if Mr. Holmes hadn't seen my distress and come to my rescue, for which I am profoundly grateful."

She pursed her lips. "The Hall of Transportation?"

"The Hall of Transportation, indeed. And a very educational place it is, Miss Williams. I'd be pleased to suggest it to your attention, if you decide to visit the White City yourself before it closes."

Behind the apothecary jars the rustling and clinking was again audible. A few moments later Holmes reappeared. He was holding a paper twist similar to the one he had given me the previous day. "Here you are, my friend. The mixture as before. I trust it will prove equally effective."

I took the twist. "How much do I owe you, Mr. Holmes?" I asked.

"Seventy-five cents will be adequate, sir." He accepted my dollar bill and handed me back a quarter. "Would you like to take that right this minute?" he asked solicitously.

"I surely would, if it wouldn't be an imposition."

"Then come with me, and we'll get you a glass of water." He took my elbow and escorted me behind the counter with the apothecary jars. The room-sized space contained a deal-topped worktable crowded with apothecary scales, retorts, and other paraphernalia, a straight kitchen chair and a threadbare armchair, a small bookcase, and a wall lined with open shelves full of tins and bottles. There was a sink in the corner. Gesturing toward the armchair, Holmes filled a water glass from the faucet and handed it to me. "Here, this will wash it down," he said. "Salud!"

"Salud!" I echoed, and then swallowed the white powder and followed it with half a glass of water. The bitter aftertaste was more noticeable than it had been the first time — no doubt due to the substitution of water for the original pilsner, I thought. I sighed, closed my eyes, and prepared for the medicine to do its work.

"I must thank you for your tact, my friend," Holmes said in a low voice. "It wouldn't have done for Minnie to think our meeting had taken place at the Streets of Cairo. For some reason she's formed an unreasoning hostility to the performances there."

"I gathered that. In the light of which I can't

help wondering whether you're still hoping Little Egypt will decide to take up residence with you."

He blinked. "I beg your pardon?"

"Yesterday you told me you knew her, and you hoped she would move in to the house you own across the street. I was impressed."

He frowned and twisted one end of his mustache into a point. "I told you that, did I? Fehreda Mahzar — a lovely, lovely person. Umm. Well, I doubt that eventuality will come to pass, my friend. What with one thing and another, it doesn't seem to be in the cards."

I said I was sorry to hear it, and he nodded gravely. I put my head back and felt the knotted muscles at the base of my skull loosen, and the pressure behind my eyes abate. "Ahh, that's better!" I sighed. We sat in silence a moment, and then, to keep the conversation going, I asked, "I don't suppose you have much trouble renting out your rooms now that the Exposition's on?"

"Oh, I manage to find as many tenants as I want. I don't need to keep it packed to the ceiling — the money's not really that important to me. I'm more interested in having congenial spirits there."

"Like Fehreda," I said.

He cleared his throat. "How's the head, Mr.

— I'm sorry, but I'm afraid I don't remember your name."

"Moretti — Paddy Moretti. And the head feels wonderful. Like it's gone away somewhere, which is the best thing for both of us." I stretched my arms and legs, luxuriating in a newfound feeling of release. I seemed to be floating above the chair, supported on a cushion of air. Lazy thoughts flitted through my mind: Little Egypt moving into Holmes's building, Alison Markey searching for three young women who had come to her for help, Velma LeSeure leaving her room at the Palmer House without a word . . . Without knowing why, I said with a kind of childlike solemnity, "Boz Markey says disappearing women aren't news in Chicago."

"What's that?" Holmes's voice seemed to come from some distance away.

"My friend Boz Markey. He says there are hundreds of girls who come here to make their fortunes and are never heard from again. Isn't that sad? And it's even worse because of the Exposition. I hope Little Egypt doesn't disappear." I opened my eyes and looked at him, sitting in the kitchen chair by the deal worktable, regarding me with a thoughtful expression on his face. "Not like the other girls."

"What other girls?" he asked easily.

I waved one hand and closed my eyes again. "Those girls Alison was helping. They were whores, but they were going to quit and live decent lives. Isn't that ironic? Disappearing just when they were turning over a new leaf. Terrible."

"Terrible," Holmes agreed.

"My girl disappeared, too. Right out of the Palmer House. Somebody else was in her room. They said she hadn't even left me a note." I was suddenly distressed, and rolled my head from side to side. "But disappearing women aren't news in Chicago."

"But you're interested in those women, you and your friend Boz?" Holmes asked in a sympathetic voice.

"Oh, yes. Boz is going to help find out what happened to them. Boz is a good reporter when he's not drunk. He knows who to ask." I opened my eyes again and looked up at the ceiling, which seemed misty. "Is this the same medicine you gave me last time?"

"Doesn't it feel the same?"

"It feels different. It feels . . ." I giggled. "It feels better. Whee! Like I'm floating!" I turned to look at him. "It *is* different, isn't it?"

He shrugged. "Perhaps a little. But as long as it takes your headache away —" His fingers tapped lightly on the deal table. "Your friend

Boz. Who's he going to ask about the disappearing women?"

"Some woman who thinks she's the Queen of the Tenderloin. Boz says she's half crazy, but nobody knows which half. I forget her name." Suddenly I felt a pang of impatience. Why was I wasting my time in the back of some druggist's shop on the South Side, when Boz and I had work to do downtown? My headache was gone what else was keeping me here? I shook my head to clear it and straightened up in my chair. "Which reminds me, Mr. Holmes, it's time for me to be on my way. So I'll be thanking you kindly for your ministrations, and heading back to the marts of trade."

He rose with me. "You're sure you don't care to rest for a few minutes, Mr. Moretti? It's really no bother —"

"Not a bit of it. I've taken up too much of your time already." I took a step toward the front of the store and then stopped to check my balance, which seemed slightly unsteady. "Your powders pack a mean wallop, Mr. Holmes."

He asked me again to rest a few more moments, and I refused. We walked into the front of the shop. The woman was sitting where we had left her, bent over the account book. "And good day to you, madam," I said. She looked up quickly. The expression on her face was compounded of watchfulness and disdain. Her lips were parted, and I could see the pink of her tongue. "Good day," she said huskily.

Holmes accompanied me to the street door and held it open. I paused on the stoop and nodded toward the house directly across the street — a rambling two-story frame building with a surprising number of dormers, chimneys, and bay windows, an abundance of gingerbread, and a crenellated tower in one corner. It was surrounded by a grassless yard strewn with scraps of wood and tar paper, and conveyed an impression of raw pretentiousness-on-the-cheap.

"Is that your place?" I asked.

Holmes nodded. "A rather impressive addition to the neighborhood, you must admit," he said proudly. With a quick glance at me he added, "Perhaps you'd care to reconsider your decision about taking a room there, Mr. Moretti. You'd be in walking distance of Washington Park, and I'd be glad to make you excellent terms . . ."

"Thank you, no, Mr. Holmes, I'm snug enough where I am, and I'll only be in town for two or three more days. It wouldn't be worth the bother." I put out my hand. "But thank you for the kind invitation, sir. Maybe next time

I'm in Chicago I can arrange it. And thanks particularly for your marvelous medicine. It's made a new man of me."

We shook hands, and I walked off toward the lake. At the corner I glanced back. Holmes was still standing in his doorway, watching me. I waved, and after a moment he waved back.

As I approached the Tuscany Hotel I saw a figure I recognized leaning in a doorway across the street. It was a man whom I had last seen holding a cut-down baseball bat, while his companion brandished an ice pick beside my bed.

I was passing the open door of a butcher shop. Without a moment's hesitation I entered and then turned to inspect the street through the grimy plate-glass window. Immediately I saw the ice pick man; he was farther down, squatting against the wall of a Chinese hand laundry and honing his favorite weapon on a whetstone. There were two more men beyond him who seemed to have little reason for being on the street, one turning the pages of a newspaper, the other inspecting an assortment of hardware in a shop window. *And how many on this side of the street?* I wondered.

Behind me the butcher asked, "And what'll it be for you today?" I turned and pretended to inspect the meats displayed on the countertop. I poked at a scrawny chicken, brushed a fly off a stack of pork chops, sniffed a pinch of sausage. "I don't know, man — most of it looks either dead too long or hardly dead at all," I said doubtfully. "Don't you have anything sort of *middling* deceased?"

This resulted in an outraged rebuttal, during which I tried to sort out my situation. The approaches to the hotel were watched, in sufficient force to suggest that the purpose of the watchers might be more than the gathering of information — that it might be, in fact, either my abduction or worse. Under the circumstances, a rapid withdrawal was indicated.

I pointed to the sausage, which was gray in color and of a gelatinous consistency. "Scoop me up a pound of that. I'm sure it'll taste grand." As he made me a package of the stuff I dug a quarter from my pocket and handed it to him. "You mind if I use the back way out?"

He tucked the coin in a pocket of his stained apron and handed me six cents change. "Why?" he asked suspiciously.

"An affair of the heart, my friend. There's a husbandly fellow out there that wants to meet me just as much as I *don't* want to meet him. A man of the world like you will appreciate my situation." I gave him a wink and trotted around behind the counter and through the back room that confirmed everything the merchandise on the counter had suggested.

In the alley I deposited my sausage with two doubtful cats and walked briskly eastward toward State Street, where I caught a car heading north. After changing cars, twice, I arrived at Huron Street thirty minutes later.

I could hear voices arguing inside as I knocked on Boz Markey's door. A moment later the door swung wide and I found myself looking into the face of Alison Markey. She was just as thin-lipped and angry-eyed as she had been before. "Oh, God! Now what do *you* want?" she cried in a tone of desperation.

I smiled in what I hoped was a conciliatory manner. "Well, if it's not too much trouble, miss, I was hoping I might have a word with your brother. And" – I held up my hands, palms toward her – "I swear there's not a solitary drop of whiskey on me person, inside or out."

Her expression didn't soften. "Well, you can't have a word with him. Nobody can. He's under doctor's orders to stay in bed and rest. So if you'll excuse us, Mr. –"

"Moretti, miss. What do you mean, he's under doctor's orders? Is he sick?"

"Sick? It's a miracle he's not dead! Knocked

down in the street, stepped on by a horse, and run over by a wagon — they say God watches out for fools and drunkards, and I believe it!"

Boz Markey's voice came from the bedroom. "Is that the Moretti? Then hurry up and search him for concealed spirits and send him back here, sissie!"

"I will not! If you want to talk to him, you can meet him in some saloon in two weeks! I don't intend to be a party to your irresponsible self-destruction!"

"Alison," Boz's voice growled, "if you don't let him in here instantly, I'll get out of this bed and waltz out there on my points!" There was a moment of silence, then: "All right, I warned you!" followed by the opening measures of "The Dying Swan" theme, determinedly off-key.

"No! Stop! You — you —" At a loss for words, Alison surrendered. Stepping back from the doorway, she gestured to me angrily to enter. Her color was high and her lips were narrowed to a knife edge. "Very well, come in, then. You can only stay for five minutes. Try not to do him any more damage than you have to."

I went into the bedroom. Boz was stretched out in a canopied double bed with a sheet up to his chest. His left arm was in a splint, and there were bandages around his head and under his chin. The small area of his face that showed was swollen and discolored. He looked past me to Alison. "I wasn't really going to dance," he said. "Not to Tchaikovsky. He's *much* too sentimental."

"Oh, be still," she snapped. "Five minutes, that's all. I'll be in the front room." She closed the door forcefully behind her.

Boz and I looked at each other. "Well, Paddy," he said.

"Well, Boz," I answered.

"I suppose you think this is attributable to demon rum," he said.

"Isn't it?" I asked.

"If pigs can fly," he growled. "Paddy, that goddamned beer wagon came up on the sidewalk to get me! Right here on Huron Street, not half a block from my apartment — and me as sober as the day I was christened."

I sat down on a straight chair beside the bed and regarded him thoughtfully. "That's mighty suggestive," I mused.

"How so?"

"Because a fellow with an ice pick and some friends of his were waiting for me outside my hotel not an hour ago."

"The hell you say!" He struggled toward a half-sitting position, resting his weight on his good arm. The exertion drained the blood from his face, turning his complexion grayish-green. "We better compare notes while we still can."

I told him about the nocturnal visitors in my hotel room, and about my unsatisfactory attempt to report the event to the police this morning. Boz listened intently, interrupting with questions about the appearance of the two thugs. When I mentioned Detective Arbuckle, he made me repeat the name, and then shook his head in concern. "Arbuckle – I don't like that," he muttered.

"Why? Because the man doesn't give a tinker's damn for a poor visiting civilian in trouble?"

"No, because normally the man *would* give a tinker's damn. Arbuckle's no knight in armor, but he's as straight as any officer on the force, for whatever that's worth. On his own, it's hard to imagine him acting that way."

"Well, he did."

"I believe you. That's what bothers me." He sighed and lowered himself back to the horizontal. "Jesus help me, I'm one big sore from my head to the bottom of my feet. Two ribs broken – I'm bandaged up like a mummy – and God knows what unspeakable things have happened to my liver and lights. Would you have the common decency to fetch me the bottle you'll find under the dirty laundry in the bottom drawer of that bureau there?"

I rummaged through his soiled linen and produced a pint of rye whiskey, uncorked it, and handed it to him. He raised his head from the pillow and swallowed two or three ounces, then motioned for me to recork the bottle, which he concealed beneath the sheet. "Ahhh. It's barely possible I may live," he sighed.

"What did you do today that brought the beer wagon down on you, Boz?" I asked impatiently, for I expected Alison to come back and escort me from the sickroom at any minute.

He replied that he had asked a number of reporters at the *Tribune* if they had recently run into any unusual female disappearances, or more than the usual number of ordinary ones. Their answers had varied; some said yes, some said no, and some looked nervous and answered ambiguously. Then his editor had called him in and told him firmly to cover his assignments and forget about chasing will-o'-the-wisps on *Tribune* time. Boz had accepted the order, but during the rest of the day had continued to press his inquiries with policemen, prostitutes, pimps, bail bondsmen, saloonkeepers, and anyone else likely to be in possession of information.

"And there's no doubt about it, Moretti —

women are disappearing in Chicago at an almost newsworthy rate," he said.

"But what about the beer wagon? Who put them onto you? Do you have any idea?"

"Not a glimmer. Of course, various possibilities suggest themselves." He closed his eyes and groaned, and fumbled under the sheet for his bottle, which he uncorked with his teeth. When he had assuaged the pain and reconcealed the bottle, he continued with more animation: "Look, Paddy. The men in your room last night were two of the leading lights of the Quincy Street Gang. The lad with the ice pick is Johnny Dee, and the punch-drunk batsman is Louis Rabshaw. They do contract work for anybody who pays their fees, which are quite moderate. I didn't get a look at the fellow driving the beer wagon, but I wouldn't be surprised if he was another Quincy boy — it's their style of approach. They often arrange their murders to look like accidents; that way the police are saved the embarrassment of having to investigate them.

"All right, let's assume the Quincys are working for someone. As far as we know now, it could be anybody. But we do know *who* they're after — us — and *why* they're after us — because we're nosing around in the disappearances of some women."

"Of too many women," I pointed out.

"That's right, of too many women. I concede that. It's the volume of disappearances that's important. If this business turns out to be news, which I consider possible, but still unlikely, it'll be because of the sheer number of missing women." He pulled down on his purplish lower lip with his good hand. "From what I heard today, we may be talking about scores of them."

"Well, you told me that every week since the Exposition started, two- or three-dozen women have disappeared," I said.

"I'm talking about a good many more than that. I'm talking about half again as many as the highest normal estimate would suggest!"

The door opened and Alison Markey strode purposefully into the bedroom. She looked at me with dislike. "You've had more than your five minutes. I'm afraid I'll have to ask you to leave now."

Obediently I rose to my feet. Boz, however, struggled back up on his elbows to protest. "Sis, will you kindly transport your medical virtuosity out into the front room again? I'll tell you when we've finished our discussion."

Alison raised her chin, closed her eyes, and sniffed. "I smell whiskey!" she cried, her eyes popping open and fixing on me. "You've brought whiskey into this house! My brother may be at death's door, and you've brought whiskey to him! Get out!"

I glanced questioningly at Boz and saw that he had no intention of correcting this misapprehension; he intended to sacrifice me to protect the bottle under his sheet. I nodded to him gravely to let him know I understood. "Very well, Miss Markey, I will leave. But before I go" — I leaned over the bed and lowered my voice — "Boz, what if the Quincys come back here to finish the job?"

"I sent word by the doctor to a bruiser in Circulation who owes me a favor. He'll be here in ten minutes. Don't worry about me. But give a thought to yourself." His eyes held mine for a moment, then he sighed heavily and turned his face toward the wall.

I preceded Alison into the living room. The heroic statue behind the sofa was still flaunting its phallic prowess. *I wonder what she thinks each time she sees that barbarous thing,* I thought irrelevantly. I turned to her to make my goodbyes. "I'm sorry for your troubles, Miss Markey —," I began.

She interrupted coldly. "You may save your sympathies, Mr. Moretti. I consider that the profligate habits in which you and your friends indulge are the cause of my brother's misfortune. And when I think that you would sneak your vile spirits into the very sickroom of an injured man —"

"Now, just a minute, ma'am! You're being a bit unfair to the both of us!"

"Unfair? Do you think yourself qualified to speak to me of fairness?" Her cheeks reddened and her eyes glinted, and a lock of hair fell across her smooth brow. "Is drunkenness fair? Is debauchery fair? Fair to yourself, or your family, or the poor drabs you destroy in your heedless pursuit of sensual pleasure? If I were you, Mr. Moretti, I would omit the word 'fair' from my vocabulary."

I felt my anger rising. "Hold on, now! If you want the truth of the matter, Miss Prim-and-Proper —"

She folded her arms and tilted up her chin. "The truth, Mr. Moretti," she said deliberately, "is not in you. Now leave, if you please."

"I will not! Not an inch will I move until you understand that drink had nothing to do with your brother's accident. He's in that bed because of *you* — because he was trying to find out what happened to those disappearing trollops you were deviling him about!"

She smiled contemptuously. "Men like you will say anything. I pity you, I truly do."

"He spent the day investigating them, asking

questions at the office, talking to the police, digging around on the levee! He was warned away, but he kept on with it! That's why somebody ran him down in the street, just like somebody's looking for me this very minute with the intention of putting an ice pick in my neck!"

The color left her cheeks. She stared at me wide-eyed. "What are you saying?" she whispered.

I felt a pang of regret, but it was too late to stop now. I told her about Velma's unexplained departure and the reactions I had gotten from the hotel staff, the police, and the Quincy Gang when I questioned it; how I had overheard her conversation with Boz the day before, and had been struck by the coincidence of the unexplained disappearances; how we had agreed to coordinate our efforts, with the immediate result of my near-abduction and Boz's injury in a nonaccidental "accident." "So you see, Miss Markey, Boz's and my enthusiasm for strong waters has very little to do with the situation at all."

She had been regarding me with an expression of wonder and chagrin. Now she put one hand on mine and said, "Please forgive me. I had no right to talk to you the way I did. Sometimes I am a foolish and intolerant woman."

Her mouth, I saw, was as soft and full as I had imagined it would be. "Not a bit of it," I said gruffly. "Any lady in your position —" I was very conscious of the pressure of her cool fingers on the back of my hand. "Sorry if I've upset you, but I thought you should know the facts."

She withdrew her hand and gestured toward the sofa. "Won't you sit down, Mr. Moretti? I think we have a good deal to talk about."

I crouched and slid under the plaster of paris progenitor to take my seat, and Alison sat in an armchair facing me. "Tell me to whom my brother talked today, and to whom he was intending to talk," she began.

I repeated what Boz had told me about his activities, and listed the few specific names he had mentioned. "There was an editor who warned him off, but Boz didn't mention his name. And the only person I know he was intending to see was some woman named Bridey Tumulty. Boz called her a blind old beldam who thinks she's Queen of the Tenderloin."

"Bridey Tumulty," Alison repeated. "I know who she is. At Hull-House we've heard a good deal about her. She employed a number of our girls at one time or another. Did Boz say where to find her?"

"No, but we can ask him." I started to rise.

"No! I don't want him bothered anymore! It's

bad enough that he was injured trying to get information for me — and after the terrible things I said to him!" She squared her shoulders and straightened her back, raising her small but perfectly formed breasts into high relief. "I'll find Bridey Tumulty by myself!"

"Glory in the morning! How's an invalid supposed to get any rest in this house!" bawled a voice from the bedroom. "If you're going to gab all night, you might as well come in here to do it!"

I looked at Alison questioningly. She shook her head. "Mr. Moretti's just leaving. You go to sleep!" She lowered her voice and continued: "I'll find out where to look for the woman. You leave now. Tomorrow we'll continue our inquiries."

"We'll continue our inquiries?" I repeated stupidly.

"Certainly we'll continue our inquiries. With my brother confined to his bed, it obviously falls to me to pick up the torch, as it were." Her eyebrows drew closer together as she added sternly, "Unless they've succeeded in frightening you off, Mr. Moretti."

"Now what sort of thing is that to be saying? Frightened me off, indeed!" *They haven't made a bad start, as a matter of fact,* I thought. "No, it's nothing like that. But this is no job for a lady, Miss Markey. Who knows where the Tumulty woman is likely to be? Why, I may have to track her down in a —" I hesitated momentarily, searching for a euphemism.

"Whorehouse?" she suggested matter-of-factly. "Yes, I wouldn't be surprised. If you do, I think you'll be glad you have a woman with you. Men don't have much luck in getting straight answers from prostitutes."

"But — but it's not right for a decent woman — I mean, how could I look your brother in the eye if —" I sputtered to silence in the face of her gently mocking smile.

"My dear Mr. Moretti, do you have the least idea of the problems we deal with every day at Hull-House? A normal day's agenda may include drug addiction, criminal abortion, rape, battery, grand and petty theft, sodomy, vitriol throwing — why, if a crime is listed in the criminal statutes, we see it, and generally on a weekly if not daily basis." Her smile broadened, as if she were narrating a humorous anecdote. "Last week one of my girls was disemboweled by her pro-curer, and it fell to me to replace her organs in her abdominal cavity as best I could before she was taken to the hospital. The week before that —" She stopped, and when she resumed, her smile was gone. "Suffice it to say that the search for Bridey Tumulty should not present any unique embarrassments."

"She's right about that, Moretti," Boz Markey's voice erupted from the bedroom. "You couldn't embarrass Alison with the collected murals of Herculaneum and Pompeii!"

"Be quiet!" Alison ordered. She rose and extended her hand to me. "Could you plan to meet me at Hull-House tomorrow evening around seven? By that time I should have enough information for us to proceed. You do know where Hull-House is, don't you?"

I took her hand and held it as I assured her I knew the location of Jane Addams's celebrated settlement house. Her fingers were long and slender, and her grip was firm. "That's fine. Until tomorrow then, Mr. Moretti."

"Until tomorrow, Miss Markey." Regretfully I relaxed my fingers and allowed her hand to slip away from mine. "Good-bye, Boz!" I called. "Take care of yourself."

"Don't stand in front of any runaway beer wagons!" he called back.

On the stairway I passed a man whose flattened nose and cauliflowered ear suggested that he was the bruiser from Circulation Boz had mentioned. He was a reassuring sight.

7

The Siege of Streeterville

I headed east on Huron, toward the lake. The
moon had just risen, and lay in the sky like a
slice of yellow onion on a cerulean plate. The
lake breeze was cool and fresh, and I breathed
deeply. My thoughts remained on the two
people I had left in the apartment behind me
– the man whose bruised body and broken
arm and ribs testified to the earnestness of our
enemies, and the woman whose presence on
our side seemed to turn these enemies into an
acceptable risk. For a few moments I found
myself inventorying her physical characteris-
tics: her fine chestnut-brown hair, pale skin,
and tawny hazel eyes; the long, finely boned
face; the straight, narrow nose and full mouth;
the slender neck and lithe waist . . .

Moretti, I told myself sharply, *there are appropriate times for all speculations, and this is not
the time for that one.*

Pulling my thoughts back to the immediate
present, I studied the street ahead as I listened

for footfalls behind. The sidewalk that stretched before me to Michigan Avenue was deserted; the puddles of light that fell around the three streetlamps were as still as empty goldfish bowls. Aside from my own footsteps, the only sounds I heard were distant traffic noises, the grunts and grumbles of a great city falling asleep.

But just to be sure, I stopped suddenly beneath the nearest streetlamp and made a show of consulting my pocket watch.

The footsteps behind me, and those across the street, didn't stop until two steps later.

Controlling my instinct to look over my shoulder, I replaced the watch and continued along the sidewalk at a steady pace. Now that I knew what I was listening for, I detected the steps of my followers clearly, even though they attempted to synchronize them to mine.

I resisted the temptation to glance back over my shoulder, but from the corner of my eye I caught sight of the trackers across the street. There were two of them, one tall and narrow-shouldered with a cap pulled down over his eyes, the other chunky and bareheaded. As I watched, my face resolutely pointed straight ahead, they left the sidewalk and began to angle across the street. They were taking long steps that would bring them even with me by the time they reached the curb on my side.

I began to stretch out my own steps, hoping to keep the change gradual and unnoticed. The first of the three streetlamps was directly ahead of me, and a moment later I entered its pool of visibility. *Should I turn and face them here?* I asked myself. *Would they dare attack me in the light?*

Of course they would. Who's to see them? Who would raise an alarm?

Without hesitating I strode through the light-spill into the darkness beyond. Now there were only two streetlamps ahead of me — one on the other side of the street about seventy-five yards ahead, and the second on my side, at the intersection of Michigan Avenue, another seventy-five yards farther. As I had passed under the streetlamp the two men angling toward me had become invisible, but now they reappeared in my field of vision. They were halfway across the street, and only a few paces behind me.

The other followers, the ones directly behind me, should now be moving into the pool of light I had just left. Since I couldn't pretend to ignorance much longer, this was the time for me to look back. I glanced swiftly over my shoulder.

They were silhouetted against the light-spill — three men in a row, one broad-shouldered, thick-necked, with a heavyweight boxer's carriage, one slender and graceful, one dwarfishly short, with hunched shoulders and arms that dangled below his knees. I thought I recognized the first two from my hotel room.

I began to run. Instantly my pursuers did, too, their feet slapping a tattoo on the pavement. The two men in the street were running parallel to me, hoping to pull ahead and then swerve in and cut me off. Behind me pounded the steps of the other three. I couldn't tell if they were closing or not.

In the street the tall man in the cap drew even with me. He ran in a peculiar high-kneed gait with his elbows pumping like pistons, but he was fast. His face was set in an expression of ferocity, with his lips twisted back and his teeth clenched, and his eyes glittering under the bill of his cap. His companion labored a half-dozen steps behind him, breathing in grunts through his open mouth and swaying from side to side with each step.

The steps behind were louder.

The streetlamp on the other side of the street was now abreast, outlining the head and shoulders of the man in the cap in yellow light. He was drawing ahead of me. My pounding heart seemed about to explode in my chest, and I couldn't draw enough air into my heaving lungs. It was fifty more yards to the Michigan Avenue corner, and I saw a carriage pass beyond the streetlamp. *If I can only get to the corner — Oh, God, they couldn't get me then!*

It was at that moment that two more men came around the corner and stood facing me under the lamp.

Involuntarily I broke my stride, and instantly the man in the cap veered toward me. At that same moment I felt a hand clutch at my shoulder. At least one of the pursuers from behind had caught up. I twisted my shoulder forward and drove my legs at an even faster pace. The man in the cap reached toward me; his fingers were only inches from my arm.

I acted without conscious thought. Half turning in midstride, I grasped his wrist and jerked him toward me. Thrown unexpectedly off-balance, he stumbled over the curb and began to fall, both arms thrust in front of him. With a snap of my arm I sent him sprawling behind me. The sound of his body colliding with another and the resulting cries and curses were fierce music to my ears.

I hazarded a glance over my shoulder. Two figures were rolling together on the pavement as two others leaped across them. The man in the cap and the one Boz had called Johnny Dee were out of the running for a few seconds, but three more remained — the batsman Louis Rabshaw, the dwarf who skittered along the sidewalk like a chimpanzee, his knuckles almost scraping the ground, and the other man in the street, puffing and groaning like a leaky engine, but keeping up nonetheless.

And ahead, by the streetlamp, two others —

I tucked my head down against my chest and concentrated on maintaining my speed. The men ahead stood crouched and waiting, one near the inside of the walk and one at the curb. I was twenty yards from the corner — fifteen — ten —

"Get the bastard!" shrieked a voice behind me.

I headed between the two, as they expected me to do, until the last possible moment. Then I suddenly veered to the left, straight at the bruiser on the curb. I stiff-armed him like a college fullback, my palm smacking against his forehead at the instant I leaped into the air. The pivot to my arm served to carry me up and almost, but not quite, past him; unfortunately my right foot connected with his companion's jaw *en passant*.

The three of us hit the sidewalk almost simultaneously, with my other pursuers not more than a second or two behind. I landed on one shoulder and somersaulted forward off the sidewalk into Michigan Avenue.

I was directly in the path of an approaching carriage. For one frozen moment the horse and I stared unbelievingly at each other, and then the horse shied, rearing back with an explosive whinny, as I sprang forward into the middle of the street.

Traffic at that hour wasn't heavy, but there was enough activity to make any sensible person stop and look both ways before hurling himself into the flow. Which my pursuers did — with the exception of the dwarf. He was after me without an instant's hesitation. As I plunged across the avenue he was close behind me, clutching at my feet. I glanced back and was almost overcome by sudden horror: The face that glared at me in a rictus of malevolence had been created for a six-foot man and then attached to a three-foot body; narrow-eyed, heavy-jawed, with a long scoop of a nose, it was the face from a statue on Easter Island.

A carriage whipped past, and I had to pull back to avoid its wheels. In that split second the dwarf's hands clutched my ankle and he gave a cry of triumph. "Got him!" he screamed, his fingers biting into my flesh. "Hang on! We're coming!" called a voice from the curb, and I saw that the rest of the gang were now in the street and approaching at a run.

And so was another carriage. It was bearing down on us at a gallop, no more than twenty feet away.

I spun on my heel and lashed out with my other foot at the dwarf. The side of my shoe struck him on the temple. His eyes widened and his mouth fell open, and he slumped to one side. As his grip on my leg loosened I jerked away and stumbled backward two steps — just far enough to avoid the pounding hooves that slashed down on the twisted figure in the road.

I began running again. Behind me I could hear the mingled cries of my pursuers and the driver and passengers of the carriage: "There he goes! After him!" "You there — wait! There's been an accident!" "Bloody bastard! When I get my hands on him —" "My God — is he dead?" "Stop, you men!" "Somebody find a policeman!" *Under the light — there he goes!*

I was across Michigan Avenue, pounding down Huron Street toward the lake. It was a dark residential street, with the dim shapes of opulent town houses on both sides. There were lights in some of the windows, but the sidewalk was deserted. I could see the end of the street a block ahead: Under the low-riding moon the sand beach that began where the paving ended was modeled by a

151

chiaroscuro of light and shadow.

I threw another glance over my shoulder. Johnny Dee and his thugs were across the avenue, five of them now, all of normal height. They moved after me in a dog-trot; evidently they had concluded that since they had me pinned with my back to the water, breakneck speed was no longer necessary.

I glanced at the houses that lined the street — stone houses, rich men's houses, with locked doors and butlers who took two minutes to unlock them. No, I decided, my chances would be better on the beach, where I could find dunes to hide behind, and shadowy depressions to swallow me up.

I passed the last house, and the sound of my running footsteps changed from the crisp thud of leather against cement to a gritty rasp that told of sand drifted across the pavement. A few steps farther on the street ended with a row of sawhorses. I vaulted one and sank into sand up to my ankles. Recovering my balance, I plowed up the face of the nearest dune, over the moonlit top, and down the far side into the inky depression beyond.

Something struck my legs at knee level and I sprawled on my face. Before I could move, a weight landed on my back, and I felt a hand pressing my head into the sand. A voice whispered harshly in my ear, "Don't make a sound, hear? I'll cut you as soon as look at you!"

I nodded as well as I could, although it's not easy to nod with one's face pressed into the sand. The weight on my back shifted, and I felt a hand probing my pockets. "Let's see what we got here," the voice continued. "A watch, that's good — a bit of change — ah, here's his wallet — and the gentleman's contribution to the cause is" — a pause, then the voice changed to a snarl — "a stinking twenty-four bucks!"

I steeled myself for the blow I expected. Instead, another voice whispered excitedly, "Turk, look! There's a bunch more coming! It's like they're chasing him!"

"What? Where?" The weight on my back shifted, and a moment later my head was rotated forty-five degrees. "All right, you — who are they? Your friends?"

I spat sand from my mouth. "They're after me, trying to kill me! The Quincy Gang!"

"The Quincys? You're crazy! They wouldn't never come here to Streeterville without Cap asked 'em!"

The other voice whispered anxiously, "I dunno, Turk. That looks like Johnny Dee in the middle there. And the big one could be Lou Rabshaw. I think they *are* the Quincys!"

The man on my back swore. "And they're

after you, huh? Well, I don't reckon they're going to get you, not till Cap says so. Come on, get up on your feet!" Seizing me by one arm he dragged me erect, at the same time putting two fingers into his mouth and whistling shrilly.

For the first time I was able to look at them, their heads and shoulders emerging from the pool of shadow into the bright moonlight that flooded over the nearest dune. The man called Turk was as villainous-looking a specimen as you'd see outside an illustration for *Treasure Island* — his lumpy head was completely bald, and gleamed like a wet rock; his right eye was twisted downward by a scar that ran from temple to chin; one of his ears sported a gold earring, which the other never would because it had been whittled down until all that remained was a narrow triangle of cartilage. His companion was a boy of thirteen or fourteen, with shoulder-length blond hair, heavy-lidded eyes, and a pretty mouth that was twisted in an expression of alarm.

"There's five of 'em, Turk," he cried softly in a choirboy voice, "and them Quincys are *mean!*"

Turk chuckled as he dragged me after him through the shadow pool. "Don't you worry, Lamby — ain't nobody going to do nothing until there's enough of us to do it right."

154

Keeping to the shadows, we skirted one dune and crossed the base of another. The sand was loose, and I slipped and stumbled in Turk's wake, falling to my knees and being dragged erect again. The boy followed me, whispering an anxious litany: "I can see them clear now, Turk — that's Rabshaw, all right. He's got that sawed-off ball bat of his — Oh, Jeez, Turk, I think they've seen us — Nobody must have heard you whistle — there ain't going to be nobody to help us — Turk, you won't let them hurt me, will you?" Turk's voice came back in reassuring grunts. From in front of us I could hear the murmur of the waves on the beach.

Then there was another man with us, sliding down a sandhill and taking his position beside Turk. Then, a few moments later, a second and a third. They were an unprepossessing trio — one had brass knuckles over a fist bearing only two fingers, and another had no nose at all — but their presence was immediately reassuring. Counting Lamby, we now outnumbered the Quincys.

Turk took immediate command. Crawling to the top of a dune, he observed the enemy's approach. The Quincys were deployed abreast, in a line fifty feet wide, and were moving directly toward us. The hilly nature of the terrain meant that at any time some of them were clearly visible in the moonlight, while others were hidden from us, and from each other, in the shadows. Turk, in the tradition of Alexander, Hannibal, and Napoleon, chose to concentrate his forces to achieve numerical superiority over a minority of the enemy. He divided us into two groups of three, and each group concealed itself behind a dune and awaited the arrival of one of the Quincys. Thus our total force would envelop only the right flank of the enemy, giving us the opportunity of annihilating it before it could be reinforced.

It worked as well for us as it had for Bobbie Lee at Chancellorsville.

The thin man with the cap, who had run beside me down Huron Street, came wading over the sandy crest and down the slope toward us in the shadows. When he reached the bottom of the dune Turk rose up beside him and wrapped one arm around his neck, Lamby kicked his feet out from under him, and I punched him in the nose. He fell to the sand under all three of us. He was able to get out one bleat of warning — "Johnny!" — before Turk shut off his wind. Lamby applied himself so vigorously to his face and body that I felt justified in crawling out of the writhing mass of arms and legs and placing myself in reserve. Then Turk ended the scrimmage with a booming clout behind the ear, and the thin man lay unconscious in the sand.

From the sounds of the other engagement fifteen or twenty feet away, our forces were carrying the day there as well. In ten seconds the cries, curses, and thuds had subsided into congratulatory whispers.

Then the inevitable counterattack hit.

The remaining Quincys struck our three allies from the flank, and the congratulatory whispers turned back to thuds and curses. Instantly Turk led us to the rescue; we swarmed into the melee and threw ourselves onto the struggling bodies. I found myself on top of Johnny Dee, with one arm around his neck and the other wrestling his right arm behind his back, in case there was an ice pick in it. There wasn't, but I kept him engaged until my ally No-Nose could deliver enough punches to his head and body to render him *hors de combat*. Meanwhile Turk and Louis Rabshaw were struggling over the sawed-off ball bat while the man with the brass knuckles belabored Rabshaw about the ribs and kidneys, and Lamby kicked him in the knees, and our third ally pursued the chunky, bareheaded Quincy around a sand dune and out of sight.

No-Nose and I joined the battle against Rabshaw, but even with five of us against him the man refused to go down. He stood like a Titan in the silvery moonlight, absorbing the blows of fists, brass knuckles, and boots, and striking back with one hand as he tried to wrench his ball bat free with the other. For half a minute we struggled against each other, bound together like the figures in the Laocoön. Then with a roar Rabshaw flung Turk away from him and freed his weapon, which he swung in a savage arc. The club missed Turk by a few inches, but connected solidly with No-Nose's head, tumbling him backward on the sand. The return swing struck me on the right shoulder, spinning me away to land on my knees in the shadow, my arm completely numb.

With a third swing Rabshaw freed himself of Brass Knuckles and Lamby, and immediately scooped up Johnny Dee under one massive arm. Facing us, his club weaving a murderous figure eight in front of him, he backed around the nearest dune.

We let him go. None of us was anxious to continue an engagement we had clearly won, not against such an antagonist as Louis Rabshaw. Instead, Turk decided to collect our prisoners and "let old Cap take a look at 'em."

We had to be content with a single prisoner, however; when we returned to the scene of our first encounter we found that the thin man with the cap had disappeared; likewise the chunky, bareheaded gang member had made good his escape. The Quincy we frog-marched across the beach was the one our three allies had overcome before Johnny Dee's flank attack; he was a lop-eared thug with browridges like an ape, a flat nose, and a receding jaw — Turk recognized him and called him Chimp.

When we had covered a hundred yards of sand I tugged at Turk's sleeve. "We're heading toward the lake," I said. "Where are we going?"

He glanced at me in surprise. "Streeterville — where d'you think?"

"Streeterville?"

"Hush up. We're about there."

From the top of the next rise we could look down on surf rolling and breaking on the beach — and only a few feet back from the water, a dozen shacks and lean-tos. Most of them had lights showing, and there was a bonfire on the open sand.

"Streeterville," Turk grunted. We passed near the bonfire, Turk exchanging greetings with some of the men taking their ease around it, and continued toward the largest shack, a perilous construction of lumber, tar paper, and tin sheets. Turk knocked on the door, and the knock was answered by a summons to enter. Pushing the door open, Turk thrust his prisoner in front of him into the lighted room, and the rest of us followed.

The two occupants of the room sat on either side of a round oak table upon which were spread, among other things, legal documents, newspapers, inkwells and penholders, a wooden decoy duck, three or four empty and near-empty whiskey bottles, a one-armed rag doll, a Colt Peacemaker revolver, a church-warden pipe, a bronzed baby shoe, a satin pillow with the inscription, "Greetings from the Columbian Exposition," a cast-iron penny bank in which a hunter shot coins into the body of a bear, a rattlesnake skin, a knitting bag, a dried corsage, a jar of horehound cough drops, a (presumably human) scalp, and a coal-oil lantern which illuminated this treasure trove and its proud possessors.

The lord of the manor, George Wellington Streeter, called Cap in deference to his erst-while position of captain of a lake excursion boat, was seated to the left of the table; his lady was to the right. They both stared at us imperiously. Cap Streeter was dressed in trousers, shoes, a dickey with a high stiff collar and a cravat held in place by an enormous artificial pearl pin, and a tall beaver hat. His arms were bare from the shoulders down. He appeared to be about fifty years of age; his bushy mustache was shot with gray hairs. His eyes, which glared from either side of a somewhat bulbous nose, were crossed.

His wife Maria, better known as Ma, was a rawboned woman of five foot nine or so, whose expression was as maternal as that of a guard on a Southern prison farm. Her lips were thin, her jaw was broad, and her eyes were so much like ball bearings that one imagined one could hear a metallic clinking when they moved. Only when her gaze turned toward her husband was there any softening of her fierce demeanor.

"Whatcha got there, Turk?" Cap Streeter demanded. "Which it looks to me like somebody I seen once with the Quincys, am I right?"

"That's right, Cap." Turk looked at his prisoner thoughtfully a moment, and then kicked his feet out from under him. The man fell heavily on one hip, and Turk held him down with a hand on the shoulder. "He come in with four others, chasing this guy here." He nodded toward me. "Come right onto the beach. Didn't ask no permission nor nothing. Johnny Dee and Lou Rabshaw was two of them." He went on to explain how he and Lamby had surprised me near the Huron Street barricade and been interrupted in their acquisition of my belongings by the approach of the Quincys. "We asks him if they're his friends, and he says they're trying to kill him. Well, of course we ain't going to let no South Side bozos sashay out on our beach without you give the nod, Cap, let alone do their heavy work out here, so I whistled up Knucks and Dingo and Cincinnati, and we bushwhacked 'em." He glanced at me and added grudgingly, "This guy, he helped some."

I bobbed my head to Cap and Ma. "A pleasure it was to be of assistance. And a pleasure it is to be talking to the famous Cap Streeter and his lovely bride, if I may be so bold."

Streeter and his lady ignored me. As he began to question Turk's prisoner, I inspected him covertly and tried to remember what I had heard about him from local members of the Fourth Estate.

A few years before, Cap Streeter had run his excursion boat aground on a sandbar just south of Chicago Avenue. Instead of floating it off, he decided to live aboard, and built a breakwater connecting the boat to the shore. Immediately the breakwater began to trap sand, and within a surprisingly short time, the sand covered the whole distance from the boat to the shore. Soon Streeter found he had created twenty acres of new beachfront where there had been only restless waves before.

Streeter considered the land his own (with good reason, it seemed to me) and proceeded to sell lots in "Streeterville" to anyone with fifty dollars to spare. Unfortunately the first arrivals were an assortment of derelicts, drunkards, and lamsters who set a social tone for Streeterville that discouraged subsequent investment by more bourgeois buyers. The result, as the years passed, was that Cap Streeter became the *patroon* of a shantytown that defaced some of the most valuable real estate in the country.

I remembered hearing that the financial moguls of the North Side, Fairbanks and McCormick and Potter Palmer, and others of their ilk, upset at the sight of the growing squalor outside their east windows, had sought to have Streeter ousted, but to no avail. The ex-excursion boat captain literally held his ground against police forays and law court finagles, and nothing the merchant princes of Chicago had come up with offered promise of evicting him.

Streeter was interrogating the unfortunate Chimp, while Turk encouraged his response by twisting one hand behind his back. "How come Johnny Dee crossed the barricade? What was he chasing this bird for?" he questioned.

Chimp groaned. "The word came down, that's all I know."

"Come down from where?" He nodded curtly to Turk, who applied increased pressure.

"I don't know! Sweet Jesus, I don't know! Johnny just said we was gonna get him, that's all!"

Streeter turned to his wife thoughtfully. "Which it ain't like the Quincys to come in uninvited. I don't like it, my love. It argufies an upset in the statue quo."

Ma Streeter folded her muscular arms across her bosom and rested her hard eyes on me. "Ask *him*," she said.

Before Turk could decide to assist my memory as he was assisting Chimp's, I cried, "And delighted I am to have the opportunity of putting the smidgen of knowledge I have at your disposal — although the truth of the matter is that I'm as ignorant of the reasons behind this recent brouhaha as a newborn babe."

"And if he's smart," Ma Streeter added coolly, "he'll drop that phony brogue before he makes somebody mad with it."

Acting upon her hint, I gave a brogueless account of Boz's and my enquiries into the disappearance of women in Chicago, and the reaction those enquiries had produced. As I talked, Streeter listened attentively, his eyes focused on the end of his nose. When, in the course of my explanation I mentioned that I was a journalist, he suddenly stopped me.

"And which of the lying, libelous rags do you work for? Which of the robber barons do you kowtow to?" he demanded, his mustache bristling.

"I don't work for any of the Chicago papers. I work for a New York newspaper called —"

"A New York newspaper!" he interrupted excitedly. "You mean you're not under the thumb of any of these plutocratic pimps hereabouts?" I assured him my paper was free of any local control. "Then you could write the truth about Streeterville if you had a mind to — you could tell how these here sneaky horse thieves are trying to take my town away from me!"

"Whatever my paper chose to print," I answered carefully, "you can be sure would be outside the control of any Chicago publishers or politicians." I didn't feel it was necessary to add that the only way Streeterville would ever be mentioned in *The Spirit of the Times* would be if Cap opened a racetrack on the beach.

This information improved my position immediately. Streeter pulled up a chair for me at the table and poured me a drink. Then, while I sipped gratefully and uncritically, he turned to the others in the room. He ordered Chimp's release, instructing him to inform Johnny Dee that any further incursions on Streeterville territoriality would result in serious hostilities. He excused Turk and his associates with thanks, and ordered that he be immediately informed of any further incidents that might occur during the night. Then he poured drinks for his wife and himself and resumed his seat at the table.

"Which it might be of value to you if I was to disperse on the historical rudiments of Streeterville, so to speak," he began, wiping an amber drop from his mustache with the back of his hand. "To look around you at these here rolling sands, lapped by the benevolent waters of the lake and warmed by the refulgent rays of the sun, what unsuspecting visitor could dream this garden spot would never have existed without the vision and resolvedness of George Wellington Streeter?" Ma Streeter coughed dryly, and Streeter gave her a courtly nod and added, "Which is to say, Mr. *and Mrs.* George Wellington Streeter, of course, since what successful man ever got to first base without the sustentation of a good woman?"

Streeter continued to discourse on the origin and growth of his realm, while his wife took tight-lipped sips of whiskey and regarded me coldly. Every so often I tried to interpolate a comment or question about women disappearing in Chicago, but to no avail; Streeter's fascination with his destiny as a real estate entrepreneur, and the machinations of those who would thwart it, precluded any digression. I sat back in my chair and listened with half an ear as the captain brought his narrative up to 1891. *Well, it's better than spending the night on the streets running from the Quincys,* I reflected.

As if that thought had been a catalyst, the door burst open and Lamby stuck his tousled head into the room. "Turk says they're coming back!" he cried. "He says there's about twenty of 'em!"

"Thunderation!" Cap Streeter growled. He fumbled amid the chaos on the table and produced a policeman's billy, the thong of which he looped over his wrist. "No sense of protocol at all! They must want you pretty bad, Moretti." He rose from his chair and started for the door.

"Your coat, George," Ma Streeter interposed as she selected an eighteen-inch knitting needle from the table and threaded it downward through the lapel of her jacket.

Streeter stopped obediently and slipped a suit coat over his dickey and bare arms, pulling the billy through the sleeve. "Why don't you stay here, Mother?" he asked solicitously. "Which there's no reason you should expose yourself to the vicissitudes of this here upcoming adjudication."

Ma Streeter sniffed. "Can't be letting every plug-ugly in Chicago come on the beach without permission. Get a move on, George."

We hurried outside, where Turk and Lamby were waiting with a dozen men. Streeter quickly delegated responsibility to Turk and two other lieutenants, and by the time we moved toward the enemy, our ranks were expanded by another dozen recruits. We moved in three groups. Cap, Ma, and I were in the center, in the largest group, under the tactical command of Turk. The other groups swung wide to left and right, and in a few moments had disappeared from view. The moon was now at its zenith in the sky, but scudding clouds moved across its face, so that the sands were sometimes brightly silvered and sometimes plunged into sudden darkness. Behind us the lake rumbled and sighed.

We slogged across the sand for five minutes before we heard the sudden explosion of curses and cries that announced an encounter on our right flank. Turk led us at a run over the intervening dune at the moment the moon burst out from behind the clouds, and we saw our flanking force engaged in an unequal contest with at least twice as many Quincys.

We struck them unexpectedly, and a minute later our left flank group arrived and added its sudden weight to the battle. This time the strategic picture more closely resembled Second Bull Run than Chancellorsville, but the result was the same: another victory for the Lost Cause.

The battle comes back to me as a series of vignettes, lit by cold white light, sounding of cries and groans, tasting of sand. I see the redoubtable Louis Rabshaw borne down beneath a half-dozen pummeling fists; I see Johnny Dee fighting back-to-back with another Quincy, and then taken from behind when his partner is struck down; I see the thin man in the cap, his face still distorted from our previous encounter, crawling for safety as kicks rain down on his head and torso. I hear the squeal of pain that comes when Ma Streeter's knitting needle finds its first target, and Cap Streeter's roar of outrage as his tall beaver hat flies from his head and is instantly flattened.

It was my intention to stay well back from the center of the fray, shadowboxing furiously to give an impression of bellicosity. Unfortunately an impetuous ally collided with me from the rear and sent me careening into the mélee. Suddenly a huge figure rose in front of me, and a fist like a keg of nails smashed into my cheekbone. My head rocked back, but my body kept its momentum forward, and an instant later I sprawled against the brute and wrapped my arms around him to keep my balance. I gasped for air and was almost overpowered by miasma of garlic, stale sweat, and dental decay. *Ah, this time they've got you for sure, Moretti,* I thought hopelessly as I felt two great hands clamp around my neck.

He bent me backward as he throttled me, and my head must have been within a foot of my feet when his iron grip suddenly relaxed, and he slumped forward on top of me, unconscious.

I gulped air into my lungs and began instinctively to slide out from under his dead weight. Then I thought, *Do you really want to get back up there and have your neck stretched by some other gorilla? Better rest a bit and think about it.*

I shifted my body into a more comfortable position and thought about it for five minutes.

By that time the sounds of battle had changed to post-pugilistic conversation, as the Streetervillians bragged about their prowess and their wounds against an obbligato of moans from the few defeated Quincys who still remained at the scene. Pushing my former antagonist to one side, I struggled to my feet. Cap Streeter, attempting to reshape his beaver hat to its former symmetry, peered at me with cross-eyed concentration.

"Ah, there you are. I was afraid they'd gotten you back." He poked the horizontal body on the sand with his toe. "You picked yourself a big one to tangle with, I'll say that for you."

"He just happened to be the one in front of me," I replied truthfully.

Streeter oversaw the tidying up of the battlefield, directing the Quincys who were ambulatory to carry off those who weren't. As the last two walkers struggled away with my late antagonist, now groaning and rolling his head from side to side, Streeter called after them, "Which you might tell Johnny Dee when you see him that that there example of pure mayhem was accomplished by none other than my friend Paddy Moretti — and there's more on tap from the same source any time he's in the mood."

"Not that he's to take it as a challenge," I added quickly. "Tell him I'm an absolute stranger to hard feelings."

Streeter put one arm around my shoulders and adjusted his bent beaver with the other. "Your Christian sentiments does you credit, but you're wasting them on them vermin." He raised his voice. "Ma! Where are you, Ma?"

"Right here, George." Mrs. Streeter joined us, her knitting needle back in her jacket lapel, and her appearance no more disarrayed than if she had just completed a stroll down Michigan Avenue.

We walked back to Streeterville, with the rest of our forces straggling behind us in the moonlight. When we were seated at the table in Streeter's shack and the captain had poured us fresh glasses of whiskey, he said, "Which, if I'm not mistook, brings the saga of Streeterville up to the year 1891. Listen close, now, Moretti — we're getting to the important part."

It was a long night.

8

The Lady in the Veil

"I know they don't pay you much on that blute you work for, but can't you even afford to get your clothes cleaned? You're lowering the tone of the newspaper business, Moretti, and that's not easy to do!" Detective Arbuckle regarded me sardonically across his bare desk, sandy eyebrows arched over colorless eyes, ears jutting like handles from his pale, freckled face.

"If you'd spent the night in Streeterville, fighting for your life against an army of thugs and murderers, you wouldn't look like you were leading the grand march at the Debutantes' Ball yourself!" It was eight o'clock in the morning, I hadn't had breakfast, and Cap Streeter's whiskey was dying in me.

Arbuckle shook his head. "Thugs and murderers again," he said sympathetically. "You certainly seem to have made some lasting friendships in this city." Before I could reply, he raised his hand. "All right, all right, I'll listen. It's what they pay me for."

I gave him a quick account of the events of the past twenty-four hours, beginning with my discovery that the Tuscany Hotel was under the observation of the Quincys. I hold him how Boz Markey had been run down by a beer wagon in circumstances that could hardly have been accidental, and how Johnny Dee and his men had chased me into Streeterville, and, meeting resistance, had returned with reinforcements and fought a pitched battle on the beach.

"Interesting," he said. "And then after the hostilities you and Cap sat and talked the night away? You must be a hell of a reporter, Moretti — that cockeyed old crock won't give the time of day to any local newspapermen."

"It's because all Chicago newspapers are under the control of plutocratic pimps. Cap Streeter explained it to me."

"He could be right." Arbuckle looked at me thoughtfully a moment, then squared his narrow shoulders and straightened his back. "Well, it was kind of you to drop by, Moretti. If you're ever back in the city again, which might not be the smartest move on your part —"

"Oh, no. No you don't. Not again." I was grimly aware of my returning headache, the dull ache in my thighs from Louis Rabshaw's bat, the throbbing pain in my cheekbone that intensified each time I gritted my teeth, and the other physical reminders of my Chicago lakefront outing. I stood up and leaned toward him across the desk.

"Something more I can do for you?" he asked innocently.

"You can unstick yourself from that chair and come back to my hotel with me, that's what you can do! Saints alive, man, they're waiting for me there! They're lined up along Twelfth Street like the teeth on a buzz saw, and not a one of them that doesn't have blood in his eye! After last night, what do you think they'll do to me today?"

"You want me to escort you to your hotel? Is that it?" Arbuckle frowned, as if trying to make sense out of a wildly nonsensical request. "These people lining the street — you've seen them this morning?"

I gaped at him unbelievingly. "Of course I haven't seen them this morning! Do you think I'm crazy? I came straight here from Streeterville!"

"Then how do you know they're there?" he asked patiently.

"Why, where else would they be? They were there yesterday, waiting for me. They don't know I spotted them — they picked me up later on Huron Street, when I left Boz Markey's place. So they'll be outside the Tuscany Hotel waiting for me to come back, right this minute!"

"Assuming they are, what do you want from me?" Arbuckle asked.

"What I'd really like is for you to descend on Twelfth Street with a half-dozen Black Marias, and round up the whole bloody bunch, and lock them up till after the derby!" He waited in silence, so I went on: "But I'll settle for you walking to the hotel with me and waiting while I change my shirt, and letting them see us together. And maybe if you feel like it, you might drop a word to the effect that the police department has taken a fatherly interest in my welfare. You could tell Johnny Dee you'd be personally upset with him if anything happened to me."

"I could, could I?" Arbuckle shook his head. "But that wouldn't be true, Moretti. You wouldn't want us to lie to the public, would you?"

"Don't think of it as a lie – think of it as a slight modification of the truth. My God, Arbuckle," I cried, "this is my life I'm talking about! Is it my blood you're wanting on your hands?"

The detective sighed and rose to his feet. "All right, Moretti. I'll walk over to your hotel with you. If we see any of these thugs and murderers of yours, maybe I'll even exchange a few words with them. Call it special attention to out-of-state visitors. Come on."

He led the way into the crowded hall and turned toward the street entrance. For a short, skinny, unathletic man he walked briskly, with unusually long strides; although almost a foot taller, I had to push myself to keep up. We were nearly to the door when a voice called, "Arbuckle, have you got a moment?"

We turned to face the speaker, a stocky, middle-aged man in his shirtsleeves, with his cuffs turned back, wearing black rubber gloves. There was an expression of concern on his blunt-featured face.

"Sure, Doc," Arbuckle said. "What can I do for you?"

"It's this Crossman killing. You people say it happened Tuesday night, but I don't believe it. It was longer ago than that – it had to be."

"We got witnesses, Doc. Crossman was eating dinner at Henrici's at seven o'clock Tuesday night."

"I don't care what you've got. It couldn't have happened Tuesday. Decomposition is much too far advanced."

"Remember it's summertime, Doc. Doesn't take long for meat to turn ripe in this weather."

The man looked familiar, but for a moment I couldn't place him. Then, as he thrust out his lower lip truculently, I remembered where I had seen him before – at Washington Park racetrack, extracting a gobbet of chicken from the windpipe of Bathhouse John Coughlin. Menifee, his name was – Doc Menifee, the police medical examiner.

"I know it's summertime, Detective," Menifee snarled. "I also know everything I need to know about aging meat. And I tell you anybody who says Crossman was alive Tuesday night is handing you vintage baloney."

Arbuckle raised his hand pacifically. "All right, Doc – if you say so, we'll double check the witnesses. If the time of death moves back a day or two, maybe an alibi blows up, and then maybe a certain somebody is sitting way out on a limb." His colorless eyes narrowed, and one corner of his mouth twisted upward momentarily. "Thanks, Doc – maybe you've given us a hand."

Menifee gestured impatiently. "Just hate sloppy work, that's all." He nodded and turned away.

"Excuse me, Doctor," I called after him, "but I saw you return Alderman Coughlin to the land of the living at the track day before yesterday, and I want to tell you it was a slick piece of work, for a fact."

He turned and peered at me. "Oh? Do I know you?"

"Paddy Moretti's the name, Doctor. I'm a correspondent for *The Spirit of the Times,* always on the lookout for human-interest stories to spice up the tiresome parade of racing reports, and anxious to give you a bit of professional publicity for your brilliant bit of lifesaving, if that's all right with you." I smiled ingratiatingly as I whipped my notebook and pencil from my pocket.

Menifee frowned in momentary perplexity. "What's that? You want to write about me in the paper? Why would you want to do that?"

"For human interest, Doctor. Against the racing background, with Coughlin an alderman, and you a police surgeon, and —"

"No!" he cried. "I won't have it!"

"Just a mention of your quick thinking and devotion to duty. I assure you it'll be handled in the very best taste —"

Menifee's face darkened, and his eyes seemed to bulge from their sockets. "I won't have it, I say! You have no right to use my name without my permission! I'll have you sued! I'll see you in jail!"

I took an involuntary step away from his sudden rage. "You misunderstand, Doctor!

There'd be nothing for you to object to in the story! Why, you'll want to cut it out and show it to your friends!"

"*No!* Can't you understand English?" He opened his mouth to continue, then, controlling himself with an effort, passed his hand across his face instead. After a moment he said to Arbuckle in an unsteady voice, "I expect you to look after my interests, Detective. For the department's sake, I don't want my name bandied around in some cheap horse-race newspaper."

Arbuckle raised one eyebrow slightly. "Certainly, Doctor. I'm sure Moretti will respect your wishes." He shot a glance at me. "If he's got any sense, he will."

I assured the doctor that under no conditions would I write a single word that he hadn't authorized. Menifee nodded curtly and walked away without comment.

"What was that all about?" I asked.

"This may come as a shock to you," Arbuckle answered sardonically, "but everybody in the world doesn't consider it an honor to get written up in a yellow sheet for touts and bookmakers." Ignoring my protests at this calumny, he led the way out of the station and onto Twelfth Street.

The Quincys were still watching the

Tuscany. As we approached the entrance, Arbuckle spoke to an unsavory fellow leaning against the brick wall and cleaning his fingernails with his teeth. "Hello, Mule — when did you get back on the street?" Without waiting for an answer, he continued, "Johnny Dee around?"

Mule spat out a small clot of dirt. "You wanna see him?"

"Not really. Just tell him I was here with my friend Moretti. Tell him I'm watching out for Moretti while he's in Chicago. Me personally. You got that?"

Mule began nibbling the edge of a fingernail with large yellow teeth. "I got it," he said through grinding jaws.

Arbuckle entered the lobby, and I followed. The first thing I saw was a familiar suitcase standing at one end of the desk. It had been packed so hastily that two inches of shirt protruded from it.

"Isn't that my suitcase?" I asked the young clerk with the unfortunate skin condition. "What's it doing out here? Why isn't it in my room?"

The clerk regarded me coolly. "Mr. Moretti, was it?" he asked as if I were deceased. "I'm sorry, Mr. Moretti, but you don't have a room."

"What do you mean, I don't have a room? Of

course I have a room."

"I'm afraid not. You *had* a room, but only until today. It was reserved, you see. We've had to vacate you."

"Reserved!" I cried in disbelief. "You've never had a room reserved in this fleabag since it was built!"

"Trouble, Moretti?" asked Arbuckle.

"You could say that," I said bitterly. "On top of everything else, the management of this wretched doss house has decided I'm not to have a place to lay my head. They say my room is reserved!"

Arbuckle shrugged. "So have them move you to another room."

The clerk shook his head. "I'm afraid that's not possible. Every room in the hotel is occupied."

"The hell you say!" I exploded. "The only reason anybody ever comes here is because there are always empty rooms! Every other hotel in Chicago could close and they'd still have rooms!"

Arbuckle looked at the clerk. "All the rooms are occupied?" The clerk nodded. "Well, I guess you're out of luck, Moretti. You'll have to find some place else to hang your hat. Blame it on the Exposition." He pursed his lips as if to prevent a smile.

I thought about raising an argument, but immediately realized the futility of it. I felt the strain of my night's adventures catching up with me. My head began to throb. I bent over and picked up my Gladstone bag. "All right, you win," I mumbled, turning away from the desk.

"Oh, just a moment, Mr. Moretti," the clerk called. "You have a telegram." He drew a folded yellow sheet from a pigeonhole behind him and handed it to me.

"A telegram?" I asked dully. "I wonder who it's from?" — although I knew very well.

PADDY MORETTI TUSCANY HOTEL CHICAGO ILL WHATEVER YOU ARE DOING STOP IT STOP THIS PUBLICATION DEPENDS ON THE GOODWILL OF ITS FRIENDS IN OTHER CITIES STOP YOUR JOB IS TO REPORT DERBY STOP SUGGEST YOU RESTRICT YOURSELF TO THIS UNLESS YOU ARE NOW INDEPENDENTLY WEALTHY STOP YOU ARE NEVER FAR FROM OUR THOUGHTS

HOCHMUTH

It needed only this, I thought, as I folded the telegram into a small square and thrust it into my pocket.

Arbuckle eyed me speculatively. "Bad news, Moretti?"

183

"Comme ci, comme ça," I answered bleakly. "This is some town you have here, Arbuckle. It seems to reach all the way to the East River. How far west does it go? To the Golden Gate?" I shook my head and hefted my suitcase. "And I thought Tammany Hall knew about organization! What a civics lesson!"

I walked out of the dingy lobby and into the sunny street. Arbuckle walked beside me, frowning thoughtfully. "Where do you plan to go now? Going to try for another room around here?"

I thought about it. "No, I guess I'll move out near the track. There's no reason for me to stay downtown now, and a friend offered to put me up at his place on Sixty-third Street."

"Oh?"

"Well, not really a friend — an acquaintance, is more like it. A pharmacist named Holmes, has a shop at Sixty-third and Wallace and owns the house across the street. I think I'll take him up on his offer. It'll be convenient, anyway."

"Yes, I guess it will." Arbuckle stopped and turned to me. "Well, Moretti, I'm sorry you lost your room, and I'm sorry you lost your girlfriend, and I'm sorry you got yourself chased around the beach last night. I don't think you'll have to worry about the Quincys anymore, as long as you keep your nose clean

184

and don't make any more trouble. Try to stay away from police stations." He put his hand out. It was rough, ropy, and dry, like the skin of a snake that has been sunning itself.

The prospect of fighting for standing space on a succession of Mr. Yerkes's streetcars was so unappealing that I decided to take the train instead. This necessitated a trip to the Exposition grounds, but that was an agreeable prospect; I had intended to visit the White City again before I left Chicago, and I doubted I'd find a time I needed the entertainment more.

The fairgrounds were aswarm with pleasure seekers and the professionals who preyed on them. Bands were playing, gondoliers were singing, guides were chanting their spiels and hucksters were hawking their wares, the great white buildings rose above the teeming crowd like a plaster of paris Acropolis, and above *them* the huge Ferris wheel swept its thousand-odd shrieking passengers up to the skies and then down again.

The Ferris wheel. Without making a conscious decision, I found myself standing in line by the ticket booth, Gladstone bag in one hand and admission fee in the other. As each car on the wheel reached the bottom and unloaded, thirty new passengers scrambled aboard, and the remainder of the line advanced fifteen feet toward the turnstile. Ten cars were unloaded and reloaded before I reached my seat, and another six thereafter.

Then we began to ascend with what seemed like breathless speed. The grounds receded below us, and people contracted into tiny heads and shoulders; buildings became mostly roofs, and the view widened to include the lake to the east and the Woodlawn neighborhood to the west. My fellow passengers gasped and gabbled and pointed, our car swayed and creaked on its hinges, and we continued to rise as if we were in a balloon.

My car reached its apogee and began its descent, causing renewed screams and sudden feelings of nausea. We swung out and down, then in and down, and in a few seconds were back a few feet off the ground and beginning our second orbit. This time I knew what to expect, and was able to relax my death grip on the handles of my Gladstone bag, sit back, and enjoy the view.

And what a view it was! The top of the wheel was two hundred and sixty-five feet from the ground, the equivalent of a twenty-five-story building. The Masonic Temple, the tallest building in the world, was twenty-two stories, and from the window of my car I was actually *looking down* on it! To the north, beyond the central city, the lakeshore angled westward until it disappeared in a late-morning haze somewhere about Belmont Avenue, and to the south the shoreline curved past Lake Calumet toward the Indiana Dunes. Westward the stockyards sprawled cross the middle distance, and to the east was the faintest suggestion of the Michigan shore. The lake sparkled like blue diamonds in the sun.

Chicago! I thought, *immense, brutal, beautiful, sordid Chicago! Where lots of things aren't news, least of all disappearing women and murdered newspapermen! Where business is business, and devil take the hindmost. And God, isn't it something to see, when you're high enough up to hide the seamy details!*

After a half-dozen revolutions the Ferris wheel stopped to unload and reload the eighteen cars on the other side, and our car hung suspended for five minutes, affording me the opportunity to search for familiar landmarks. I located the Palmer House, and the block where I calculated Boz Markey's apartment must be, and the arc of sand that constituted Cap Streeter's domain. I found the Twelfth Street station, and just to the left of it the small rectangle that represented my erstwhile home away from home, the Tuscany Hotel. To the west the Midway Plaisance extended a mile to Washington Park, the track coiled in front of its grandstand like a snake eating its tail. Sixty-third Street ran past the south end of the park, and a few blocks farther I could make out, I was sure, the tiny Gothic *grotesquerie* of my friendly pharmacist H. H. Holmes's mansion. *Where I'll soon be taking up residence.*

When I finished my ride on the Ferris wheel I sauntered along the midway toward the Streets of Cairo. But when I reached it, I found to my surprise that I didn't want to join the line. *Some experiences,* I thought to myself, *are too special to repeat. After what Little Egypt and I had together the first time, I wouldn't want to risk an anticlimax.*

So instead I visited the Dahomey and Eskimo villages, watched the Javanese dancers and the Wild West marksmen, enjoyed a therapeutic glass of lager at the Austrian rathskeller. Then, regretfully, I picked up my valise and left the fairgrounds in search of shelter.

I stopped in the doorway of Holmes's pharmacy to give my eyes a moment to adjust to the dimness inside. The air was stale and medicinal-smelling; I could make out iodine, ether, and orris among the combined odors. The bell tinkled briefly at the back of the shop, and was followed by a few moments of silence. Then, as my eyes became accustomed to the gloom, I saw Holmes emerge from behind the tall counter topped by the apothecary jars. He was again in his shirtsleeves, and brushed his hands together as he approached me.

"Yes, sir! What can I do for — Why, it's Mr. Moretti, isn't it? This is a treat, sir! Out for an afternoon at Washington Park, are you? Well, you've picked a hot day for it! Now how can I be of service, Mr. Moretti? I hope your headache's not still giving you trouble." As he spoke he took my elbow solicitously and guided me into his shop.

"I could do with another dose of your medicine, and that's a fact. But that's not the main reason I came." I raised my Gladstone by way of explanation. "I'm afraid I'm in need of a room, and I remembered your offer yesterday, and thought if it's still open maybe I could take you up on it."

"Why, that's capital!" He clapped his hands together. "Yes, sir, the offer is still open, and I'm delighted to hear that you're interested. I'm sure you'll find the accommodations will fit you to a T. We'll go have a look directly — but first, why don't we splice the mainbrace, as our nautical friends would say? You have time for a snifter, I hope?"

"Well, it's a little early to go to a saloon —," I said doubtfully.

He gave a rich laugh. "Who said anything about a saloon? When you're a pharmacist, my friend, you have access to purer waters than any saloonkeeper, and stronger, too! We'll enjoy our cup that cheers right here in back!"

He led me to the rear of his shop and seated me in the threadbare armchair. As he rinsed out two glasses at the sink in the corner I said, "The lady who was here yesterday — is she off today?"

Holmes chuckled. "You're thinking that if she were here we wouldn't be having a drink at eleven o'clock in the morning, aren't you? Well, you're right. Minnie takes a highly moral view of the world, and I must admit I indulge her in it to a degree. In other words, she'd flay the skin off my back if she caught me!" He leaned toward me and gave me a comradely tap on the shoulder. "Today, however, she's off for a visit to the Exposition, so we don't have to worry. Something you said yesterday about the flying machines at the Hall of Transportation caught her attention. And after that, she plans to visit friends."

He poured two glasses half full of a light-green liquid from a frosted bottle, and handed one to me. I looked dubiously at the stuff, which was viscous and beaded on the glass, like very old brandy. "What is it?" I asked.

"Pure alcohol, chastened and inspired by the addition of certain rare flavorings and aromatics. My own formulation. I don't believe you'll find anything even remotely similar anywhere in the world." He raised his glass to his lips and took a swallow, his eyes dancing at me across the rim.

I followed suit. The liquor was indescribable — bittersweet, with a fragrance of oranges and sandalwood, cool as crème de menthe and razor-edged as akvavit. It rolled down my throat like liquid gold, and crackled through my blood. When I could speak, I asked what he called it.

"I've never called it anything, because I've never thought of a name to do it justice," he replied. "You're a writer — if you have any suggestions, feel free to rise to the challenge." He took another sip and set the glass aside. "Now, before I forget, I'll get you your headache powder." He rummaged in a drawer in the deal worktable and produced a twist of paper similar to the others he had given me. "Here we are — I thought I had another one there." He unscrewed one end of the twist and sniffed the contents. "Yes, this is it. The mixture as before. Would you care to take it now? I'll get you a drink of water — you wouldn't want to waste the elixir by using it to wash down medicine." He found another tumbler, filled it with water from the tap, and set it before me beside the paper twist.

"I don't suppose the combination of the medicine and the, er, elixir is anything to worry about?"

"Gracious, no! There is no categorical impingement whatever. Physiologically, they function in separate spheres." He smiled benignly and folded his hands across his chest. "To your very good health, Mr. Moretti."

I sprinkled the white powder on my tongue and swallowed a mouthful of water. Once again it tasted more bitter than I expected. I put my head back and closed my eyes.

"A little bitter? Have a taste of the elixir," Holmes suggested. I took a sip of the green liquor and immediately the harsh taste disappeared, leaving in its place a pleasant tanginess. We sat in silence for a few seconds, and I turned my attention inward as the sensations I had felt the previous day repeated themselves; the knotted muscles at the back of my neck loosened, the pressure behind my eyeballs eased, and a delicious languor began to spread through my body. I sighed.

"That's right — just let the tensions dissolve.

Breathe deeply. Pretend you're floating on a cloud." His voice was measured, monotonous, distant.

"That's just what I do feel like. Remarkable. Like the Ferris wheel. Or maybe a magic carpet. I'm floating on a magic carpet, like in The Arabian Nights. Whooo! I could look over the edge and see the whole world, but I don't want to. Can't be bothered." I snuggled deeper into my chair. "Just stay up here, floating."

"Good, good." There was another interval of silence, and then his voice continued, deep and resonant: "Those disappearing women you told me about, Mr. Moretti — have you and your friend Boz found out anything more about them?"

My flying carpet took a lurch. "Poor Boz. Run over by a beer wagon. Broken arm, terrible bruises. In the midst of life. Who knows where the Reaper lurks?" I rolled my head from side to side. Holmes patted my arm and I stopped.

"Your friend was in an accident? How unfortunate. I imagine that will curtail his investigations for a while. It's an odd coincidence, isn't it, Mr. Moretti — that he should be injured just when he began poking around in this business of yours."

"Disappearing women aren't news in Chicago," I quoted. "Police don't even care about them. Not even my friend Detective Arbuckle."

"Apparently not." He made a sound that might have been either a cough or a chuckle. "Well, sir, since your headache's gone," he went on briskly, "we might as well move you into your new room." He rose to his feet, drained his glass of green liquor, and picked up my Gladstone bag. "Come, come, Mr. Moretti. Let's get you comfortable."

I rose from my armchair with regret, but found that my delicious feeling of insubstantiality was still with me. In fact, it increased, and I felt myself swaying on my feet. As Holmes took my elbow and led me toward the street door, I said, "Detective Arbuckle is sorry. He told me so. Sorry about Velma. Sorry about them chasing me on the beach. Sorry about me losing my room."

"Of course he is," Holmes said soothingly.

"But he's glad I can get another one here, close to the track. He wants me to take care of myself."

"Oh?" Holmes's voice became even more sympathetic. "You told him you were moving to the South Side?"

"Told him I was moving right here on Sixty-third Street. Told him my friend Holmes had a rooming house right across from his pharmacy. He was glad."

Holmes stopped, and his fingers on my arm tightened slightly. "Oh, you mentioned me. How flattering. And my drugstore, too. Well, now." His head moved close to mine, and he peered into my eyes. "Just as I suspected. Mr. Moretti, I believe you are experiencing an unfavorable reaction to your headache medicine. Perhaps there is a categorical impingement with the elixir after all. In any case, immediate remedial measures are called for." He drew me back behind the tall counter and stood me before the sink. "Wait there, Mr. Moretti. I won't be a minute."

I stood swaying and staring at the wall, while he bustled busily behind me. In a few moments he pressed a glass into my hand. "Drink it right down, hear? Every last drop, that's a good fellow." I raised it to my lips, hoping for another taste as pleasing as that of the green liquor. Instead, after one swallow of the nauseous mess, my gorge rose to meet the next swallow in mid-passage. I barely had time to move the glass to one side before I spewed a mouthful of liquid into the sink.

"Drink the rest. Drink it all down. Hurry."

I tried to swallow, but gagged instead. My mouth filled, my cheeks swelled, and the foul stuff raced up my sinuses and dripped from my nose. I collapsed over the sink, retching and gasping and retching again, until my esophagus was as clean as a new gun barrel.

"Ipecac," Holmes murmured in my ear. "A heroic remedy. Better to be safe than sorry, wouldn't you agree?" I gagged in response. He patted my shoulder. "I knew you would." He reached past me to turn the faucet on, and I watched bleakly as the water washed the sink clean. Then, shaking my head to clear it, I stood up.

"Well, I *hope* there was a categorical impingement," I said. "I'd hate to have gone through that for nothing." I shuddered. "I think I'd like to go to my room and lie down."

Holmes's pleasant features drew downward in disappointment. "I'm sorry, Mr. Moretti, I'm afraid I have unhappy tidings. There are no vacancies at my establishment."

My mouth dropped. "But you said —"

"I know, I know. I don't know how I could be so forgetful. I rented the last empty room to a gentleman yesterday afternoon. It completely slipped my mind — or perhaps I anticipated the pleasure of your company so much I wiped the other memory from my thoughts; who knows the subtleties of which the human brain is capable?" He smiled ruefully and spread his hands. "However, the fact is, there is no room for you at my establishment. I'm sorry. I'm afraid you must make arrangements elsewhere." With a commiserating look, he handed me my Gladstone.

"But — that is —," I stumbled. "Well, could you give me any suggestions?"

"Perhaps a few blocks east. There are one or two hotels there. I'm sure you won't have too much trouble." He put one arm around my shoulders and drew me toward the front door. "It was nice seeing you again, sir. I'm sorry we had this little mix-up. Have a safe trip back to New York. Good-bye, Mr. Moretti, good-bye!"

The shop door closed firmly behind me, and I was on the sidewalk.

My headache was back.

I found a room in a small hotel on Sixtieth and State. The lobby was dank, and my room was small and airless, but as far as I could tell, nobody connected with the place had never heard of *The Spirit of the Times*, and that was certainly worth something.

I sent the bellboy out for a pint of whiskey and lay on the bed until he came back with it. I passed the time in mentally composing telegrams to my editor. The problem was to prepare him for the possibility of a bigger story than he was expecting without promising him anything. I wanted him to sense the looming of an untold drama, to hope to be a witness to its resolution, and yet not to use its failure to materialize, should that be the outcome, as a stick to beat me with.

The bellboy returned with the bottle. I tipped him, sent him on his way, pulled the cork and poured myself a stiff drink, which in no way approached Holmes's green elixir, but nevertheless eased my throbbing head. Then I lay back on the bed with the glass balanced on my chest, and reworded more mental telegrams.

It was no good. There was no way I could manipulate Otto Hochmuth in the way I hoped. I was trying to do two mutually exclusive things, and I might as well give it up and study my notes on tomorrow's American Derby, and prepare to do the job I was paid for.

"Yassah, boss, yassah!" I muttered, putting my stockinged feet on the floor and emptying my glass. "Disappearing women ain't news nohow. Hee, hee, hee!"

I got to the track half an hour before the first race, and went directly to the betting ring. The odds on the derby had shifted. The favorite, Anton Birkmann's Mustafa, had dropped from eight to three to three to one, while Paul Vannatta's Home Free had moved up to four to one. Not a dramatic change, I reflected, but one worth thinking about.

The first two races were uneventful. While waiting for the third I walked through the reserved boxes. Anton Birkmann's was empty, but Vannatta's was occupied. A reporter I recognized was interviewing Vannatta, and the other occupants of the box were passing the time until the next race according to their respective interests: Razor, one gleaming shoe propped up on the rail before him, was studying the racing page through mismatched eyes, his reptilian lips pursed judiciously; the Loogan was staring at an attractive young woman in a nearby box with unabashed lust; and Mrs. Vannatta, gracefully erect in her chair, was effortlessly managing the close stitches of her needlework in spite of her heavy veil. . . .

In spite of her heavy veil . . . The thought echoed through my mind with growing resonance. A heavy veil! Wasn't that unusual? Were heavy veils a fashion item this summer? I wasn't sure, but I doubted it. Surreptitiously I glanced at the ladies in the neighboring boxes. Not another veil in sight. I looked back at Mrs. Vannatta, this time studying her figure and the way she carried it. Her shoulders were of average width, but squared, her waist was narrow, her back straight — and her bosom, judging from what I could see of it beneath her forearm, superb. Her hair was completely concealed by her veil, and white gloves covered her hands.

I closed my eyes and drew a deep breath. Was it possible?

And who was it first mentioned Paul Vannatta, there on a green plush seat in the B & O Pullman an hour out of Chicago? And who switched us back to Vannatta every time I tried to develop more promising conversational gambits?

A tingle of excitement ran through my body. Deliberately I walked down the aisle away from the Vannatta box. When I was thirty feet past it, I stopped and leaned against a pillar and pretended to consult my notebook. I waited until the reporter finished his interview with Vannatta and left the box. Then, just as the bugle announced the third race, I sauntered back.

There was no use of calling attention to myself until I had a plan. How was I going to get under the veil? That was the question I had to answer. Once I answered it, I might be at least partway along the path to an explanation of Chicago's biggest nonnews story — or, on the other hand, I might not be.

In any case, I had to make the attempt.

But it had to be an attempt that would not result in my own apprehension. I was in no position to create a scene in the Washington Park boxes, involving the wife of a prominent owner on the day before the running of the derby. The very thought of such a debacle made the sweat pop from my forehead. No, I should have to find a way to penetrate the veil without exposing myself as the penetrator. But how? How?

As I cudgeled my brain for a plan, the horses lined up at the post for the third race, and a moment later were thundering down the track. Instinctively the crowd swayed forward, and I found myself pressed against the bar that formed the rear of Vannatta's box; on both sides and behind me the aisle was jammed with excited spectators. Mrs. Vannatta was leaning forward in her seat, and the back of her hat was a foot beyond my farthest reach.

The horses moved into the backstretch, and the crowd's excitement increased. Vannatta had a pair of binoculars to his eyes, Razor had his elbows on the railing instead of his feet, and the Loogan had forgotten the woman in the nearby box.

I looked around for something that could serve to extend my reach. The man on my left had a rolled-up newspaper thrust into his jacket pocket. I leaned against him and simultaneously grasped the paper and eased it from its position. I held it against my right thigh, ready for action, as the leading horses swung around the last turn and entered the homestretch.

Vannatta, Razor, the Loogan and Mrs. Vannatta were all on their feet now, the crowd was roaring, and three horses were almost neck and neck as they approached the wire. Leaning as far forward as possible, with the railing cutting into my thighs and only the tips of my toes on the ground, I raised the paper and began beating time to the roaring of the crowd. As the winning horse crossed the line a thousandth of a second ahead of its competitors, as the crowd swayed forward, every eye glued to the dramatic and hard-fought finish, I snapped the newspaper up under the brim of Mrs. Vannatta's hat and flipped it forward.

It seemed incredible that the single-minded concentration of the crowd could dissipate so quickly. Before the platter-sized leghorn straw chapeau, weighted down with ribbons, bows, ostrich plumes, artificial poppies, and enough black veil to protect a double bed from mosquitoes, could reach the ground, the roar of the throng had subsided to an orchestrated murmur of satisfaction and disgruntlement, and the shrill cry of the woman in front of me rang out like a tocsin in the night.

Pressed against the railing of the box by the

bodies around me, and incontestably identified as the culprit by the rolled-up newspaper in my hand, I could only stand and confront one of the most painful sights of my life.

Mrs. Vannatta turned instinctively to face me. For an instant we stared at each other, and then she clapped her gloved hands over her face and sank into her chair, her back bent and her head almost touching her thighs. Only an instant — but more than time enough to engrave her features on my memory forever.

She must have been beautiful once, before the acid did its work. Now the left side of her face, from brow to chin, was a puckered, purple sweep of scar tissue; her left eye, white and sightless, drooped at its outer corner to show the eyeball's inward curve; the upper lip drew back from the teeth in an involuntary snarl; most terrible at all, the left side of the nose was gone entirely, and only a dark hole in the face remained for breathing.

I opened my mouth and tried to speak, but no words came. I was still struggling to find my tongue when Razor and the Loogan reached me.

I barely had time to cry out, "I'm sorry!" before Razor seized my arm and dragged me over the railing. I hit the floor of the box facedown. The Loogan's knees landed on my back and his hands grasped my head, which he drew back and slammed down on the cement in a rapid one-two rhythm until all the sounds around me receded into the echoing distance.

"That's enough. Don't kill the son of a bitch." It was Vannatta's voice, harsh and far away, and then growing closer. "Goddamn dirty rotten sneaking miserable *bastard!*" he continued, as a pointed shoe struck my ribs. "Turn him over! I want to see his face!"

The Loogan rolled me on my back and anchored one arm with his knee, and Razor pressed his heel against my other elbow. I stared up into the circle of faces that cut off most of the sky. There was Vannatta, white-faced with rage, and Razor, grinning in wolfish anticipation, and the Loogan, impassive and sleepy-eyed – and Alderman Bathhouse John Coughlin, with his roast-beef face and sergeant-major's mustache, resplendent in a mulberry frock coat and a bottle-green silk vest, flanked by two young women with wide eyes and mouths shaped like red *O*'s and half a dozen spectators whose expressions reflected varying degrees of enjoyment or outrage. And the policeman who had told me where to find Vannatta's box the first time I visited the track.

Mrs. Vannatta stood behind her husband. Her hat was on her head, and her face was invisible behind her heavy black veil.

Struggling to raise my head from the floor, I called to her, "I beg your pardon, ma'am. It was an accident. Forgive me, it was the crowd that pushed me."

Vannatta stepped back to kick me again, but Alderman Coughlin intervened. "Now, now, Paul, we don't want any more trouble, do we? Let me handle this." He turned to the policeman and said magisterially, "Take care of this for us, me lad —"

"Yes, sir," the officer answered eagerly.

"Take this spalpeen and run his tail out of here, and give him a little something to remind him not to come back — would you do that for me?"

"That I would, Mr. Alderman!"

"Wait a minute, Bath," Vannatta interrupted. "I know this man. He's a racetrack reporter named Moretti. He's bothered me before, and I want him barred from the track."

"Well, that's easy enough. Take him by the steward's office on your way out, lad, and tell them there that Alderman Coughlin would take it as a favor if they would bar the bugger for life."

"Wait! You can't do that!" I cried. "You can't deprive me of my livelihood!"

"Oh, can't I now! Why, half the things I can

do I ain't even thought of yet!" He shook his head unbelievingly and repeated, " 'Can't deprive me of my livelihood.' Would you listen to the man! Take him away, lad."

My arms were released, and the policeman tugged me to my feet and dragged me out of the box. With an iron grip on my arm he led me through the crowded aisle toward the steward's office. My head throbbed like an abscessed tooth. People drew away from me as if I were contagious. I saw a reporter I knew, and he avoided my eyes.

"Officer, you don't really need to do this," I pleaded hopelessly. "Just take me out of the gate, why don't you? I've learned my lesson, I swear I have."

"Shut up."

"I have a friend on the force — maybe you know him? Detective Arbuckle?" I improvised. "We're working together on a case —"

"Shut up, I said!" He clamped down on my arm until it hurt even more than my head. "You're getting off easy, if you want to know! If Mr. Vannatta or the alderman was to give the word, you'd end up in the Chicago River, and no great loss to anyone! Now shut your gob till we get to the steward's office!"

The steward, a pompous old soak with dewlaps and basset eyes, told me I was a disgrace to my profession. He ignored my pleas and promises, and banished me from Washington Park forever.

At the gate the policeman hesitated, apparently debating with himself whether or not to speed my steps with corporal encouragement, as Alderman Coughlin had suggested. Reluctantly, due to the crowd around us, he decided not to. "There's the gate, and for you it only works in one direction," he barked. "Let's see the back of you — and if you're smart, you'll never show your ugly mug to me again as long as you live! Now march!"

I marched.

9

Advantages of a
Whited Sepulcher

I knocked on the heavy oak door of Hull-House at seven o'clock exactly. The woman who opened it was at least seventy and had a face like a hot cross bun. When I identified myself and asked for Alison Markey, she stepped aside and allowed me to enter. "She's waiting for you in the small sitting room. But you can't stay for dinner. We got a full house tonight."

I assured her, truthfully, that I had already eaten. She sniffed, and her expression indicated disapproval of the two large brandies with which I had topped off my spaghetti supper. *She doesn't know the demands of true desperation or she'd be more forgiving,* I thought.

She led me down a long hall to a closed door flanked by two paintings, one showing a push-cart on a slum street, the other of a girl working over a sewing machine in a dimly lit sweatshop. Opening the door, she stepped aside and motioned me to enter. "Here's the one you were waiting for, Miss Alison," she snapped.

"Thank you, Alma. Won't you come in, Mr. Moretti?" Alison Markey turned away from a window to face me, letting the curtain fall behind her. She was wearing a dress of very light-blue satin with a modestly modish amount of *décolletage*. Her brown hair, which had been severely tied back the last time I saw her, was now piled richly on top of her head, with gleaming curls framing her brows. Her eyes were friendly, and no one would ever have described her lips as thin.

She put her hand out to me without affectation, and her grip was firm. "I'm afraid I'll have to leave you for a few minutes – we're having *very* important dinner guests tonight, as you can see" – she indicated her gown with a half-embarrassed smile – "but we'll have a little while to talk first, and I promise I'll get back as soon as I can."

We sat on a settee in front of the mantelpiece. "Now tell me," she demanded, "how did your day go?"

I drew a deep breath and began my inglorious recital: "To tell you the truth, I've had better." Her eyes widened as I recounted my dash down Huron Street to Streeterville and the resultant siege, and she pressed her hand against her heart as I described the battle on the beach. Her expression changed to incredulity and then to outrage as I told about Arbuckle's brief conversation with the Quincy bully, Mule, and my ejection from the hotel.

"But they can't do that!" she cried.

I raised my hand to indicate that I had more wonders in store. "So then I went to see a druggist fellow on the South Side who had offered me a room in his house. At first he was tickled to death to have me, and then he must have gotten downwind of me or something, because he changed his mind and couldn't wait to get me out of his shop."

She frowned. "What had you said to him to make him change his mind?"

"Not a thing, that's the devil of it! We were having a little, ah, conversation, and then I had some kind of reaction to the headache powder he'd given me, and he made me swallow ipecac to empty my stomach — and the next thing I knew he was telling me he didn't have a vacancy after all, and showing me the door."

Alison stared at me. I saw that her hazel eyes had green flecks the color of emeralds. "That's very remarkable," she said.

Again I waved my hand to indicate upcoming attractions. "Here's something else remarkable I forgot to tell you. I had a telegram from my editor in New York — the clerk at the Tuscany gave it to me before he threw me out. Somehow he knew about the questions I've been asking."

"Who, the clerk?"

"No, Hochmuth, my editor. He told me to stick to horse race-reporting unless I was independently wealthy. From New York he wrote me that!"

"Remarkable indeed," she said. She smoothed the fabric over one knee with slender tapered fingers. "News of your inquiries spread rapidly, Mr. Moretti. What happened after you left the druggist's?"

I told her I had found myself another room and then gone to Washington Park to do the job I was paid for.

After a pause she asked, "And did you?"

I found I had difficulty speaking. She waited a moment, and then repeated gently, "And did you?"

"I wish to God I had!" My hands were clenched together between my thighs. I thought how clumsy and coarse they looked. I raised my eyes to her face.

"Tell me," she said quietly.

I blurted out the whole grotesque story — my sudden suspicions of Mrs. Vannatta's veil and my determination to see beneath it, the business with the rolled-up newspaper and its shocking denouement. It was all I could do to describe the woman's face.

"Oh, how terrible!" Alison gasped. "How terrible for you!"

"For *me*!" I cried. "Oh, God, how terrible for *her*!"

"For both of you!" Her face was white, with two spots of color over her high cheekbones. "What happened then? What did they do to you?"

I told her about being dragged through the crowd to the steward's office and being tongue-lashed and barred from the track. "Which does not seem inappropriate under the circumstances," I finished, trying for a lighter tone, "although it presents a bit of a problem to a man who's paid for writing eyewitness reports of horse races."

"Oh, Paddy! What an awful mess!" She reached out her hand and placed it on top of my two clenched ones just as I realized she had called me by my first name. "My brother run down by a wagon in the street — you set upon by toughs and threatened with ice picks and barred from your work — and I'm afraid it's my fault! If I hadn't gone on about those missing girls —"

"No, it didn't begin then," I reminded her. "It began at the Palmer House. There was something going on before I even talked to Boz about the other girls —" I paused guiltily. "And how is Boz? I've been so full of myself I haven't had the manners to ask."

"As well as can be expected. He'll be in bed for a while, and he hates it. It makes him harder to be around than usual. Fortunately the men from the circulation department have most of the invalid-sitting responsibility. I don't believe I could handle it by myself."

"There are men with him all the time?"

"Around the clock. We've made sure of that."

"Armed?"

She smiled crookedly. "I'm afraid so. As disagreeable as it is to think of firearms in the apartment, the alternative seems worse." I didn't comment, and she went on: "I'm afraid we have involved ourselves in a desperate game, Paddy."

"Don't be saying 'we' — there's no 'we' to it! Boz and I are newspapermen, and digging into dirty stories is part of our job, but it has nothing to do with you! If newspapermen get hurt, God forbid, it's their business. Your business is staying here at Hull-House and ministering to — to whomever it is you minister to!"

"Ministering, as you call it, was what caused me to meet the women I told Boz about, the women who disappeared. No, my friend, I'm as much a part of the 'we' as you and Boz are."

We regarded one another in silence. Alison's face was composed; from her expression, she might have been discussing Theodore Thomas's last concert at the Auditorium. For a moment I felt angry that she should refuse to accept the danger we were in — and then I realized she *had* accepted it, calmly and unequivocally.

I shook my head. "I can't allow it —," I began, and was interrupted by a knock at the door. "Yes?" Alison called. The door opened and the woman named Alma thrust her head in.

"Soup's on, Miss Alison. They're waiting on you." She stood with her arms folded until her words were acted upon.

Alison smiled apologetically as she rose. "Please don't think me rude, Paddy, but Miss Addams *is* expecting me — and there really *isn't* room for another guest at the table. But make yourself comfortable here — Alma can bring you a cup of coffee if you like — and I promise to be back as soon as I can."

I refused the coffee, eliciting an I-knew-he-wouldn't-drink-anything-without-alcohol-in-it grunt from Alma, found myself a newspaper on the reading table, and settled down on the settee to wait. After five minutes, realizing I was reading paragraphs three or four times and still not comprehending them, I tossed the paper away. I inspected the titles of the books on the shelves, but found nothing that provoked interest. I studied the pictures on the walls, with similar result. Finally I paced the floor.

When Alison returned, she was accompanied by two men. Both appeared to be in their late thirties, but there any similarity between them ended. One was clean-shaven, with straw-colored hair that hung lankly over one eyebrow, and deep wrinkles that radiated from his narrow eyes. His clothes were of good quality, but poorly cared for; his collar was definitely on its second day, and there was a food spot on his tie. His companion, bearded and dark-visaged, with angry eyes and an imperious chin, was immaculately dressed; the creases in his trousers were knife-sharp, and his shoes gleamed with a hard brilliance.

The men paused at the door as Alison approached me. "Paddy, I hope you don't mind, but Mr. Darrow and Mr. Sullivan and I got talking about this mess, and I thought it might be a good idea if you talked to them, too."

Darrow I knew by reputation — he was the brilliant lawyer who was leading the campaign to free the Haymarket survivors from prison. Sullivan, Alison explained as we shook hands, was an architect, a partner in the firm of Adler and Sullivan. "I fear my knowledge of crime and violence is minimal, Mr. Moretti," he said sternly, fixing his eyes on me as if his lacking were my fault. "But my attention was captured by Miss Alison's remarks to Clarence, and I pushed my way shamelessly into the conversation."

"Louis is always happy to join any conversation, so long as it isn't about the Exposition," Darrow drawled, shooting a mischievous glance at his friend.

The gibe obviously hit a nerve. Sullivan's face darkened, and his pointed beard jutted forward like a weapon. "A whited sepulcher, full of the stinking bones of long-dead civilizations, and not even a well-made sepulcher," he snarled. "Don't get me started, Clarence!"

Darrow raised his eyebrows innocently. "Not for the world, friend. Let's talk about disappearing women instead." He pushed his lank forelock up on his brow, and it immediately fell back to its former position. "Your experiences, Mr. Moretti, and those of Miss Alison's brother, have elements of considerable interest. If you can spare a few minutes, I'd appreciate hearing the story from your own lips. In chronological order, please."

We sat in a circle; Alison and I on the settee, Darrow and Sullivan in two armchairs facing us. I began with my conversation with Velma LeSeure on the train. I found I had told the same facts so often that they began to sound rehearsed and unbelievable to my own ears. Only when I reached the events that had transpired today – my ejection from the Tuscany Hotel, from a room I had almost rented from H. H. Holmes, and from the Washington Park racetrack – did my account sound spontaneous to me.

Darrow and Sullivan listened without interruption until I concluded. Then Darrow pulled on his nose and wiped his hand absently on the lapel of his jacket. "Provocative, damn provocative," he said, scowling at the floor. "Particularly the telegram from New York. That puts the cap on it."

Alison leaned forward. "I don't understand, Mr. Darrow."

"It means that whatever forces are trying to prevent Moretti and your brother from continuing their investigation – assuming there *are* forces trying to do that, which I'm prepared to believe – are not confined to Chicago. They can apply pressure as far away as the East Coast. You realize that, Moretti?" I nodded.

"Very well. Now, who in Chicago could influence your paper to call you off a story?"

I thought a moment. "Any of the tracks, I suppose — the paper couldn't afford to be barred from any of them. Maybe some of the wealthy horsemen or other sporting types here have influence with the owner — I wouldn't know about that."

"Advertisers?"

I shook my head. "We don't carry enough advertising to make any difference."

"Politicians? The police department?"

"I shouldn't think so. Not unless there was a good reason for it."

"How about the underworld?" Sullivan asked.

"No chance. We've always avoided contact with them. A sporting paper can't afford to get a reputation for having underworld connections. It would undermine our credibility."

"Not even with gamblers and touts?" Sullivan challenged.

I shrugged. "Gamblers and touts go with the territory. But I meant heavy men — thieves, gang leaders, white slavers, enforcers — we have nothing to do with them." Remembering my meeting with Skeeter Huff and Ty-Ty Davenport outside the Palmer House, I amended, "Or anyway, as little as possible. In any case, I can't see Chicago hoodlums having any influence on the editorial room of *The Spirit of the Times*."

"Then that leaves us with wealthy men with sporting connections," Darrow said. "Let's go at it a different way. Who are the people who have interfered with your getting the story since you arrived in town? Let's list them — speak up if I leave any out." He began counting on his nicotine-stained fingers as he spoke. "The desk clerk at the Palmer House. The house detective. Your spotter friend, and later his associate, the heister. The Quincy Gang, who were probably also responsible for Boz Markey's accident. Detective Arbuckle. The bellboy at the Palmer House. Vannatta's men Razor and the Loogan, and Schacter, who's apparently a friend of Anton Birkmann —"

"They didn't actually warn me off the disappearance story," I interrupted. "They just indicated a general disapproval of my activities."

Darrow waved his hand in dismissal. "Close enough. And then there's your editor in New York, and the medical examiner who doesn't want any publicity, and the desk clerk at the Tuscany, and your friend the pharmacist, neither of whom want you living in their establishments — let's see, have I left anybody out?"

"I don't think so." I rubbed my temple and

wished I had another of H. H. Holmes's marvelous anodynes. My thigh and my cheekbone ached dully, and I still swallowed with difficulty. A wave of depression swept over me. "It's not what you'd call a great tribute to my popularity," I added.

"I'll tell you what it is, though," Darrow said, leaning forward to tap me on the knee with a dark-rimmed fingernail. "It's champion evidence that a lot of people are in cahoots to keep your story from being told. All kinds of people — people from the highest walks of life and from the lowest — capitalists and politicians and thugs and policemen and newspaper editors and God knows who else — all united in the single unswerving ambition of keeping you and Boz Markey from finding out what happened to some disappearing women."

"But *why*, Mr. Darrow?" Alison cried.

Darrow glanced at Sullivan and raised an eyebrow, inviting his comment. The architect folded his arms and glared at me as if I had personally offended him. "The damned whited sepulcher," he growled.

Darrow nodded. "That's right. The Exposition. It has to be. There's nothing else important enough."

"Please, Mr. Darrow," Alison implored.

"The Exposition may be a whited sepulcher

architecturally — I wouldn't argue with Louis about that — but financially it's been the saving of Chicago. Maybe living here you haven't realized it, Alison, but there's a Depression in this country. The gold reserve's fallen to below eighty million, hundreds of banks have failed, and they say more than ten thousand businesses have gone bust. God only knows how many men are out of work. Cleveland's calling a special session of the Congress to repeal the Silver Purchase Law, but even if they repeal it, which is doubtful, the milk has already been spilt. On Wall Street they think the country's in for at least another year of it, maybe two. Right, Moretti?"

"Wall Street's not my beat, Mr. Darrow, but from what I hear, it's bad and getting worse."

Darrow nodded and brushed at his forelock. " 'Bad and getting worse.' That's right — everywhere in the United States except Chicago. Here, we've got that whited sepulcher of Sullivan's."

"It's not *my* sepulcher, damn it!" Sullivan snapped.

Darrow turned to the architect and opened his mouth to say something, and then apparently thought better of it. He cleared his throat instead, and smiled. "Of course it's not, Louis. I was only teasing. Your Transportation

Building's the only decent piece of work out there. But aesthetics aside," he resumed, "the fact is, the Exposition's the only thing keeping Chicago out of the breadline today. And whether you ladies at Hull-House realize it or not, Alison, Marshal Field and Potter Palmer and Charles Yerkes realize it. *And* Mayor Harrison. *And* Alderman Coughlin. *And* the Chicago Police Department. *And* the gentlemen sportsmen who own racehorses. *And* a few hundred thousand other people whose names I can't recall at the moment."

"Including the Quincy Gang, and Skeeter Huff and Ty-Ty Davenport?" I raised my brows skeptically.

"Oh, they work on instructions," Darrow answered. "The word comes down — they wouldn't even know where it originated. We're talking about the men who make decisions. The men whose profits and power depend on a prosperous city. The men who are ruthless enough to take action when that prosperity is threatened."

Alison studied Darrow's face. "You think there's some kind of a conspiracy to prevent Paddy and Boz from digging up a story that might hurt the Exposition?"

Darrow pursed his lips and closed his eyes. "Let's say there's something getting rid of women in Chicago. Maybe it's a mass murderer, who kills them and cuts up the bodies. Maybe it's some kind of loathsome disease that disintegrates them. Maybe it's a prostitution ring that kidnaps them and sends them to Asia and a life of vice. Maybe it's a hole into the fourth dimension, and they all fall through it and can't get back — I don't know! But it doesn't make any difference what it is. The point is, women are disappearing in Chicago. *Lots* of women. Women like your wife, or your daughter, or your sister, or yourself, if you're of the female persuasion. And nobody knows why, and nobody knows how to put a stop to it.

"Now reading about it in your local newspaper in Chillicothe, Ohio, how likely are you to pack up the family for a trip to Chicago?" He grinned sardonically and pulled on his long nose.

"They're all in it, then, all trying to protect the tourist trade?" I said in awe. "Saints preserve us! And I thought things were organized in New York!"

Alison shook her head. "I'm not sure I believe it, Mr. Darrow. Oh, not that I'd put it past them, the business tycoons and the politicians and the police. Morally, I mean. I've seen the sweatshops and tenements and redlight houses; I know the way the system works. But I just can't believe they can *all* cooperate so efficiently. There's always one maverick who refuses to march in lockstep — that's the only way we reformers make any headway."

"The reason for that, my dear, is that the maverick sees an opportunity to make a profit by breaking ranks. But in this case, who can make a profit? There's not a single citizen of Chicago who won't suffer in one way or another if the Exposition stops drawing customers."

Alison shook her head angrily. "But what about all the tourists, all the men bringing wives and daughters — don't they have the right to know their women will be in danger? Don't the women have the right to know?"

"The *right*? Of course." Darrow smiled wryly. "Like they have the right to join unions and eat pure food. But apparently the right isn't enough." He drew his feet in and prepared to rise. "Thank you, Mr. Moretti, for a most interesting half hour. I wish I could stay longer, but Louis and I promised Miss Addams we'd join the rest of the guests for a discussion of the pardon issue, and we're already late." He rose and put out his hand.

As I took it Alison asked sharply, "But don't you have any advice for us, Mr. Darrow?"

The lawyer released my hand and took hold of his lapels. "Why, yes," he answered coolly.

"If you need the services of an attorney, please get in touch with me. But I doubt if you will. In any case, good luck." Turning, he slouched toward the door. "Coming, Louis?"

Sullivan, stiffly erect, gave my hand a single shake as he fixed me with his eye. "*I* have some advice for you," he said harshly. "Nobody wants to worry about problems without solutions. You've got hold of a problem here. If you want anybody to listen to you, present the solution along with it."

"I haven't a hint what the solution might be, Mr. Sullivan."

He shrugged his splendidly tailored shoulders. "Then find out." He bowed abruptly to Alison and followed Darrow from the room, his bearing as rigid as a drum major on parade.

After they had left I sat down on the settee beside Alison. "A salutary exchange of opinions, to be sure," I said glumly, "but that's all I can say for it."

"Why, Paddy, I thought Mr. Darrow's analysis of the situation was extremely helpful," Alison replied with a frown. "At least now we know who our enemies are."

"Which is to say, the entire population of Chicago."

"I can't believe that. You can never paint a

whole group with a single brush. I will not believe that everyone in the city will place material desire above the free expression of facts. As Mr. Bryant said, 'Truth crushed to earth shall rise again.' "

"Which may be one of the main differences between Truth and people," I said.

She turned toward me with a look of vexation on her long, lovely face. Her mouth was tight again, I noticed. Before she could speak I raised my hand. "All right, Miss Bluestocking, I take it back. God's in His Heaven, watching the sparrow in his fall, and all's right with the world, including Chicago."

"I didn't say that!"

"Indeed you didn't, and I'll whip the man that says you did!" My eyes moved from her flashing eyes and determined chin to the smooth column of her neck and the swelling flesh that divided at the vee of her dress. "I'm not about to get in an argument with you. You can depend on it."

She studied me for a moment and then stood up, her hands smoothing the blue satin over her hips. "In that case, I suggest it's time to leave."

"To leave?" I repeated as I got to my feet.

"Of course. In search of Bridey Tumulty,

Queen of the Tenderloin." She lowered her head and looked up at me through her lashes. "You hadn't forgotten, had you?"

10

The Blind Beldam

Alison Markey demonstrated a startling familiarity with the brothels, bordellos, and bagnios of the levee. When I commented on it, she said, "Well, after all, prostitution is my business, you know."

"In case I ever take you home to meet my mother, perhaps you might think of another way of phrasing that," I suggested.

She tilted her head and raised one eyebrow. "Why, Mr. Moretti, how the pendulum doth swing! Two days ago you came to our apartment to bury your nose in a whiskey bottle with my brother, and now you express concern at the moral image *I* project! I can only conclude that Chicago has exercised an uncharacteristically Christian influence on you!"

I raised my hand. "Peace, madam! Phrase your phrases any way you like. However you do it, they're music to my ears! Now, what's our first stop?"

We were traveling, in spite of the cabbie's

remonstrances, south on Market Street, beside the south branch of the Chicago River. It was a sinister neighborhood, with few streetlights and buildings whose windows were either dark or heavily curtained. The streets were almost deserted; the few pedestrians we passed either lurched drunkenly along the curb or kept to the shadows. Every so often a saloon appeared, interrupting the somber procession of residences, warehouses, and storefronts with glaring lights and cheerless laughter.

Alison leaned back on the cab seat and folded her hands in her lap. "We're close to Custom House Place — there's a saloon called Big Augie's on the corner of Harrison. If Bridey Tumulty's in the neighborhood, we might find her there."

I chewed a knuckle. "You think there's really a chance she can tell us anything? It seems like a long shot."

"Yes, I think there's a chance. I don't know of a better one — do you?"

I shook my head and leaned out the cab window. "Cabbie! Take us to Big Augie's, corner of Custom House and Harrison!"

The cabbie looked over his shoulder, an aghast expression on his face. "Oh, you don't want to be taking a lady there, sir! Not if you care about her at all!"

I glanced at Alison. "You heard the man."

"I heard him," she replied without interest.

"Big Augie's it is," I called out the window. "And many thanks for your advice."

The cabbie swore and popped his whip, the old horse leaned into the harness, and we clattered down the empty street. We didn't speak again until the cab pulled up in front of Big Augie's.

Alison allowed me to take her hand and help her down from the cab. As I did so I noticed that the street wasn't quite empty after all; another cab was rounding the corner of Market Street, heading toward us. *If you have the brains you were born with, friend,* I reflected idly, *you'll drive on past and head for Michigan Avenue.*

And thought no more about it.

Big Augie's was all the cabbie had implied: a big, crowded, smoky room stinking of stale beer, unwashed bodies, and cheap perfume. A third of the patrons were whores, a third thugs, and the remaining third were victims of various kinds — victims of the whores and of the thugs, and mostly victims of themselves. Some were sprawled unconscious over tables, some were laughing or singing, some stared blindly ahead or sobbed into their drinks. As we entered, we narrowly avoided colliding with an unconscious man carried between two bouncers; his head hung loosely, his toes dragged on the floor, and his trouser pockets had been turned inside out.

Alison paused in the doorway, and for a moment the cacophonous din was muted. As she surveyed the room, she might have been waiting for the headwaiter at Henrici's; she stood poised and expectant, but without impatience, her slender body in its gleaming blue satin sheath neither inviting attention nor avoiding it. I drew myself up to my full height and glared around the room as if to say *I'm the one she came with — and I'm the one she'll leave with!*

She led the way to an empty table, moving gracefully between the crowded drinkers. Once when a hairy hand closed on her wrist she removed it as coolly as if it were a burr on her dress; she was deaf to shouted invitations, and suggestive comments elicited no response from her. Walking behind her, I was aware of my heart pounding and my palms dampening; it was all I could do to keep my movements casual and my expression bored.

When we were seated she said in a businesslike way, "She's not here. You'll have to order yourself a drink."

"And why would I want to do that?" I demanded, although it sounded like an excellent idea.

"So we'll have an excuse to stay and ask questions."

"Then I'll force myself." The waitress appeared, a blowsy blonde with a four-inch scar on her right cheek. She looked suspiciously at Alison as she asked for our order.

I said I'd like whiskey with a beer wash. "Nothing for me, thank you," Alison said. "But I wonder if you could help me? I'm looking for Bridey Tumulty. Has she been in tonight, or do you expect her?"

The woman's eyes narrowed. "What was that name again?"

"Bridey Tumulty," Alison repeated patiently. "You know her. The blind madam."

The woman assumed an expression of deep thought. While she was developing her rôle I produced a dollar bill, folded it longways, and tapped it on the edge of the table. It drew her eyes like a magnet. "What do you want with her?" she demanded.

"A little conversation, nothing that need concern you. I'm a friend of hers. I wouldn't do anything to cause her trouble."

The woman's eyes flicked to Alison unbelievingly, and then returned to the bill. She licked one corner of her lips. "I don't know — I'll get your drink, mister." Tearing her eyes away, she weaved between the tables toward the bar.

"Checking with the higher-up," Alison said, watching her.

"Or with the lower-down," I amended, for the waitress had reached the bar and was leaning over it, engaged in conversation with a man whose head barely showed above the gleaming mahogany. The man's eyes turned our way. A moment later his head moved down the bar, and then he appeared around its corner.

"Big Augie in the flesh," I hazarded.

The midget moved between the tables swiftly, although he seemed to totter on his tiny feet. His face was that of a chubby and corrupt child; his fat cheeks were tallowy, and his round eyes were pouched and wary. His pale hair was parted in the middle and plastered down with some kind of heavy grease, which also caused the skin near the hairline to gleam wetly. He wore a short apron around his waist, from the top of which projected the handle of a bung starter.

He stopped by our table, resting one tiny hand upon it. "I hear you're looking for somebody." His voice was high and piping, with a mechanical quality to it. "Want to tell me about it?"

"Big Augie?" Alison asked. At his nod, she continued, "My name is Alison Markey. I work with Miss Jane Addams at Hull-House.

Angelina Crocci sends you her regards."

The midget's bulging eyes narrowed and his pouting mouth opened. He wet his lips with the tip of his tongue. "Angelina —," he repeated. "Angelina? What about Angelina?"

"Why, she wanted me to tell you that she's just fine. She has an excellent job at a better than adequate salary, and her employers are delighted with her. She's sharing a flat with another woman. It's very nice. It's outside the city — I'm sorry I can't tell you where."

"And the baby?" Big Augie asked in an unsteady voice.

"Already adopted, into a fine family. She has a promising future in store for her, God willing." Alison smiled sweetly, with a touch of Lady Bountiful in her expression. "So you see, everything has worked out for the best," she went on. "I'm so glad — for all our sakes."

The midget seemed to have difficulty speaking. He made two false starts before he managed to say, "That's okay, then. I don't have to hear nothing else about it. Tell Miss Addams thanks." He snorted and wiped the back of his hand across his nub of a nose. When he spoke again, his voice had regained a little of its former harshness. "Now what's this about Bridey Tumulty?"

"We'd like to have a few words with her — my

friend Mr. Moretti and I. Nothing that would cause her any bother or inconvenience, I assure you."

Big Augie stared up at me suspiciously. "Who's he?" he demanded.

Before I could answer, Alison answered, "A friend of mine — and a friend of Hull-House. He's helping us on another delicate problem. We need some answers, and I'm sure *you* will want to assist us." Her stress on the word *you* conveyed the slightest suggestion of indebtedness.

Big Augie licked his lips again. "How come you think I know this Bridey twist?"

"Oh, Big Augie, you know her. You didn't become one of the most important men on the levee by having a bad memory." She smiled and waited for his answer like a schoolteacher waiting for a favorite student to recite.

Big Augie gave up. "She ain't been in here in two, three months. I hear tell she's mostly at the Boots and Saddles, down at Twenty-third and Wabash. Jock O'Roark's joint. If anybody asks who told you, dummy up. Got it?" Alison nodded, and I followed suit. Big Augie turned his back to us and waved a diminutive arm at our waitress, who was watching us from beside the bar. "You Ellen, there!" he screamed in a piercing boy soprano, "bring over drinks for these people!"

The scarred blonde scooped up two glasses from the bar and hurried to our table, passing the midget en route. She placed a shot glass of whiskey and a six-ounce glass of beer in front of me, spilling some of both in the process. "Geez, I'm sorry, mister. I can't answer no questions without *he* says it's all right – you know?"

I produced the bill I had shown her before and tucked it into her hand. "It's all right," I assured her. "Your discretion does you credit."

When she had left us, I took a sip of the whiskey and washed it down with a swallow of beer. The resultant taste was so disagreeable I was contemplating reversing the order, when I noticed that Alison was tapping her fingers impatiently on the tabletop. "Sure you wouldn't like a touch of something yourself?" I asked.

"What I'd like would be to get out of this foul den before you befuddle your senses with alcohol," she said crisply.

"But it was you yourself who told me to order it!" I pointed out.

"Yes, but I didn't tell you to *drink* it. Now come on. We don't have all night." And before I could empty either glass she stood up and started for the door.

The street in front of Big Augie's was empty,

236

although there was a hansom waiting by the curb half a block away. I whistled and waved, but the driver on the seat did not respond. Assuming the cab was engaged, I looked for another. Five minutes later it appeared, and I helped Alison aboard. "The Boots and Saddles, Twenty-third and Wabash," I said, and we sank back into the musty leather seats.

In the light of the passing streetlamps Alison's face was composed and calm. She seemed as far removed from our evil surroundings as if she were enjoying a Sunday afternoon in Lincoln Park. I admired her patrician beauty for a few moments, speculating on the pleasures that might come from agitating its placid perfection. As I was trying to decide whether or not to drape a casual arm over the seat behind her, she turned and looked directly at me. "Well?" she asked coolly.

"Well —" I answered, and for a moment could think of nothing else to say. I folded my hands on my lap. "Well, I was wondering — I was wondering what all that was about, back there in the saloon. That business with Big Augie, about that Angelina What's-her-name."

"Crocci — Angelina Crocci." She sighed. "Poor Angelina. She was a part-time prostitute who also worked as a dishwasher whenever she could. For a while she worked for Big Augie.

She wasn't very bright, I'm afraid, but she was quiet and modest and had a very sweet nature. Big Augie was extremely fond of her."

"You don't mean —," I interrupted.

"Well, I don't know, not for sure. But Angelina became pregnant, that I do know. Sometimes I wonder if she even knew what caused it. She was certainly unable to name the father, but Big Augie adopted an extremely protective attitude. It was easy to see him in the paternal role."

"Not so easy for me," I said. "The mere thought of him assuming the necessary position is enough to stagger the mind."

Alison's lips thinned. "Then I suggest you avoid the thought, and others like it," she said in clipped tones. I swallowed and waited, and in a moment she went on: "The upshot was that Big Augie came to Hull-House for help. He realized, and we agreed with him, that it was unthinkable for Angelina to have her child while living and working as she was. For whatever reasons, Big Augie declined to assume the legal burden of fatherhood. Therefore we took responsibility and moved Angelina to Halsted Street until the child was born. Afterwards we were able to arrange for her and the child's relocation to one of the western suburbs, and for the subsequent adoption. One of the terms of our agreement with Big Augie was that he was not to know their address. That's all there is to it."

"Remarkable. And the little fellow – is he built along the same dimensions as his father?"

"As it happens, the little fellow is a girl. And as far as we can tell at this early age, she is perfectly normal physically. And also mentally." Alison smiled. "With luck, she may avoid both her parents' handicaps. I hope so."

"I hope so myself." Remembering my conversation with her brother in his apartment two days before, I added experimentally, "I'm sure both mother and daughter will find lives with social value, thanks to you."

Her eyes widened in surprise. "Why, what a nice thing to say! It's nothing I can take any personal credit for, of course – But I'm so glad to hear you place importance on social value, Mr. Moretti. I hadn't realized your attitude was so responsible."

"To me, social value is the very heart of the matter, Miss Markey. The *ne plus ultra* and the *sine qua non*. The polestar for all our earthly navigation. The keystone of all our human erect – edifices." I turned toward her and placed my arm along the top of the seat behind her. "You might say that social value is my middle name, Miss Markey."

239

She leaned forward just far enough to avoid contact with my arm. "Then in that regard there is a considerable difference between you and my brother. I don't believe Boz would recognize social value if he met it on the street wearing a sandwich board."

"You shouldn't be so fast to condemn the man, if you'll pardon me for saying so. After all, it was his investigations of those disappearing women of yours that put him where he is today, flat on his back on a bed of pain."

"Oh, you're right, you're right," she said in a contrite voice. "Poor Boz. Sometimes I think I may be too hard on him. His physical health isn't all it should be, I'm sure. And I believe he has financial worries – something he said about the stock market recently – I didn't understand it, and he wouldn't explain. If I were more sympathetic and less judgmental, perhaps he would begin to look more on the side of social values. Is that what you think, Mr. Moretti?"

"Well, we're all of us a little lower than angels, as they say." I leaned toward her and placed my hand gently on her shoulder. "And poor flawed creatures as we are, we must be kind to one another. Especially those of us with things in common. We must offer one another strength and forgiveness. We must love one another —"

Her eyes were wide and her lips were slightly parted. My face was only an inch from hers. I tightened my grip and drew her toward me. . . .

"Boots and Saddles," the cabman shouted as the hansom creaked to a stop. "Maybe I should wait till you decide if you want to stay or not."

I stifled a curse, and let my arm fall to my side. Alison turned her face away, but not before I saw she was smiling. "That won't be necessary, my man," I shouted back. "How much do I owe you?" He told me, and I paid him after I had helped Alison down the cab step, and he clattered off down the deserted street.

Jock O'Roark's saloon was a cut above Big Augie's, but it was a narrow cut. The smell was a trifle less oppressive and the clientele a bit better dressed, but they still appeared to be evenly divided into the three classes of whores, thugs, and victims. A number of the men looked like jockeys, and there were paintings of racehorses on the walls.

Alison's entrance caused the same muting of the noise level as it had in Big Augie's, and she seemed just as oblivious to it. She paused in the doorway and studied the crowd, her eyes skipping from table to table until they reached a black enameled screen standing a few feet out from the wall in the far corner of the room. Then she gave a curt nod. "She's here. Come on."

We worked our way across the room toward the screen. It was made of three hinged panels, each about two feet wide by six feet high; standing open, it concealed an area almost two yards square. The decoration was *chinoiserie* peacocks and pagodas, once brilliant, now dulled with age and grime.

As Alison approached the screen a man arose from the table nearest it. He had a gray, eroded face, and eyes that seemed to have a lifetime of bitterness and despair in them. His suit had been sharply tailored, but fitted his shrunken body as shapelessly as a blanket. I recognized him as an addict. He reached a talonlike hand toward Alison and said, "Hold your horses, lady. Where do you think you're going?"

Alison coolly avoided his hand and paused at the edge of the screen. "Why, back here — to talk to Bridey Tumulty, if she's here, and I strongly suspect she is."

"Unh-unh. Bridey don't talk to nobody unless it's *her* idea. Forget it." His fingers made a second approach to her arm and curved around her elbow.

"Don't worry. It *will* be her idea, when she

hears where I'm from, and why I want to talk to her." She glanced down at his hand, and continued to stare at it until he flexed the fingers uncertainly.

I was about to suggest that he unhand the lady when a voice from behind the screen cried, "All right, I give up. Who the hell are you, and why should I give a damn where you're from?"

Alison pulled her arm free and stepped around the screen. I followed, pausing only to smile coldly at the watchdog, who gave me a look of baffled resentment in exchange.

The woman sitting alone at the table behind the screen might have been attractive forty years and two hundred pounds ago — her brow was wide, her nose was straight and narrow, and her hands were small — but the appearance she conveyed today was of a great powdered frog. Her chalky skin was crammed with fat; fat globes of cheeks pressed against her smoked glasses and crowded her mouth into the shape of a tiny pink shrimp; fat folds like sausages fell from her chin to her bosom; fat hillocks strained against the gleaming black bombazine that covered her body. The fat seemed out of control, as if it were increasing visibly before one's very eyes.

Her face was powdered in a haphazard manner, so that some areas were only lightly dusted, while others were caked dead-white. Her hair, which was quite thin and showed the scalp beneath, was of an indescribable color — or rather, the residue of an indescribable mixture of colors; at various times it must have ranged from ash blond to black.

Her earrings were twin gold bird cages, with tiny birds inside that appeared to be made of silver, jade, and jet.

She turned the empty black windows of her glasses toward us and said, "Okay, let's hear it."

Alison said briskly, "Mrs. Tumulty, my name is Alison Markey, and my friend is Mr. Paddy Moretti, of New York. I work with Miss Jane Addams of Hull-House, where as you know we have been able to help many of the women in your profession. Now it seems that something terrible may be happening, and I want to ask you if you know anything about it."

"Hull-House, huh? So you work for Hull-House. Your friend from New York, is he a do-gooder, too?"

Before I could answer Alison replied, "Oh, no, Mrs. Tumulty. Mr. Moretti is an executive in the publishing business."

"He is, huh? Let him speak for himself." She turned her massive head toward me. "How're they hanging, Mr. Moretti?"

It seemed best to ignore the question. I said, "How do you do, Mrs. Tumulty."

The woman snorted and turned her face away from the sound of my voice toward Alison again. "Yeah, I know your Miss Addams. She's all right. She's helped out some of the girls when nobody else would. If she'd just quit trying to turn them back into virgins, I'd like her better though. But I don't hold it against her. A woman can't help being born decent." One fat cheek rose to allow the corner of her mouth to curl. "Is that your problem, too, dearie? You bit by the same bug? You want to save all us poor sinners from a life of deg-ree-dation?"

Alison answered evenly, "No, Mrs. Tumulty. I want to find out why a great many women are disappearing here in Chicago. Since many of them are either prostitutes or ex-prostitutes, I think you would be interested in helping."

The blind woman reached her hand unerringly to the whiskey glass in front of her and drained it. "Beau!" she called, and the man who served as watchdog slid by us and refilled the glass from a bottle on the table. She nodded her head in acknowledgement, and he stepped behind us again.

"Whores are always disappearing," she said. "They got no sense of responsibility — that's why they're whores."

"I'm talking about other women, too. Women who have started a new life, or never were part of the old one."

Bridey Tumulty shook her head, and five pounds of soft flesh jiggled. "How would I know anything about them?" she demanded.

"I'm not asking you about them," Alison said. "I'm asking you what you do know about. I'm asking you about disappearances here, on the levee. Please, Mrs. Tumulty — can you tell me anything?"

The old madam picked up her glass and held it a moment between her small, puffy fingers. She licked her lips before taking a thoughtful sip. Then she placed it carefully before her on the table. "All right, maybe there have been too many girls disappearing. What do you want us to do about it? You think the cops are interested? You think the newspapers are going to send out reporters? In Chicago? In the middle of the goddamn Columbian Exposition? Act your age!"

"What do you think is happening?" Alison pressed. "What do people say about it?"

"People say anything. You can't pay attention to what people say." She drank the rest of her drink, scowling. "Beau!" she shouted, and waited while her glass was refilled. Then she said, in a troubled voice, "Some of the girls think there's a collector working."

"A what?" I asked.

"A collector. Some crazy galoot that collects scalps. Women's scalps. Or whatever parts he wants to save. And then gets rid of the rest of them. That's what some of the girls are saying. I don't take no stock in it myself." She gave a forced laugh. "Listen, forget it. Sit down and have a drink. I don't get much chance to visit with do-gooders from Hull-House. We can talk about how the other half lives."

Alison glanced at me inquiringly. I shrugged my shoulders. She said, "Thank you, Mrs. Tumulty. We'll be glad to join you for a few minutes."

At the blind woman's order, Beau busied himself finding us chairs and pouring us drinks. His hands were shaking so badly he spilled an ounce of whiskey on the table. I took a swallow of mine; Alison left hers untouched before her. We sat for a few moments without speaking. Beyond the screen the sound of a hundred voices merged into a raucous alcoholic cacophony. Suddenly two male voices rose above the rest; one was a tenor, the other a baritone. They were questioning each other's manhood, profanely and in picturesque detail. Bridey Tumulty gave a short laugh. "Goddamn jockeys," she said.

"How do you know?" Alison asked curiously.

"Because they're all banty roosters when it comes to their precious privates. The smaller they are, the bigger they act. You hear somebody yelling about how he takes care of three different women in one night, you can bet he stands five foot tall and weighs a hundred pounds dripping wet."

Alison said, "Tell me what the girls say about the collector, Mrs. Tumulty."

The madam shook her head. "Jockeys," she continued. "There ain't nobody else like 'em. There was a couple of 'em fighting over some bitch two, three nights ago. I thought they was going to kill each other before they was through. They were both too stupid to see she was playing them off against each other. Jockeys!" she snorted.

Suddenly the memory of a conversation ran through my head. What was it Velma had said on the train, as we drank our way across Indiana? *I wouldn't know about slow jockeys — the ones I know are fast every which way.* And *You'd think I would have learned by now.* Alison was about to speak, no doubt to repeat her question about the collector, but I raised a finger to forestall her. "What night did you say that was, Mrs. Tumulty?" I asked.

248

"I don't know. What's tonight — Friday? Then it was Tuesday. Tuesday. Who the hell cares?" She swallowed half her drink and coughed. "Some of my best customers have been jockeys. Every one of them the cock of the walk, to hear them tell it. I remember once, in my house on Taylor Street —"

"Last Tuesday night — the woman with the two jockeys. You didn't hear anybody call her by name, did you? Or say anything about her personally?"

Bridey Tumulty turned her round black insect-eyes toward me and said harshly, "What's eating you, Mr. New York? No, I didn't hear nobody call her by name. And even if I did, what's that got to do with the price of fish?" She raised her glass to her nose and sniffed the raw whiskey as if it were fine cognac. "New York," she said in a thick voice. "I like your town, Mr. New York. Never should have left. They know how to take care of things back there."

With a touch of impatience in her tone, Alison returned to her unanswered question. "What do the girls say about the collector, Mrs. Tumulty?"

The madam stretched her arm toward Alison, touching her first on the forehead and then drawing her finger down to trace the outline of her nose, mouth, chin, and throat, coming to rest finally in the vee of Alison's bosom. "Hey, you're put together real good, honey," she said. "How'd you like to make some good money on the side? Some nights when you ain't working for Miss Jane Addams — I'll show you how to have some fun and make yourself a bundle besides."

Alison looked calmly into the old woman's derisive face. "You can't shock me, Mrs. Tumulty. I wouldn't be very good at my job if you could. So let's talk about the collector."

"Goddamn the collector! There ain't any collector! It's all hot air." She drank quickly, and when she spoke again, her voice was noticeably slurred. "Talking about New York. Wonderful place. Never should have left it. I remember — I remember —" She paused, and a startlingly gentle smile crossed her face. "Oh, they loved me in New York! Everybody loved me! There wasn't nothing too good for me! They knew how to take care of a girl in New York!"

"Mrs. Tumulty —," Alison said, but it was no good. Bridey Tumulty wanted to talk about the golden days of her youth, when she represented the acme of desirability to Tammany politicians, society playboys, underworld chieftains, and captains of industry. "They waited in line to buy me champagne," she remembered. "Real French champagne — I never drank nothing else."

Alison raised an eyebrow at me ruefully and sat back in her chair to wait out the rain of reminiscences. I uncrossed and recrossed my legs and toyed with my glass. Out of the corner of my eye I could see Beau, standing behind us, chew on his lip.

"— and then the Hi-Lows set me up in my own house. You wouldn't believe the parties we'd have! Everybody who was anybody come to Bridey's place! We ate lobster and pheasant and fresh strawberries, and there was always a string orchestra, and not a girl in the place went for less than thirty bucks a trick! And never a peep from the Law — the Hi-Lows seen to that!"

"The Hi-Lows?" I interrupted. "I've heard about them. They were a power back in the eighties. Operated on the East Side, north of Houston and east of Avenue A. Women and contract murder, mostly." Ignoring Alison's look of irritation, I continued, with a reporter's unselective curiosity, "What happened to them?"

"Lost their protection. Paying off the wrong man or not paying off the right one, I never got it straight." She shook her head. "Too bad, too bad. They was real gents, them Heidenreits. Classy. Louis, he was the boss. When he come by the house, he'd lock the door, throw a party, sky was the limit. And brother Hugo, he took care of the girls good as any sawbones. None of 'em got sick, hardly ever, y'know? And no trouble with the customers that way. We used to kid him — told him he ought to get out of the rackets and hang up his shingle. And Louis — what a dude Louis was! Claw hammer coat and striped pants, always wearing a fresh carnation — I could have gone for Louis myself."

"But you didn't?" I asked.

Her pink shrimp of a mouth turned down. "Never had the chance. One of the girls had him wrapped up. Girl named Wilma. A Dutchie from upstate. Never could figure out what he seen in her."

"Wilma? Was her last name Verhulst?" In my excitement I leaned forward so suddenly that Beau put a cautionary hand on my shoulder.

"Who the hell cares?" She emptied her glass and called, "Beau!" I glanced at Alison. She was looking at me, and her eyes were wide.

I waited impatiently until Bridey's glass had been refilled, and then I put my hand on her spongy wrist. "Listen, Mrs. Tumulty, this is important. The woman you were talking about, the one you said was in here last Tuesday, that you said was playing off the two jockeys against each other — was her voice familiar? Could she have been that woman from New York? Could she have been Wilma?"

For a long moment the blind madam froze in mid-motion, her glass raised a few inches from the table. Behind her smoked glasses her expression was unreadable. Then she carefully put the glass down without drinking from it. "What ya talking about? Wilma? How could it have been Wilma? I told you she worked in New York." Her voice was noticeably less slurred.

"Are you saying it *wasn't* Wilma?" I pressed.

"How the hell would I know? Who remembers voices after ten years? Listen, Mr. New York, I'm tired of you. You ask too many questions. Go away. And take your do-gooder friend with you. You hear me? Beau! Get 'em out of here. And make sure they don't come back! I'm sick of 'em!"

Beau's hand tightened on my shoulder. I began to rise, then paused. "Just one more thing, Mrs. Tumulty," I said earnestly. "The jockeys who were with that woman last Tuesday — can you tell me anything about them? It's for the sake of all the missing women I'm asking you! Won't you tell me anything you remember?"

She sat motionless, her great black insect-eyes as opaque as Fate, her gross body like a frozen waterfall. Then she said, in a voice so low I could barely hear it over the noise of the saloon, "One of 'em was named Sparrow somebody. He was a real mean bastard. The other one, I think his name was Ernie, or Eddie, or something. I can't remember."

"Try!" In my excitement I squeezed her wrist, and it must have hurt her, for she jerked her hand back with a cry. Instantly Beau's grip tightened on my shoulder, his fingers pressing into my trapezius with enough force to make me gasp in pain. I rose to my full height and took a step away from the table. "All right!" I cried.

Alison stood up. "Thank you for the help you've been able to give us, Mrs. Tumulty. If you should remember anything more, you can send word to me at Hull-House. I know I speak for Miss Addams when I say we would be grateful." The blind madam didn't reply. With a curt nod to me, Alison led the way around the *chinoiserie* screen and out into the noisy, smoky barroom. I followed, and Beau brought up the rear, his fingers locked in my shoulder muscle. This procession continued until we were half-way to the street door, at which time Beau released me and returned to his watchdog position at the table nearest the screen.

Alison moved coolly between the tables, ignoring propositions and avoiding clutching hands. I followed, rubbing my shoulder gingerly. We had almost reached the entrance when Alison spied a familiar face.

"I know that woman," she said, gesturing toward a sad-eyed and hollow-cheeked brunette sitting between two toughs. "She shouldn't be here — she's not well. I have to talk to her."

The prospect of intruding on the evening plans of the two proprietary-looking thugs was anything but attractive, and my expression must have shown it, for Alison added quickly, "I'll only be a minute or two. You go out and find us a cab."

I looked uncertainly around the noisy room. "I don't think you ought to be here alone, Alison."

"Nonsense. Places like this are where I do my work. I'm not made of spun glass, you know. Now go, please." Before I could answer, she resolutely approached the threesome at their table and, disregarding the scowls of the two men, seated herself beside them.

I gave a mental shrug and pushed my way out of the saloon. *You can always tell a lady,* I thought, *but Lord knows you can't tell her much.*

The sidewalk outside was empty, as was the

street, except for a stationary carriage half a block away. I waited impatiently for three or four minutes, but no cab appeared. Realizing I might stand in front of the Boots and Saddles for an hour and still not find one, I started walking toward State Street, where traffic was bustling.

Ten minutes later I returned. My driver pulled up in front of the saloon, and I leaped down onto the sidewalk. I was surprised to see another cab at the curb in front of us, and even more surprised to see Alison preparing to enter it.

"Alison!" I called. "Here! This is our cab!"

She hesitated with one foot on the step. "Paddy? Is that you? What do we need two cabs for?"

I trotted toward her. At that moment the door of the other cab, which had been open, suddenly slammed shut. There was a muffled order, the snap of a whip, and the cab lurched forward so suddenly that Alison almost lost her balance. I steadied her as she stumbled backward.

"Whoa there, I've got you!" I said as my arm encircled her supple waist. She allowed it to remain there as she stared at me in surprise.

"What was the matter with that man? Why, he might have killed me, starting up like that!"

I led her back toward the second cab, and seated her inside. "Let's get out of this neighborhood. Where do you want to go — Huron Street, or back to Hull-House?" She said Huron Street, and I gave the driver the address. Then, as we rattled north through the sinister emptiness of Wabash Avenue, I asked, "Now for heaven's sake, whatever possessed you to climb into a stranger's cab that way?"

"Well, he wasn't a stranger, that was the point! I mean, he said you had sent him. He said you wanted me to come with him in the cab. He was to pick me up at the Boots and Saddles and bring me to where you were waiting. He said you couldn't come yourself because you were tied up." Her eyes were very wide as she added, "He was lying. And I never even suspected."

A chill ran up my spine. I took her hand and squeezed it. "A very persuasive fellow, indeed. What did he look like?"

"I couldn't see him, it was too dark in the cab. But he sounded like a gentleman. He had a deep, soft voice, like an actor or a singer. And he sounded so *believable*. I didn't question what he said for a moment!"

The chill had spread to my arms and legs. "He mentioned me by name?" She nodded. "How about you? Did he call you by name, too?"

"No. He just said you wanted me to join you, and asked me to get in the cab. I think he called me 'My dear,' but it didn't seem presumptuous the way he said it." She was silent for a moment, and I realized she was now holding my hand in both of hers. Then she said, softly, "I'm afraid, Paddy. For the first time since I've worked at Hull-House, I'm afraid."

"Then that makes two of us."

"I'm afraid," she repeated in a stronger voice, "and that makes me *mad*. Damn him, or them, or whoever it is! I won't be frightened this way! I won't! I've never been afraid to go anywhere in this city, at any hour of the day or night, and I won't let anybody change that!" She raised my hand in both of hers and brought it down on her knee to emphasize her words.

"A certain amount of judicious fear," I pointed out, "can do wonders in saving a person's life." She turned toward me angrily, and I hurried on: "Not that I'm advocating cowardice — just a healthy sense of self-preservation."

"I won't be bullied!"

"And am I suggesting you should be? It's the farthest thing from my mind! Only — Alison, I think disappearing women are close to being news in Chicago. Whether the McCormicks and Potter Palmers like it or not. I'd like to stay alive long enough to see it happen."

"Yes — and so would I, of course. Of course I would. Only it makes me so mad —" She caught herself, and went on in a more even tone, "So you think this proves there's a connection between your Velma, and the other missing women, and what happened to you and to Boz?" She shook her head. "I don't know. It seems so, so *grandiose*, somehow."

"Like the Columbian Exposition?" I asked.

She nodded. "I suppose so, now that you mention it. Like Mr. Sullivan's Whited Sepulcher. *Grandiose* seems to fit a lot of things in Chicago. What was it Mr. Burnham said? 'Make no little plans —' That applies to everything else here, so why shouldn't it apply to murder?"

"Why indeed?"

We sat in silence as the cab rattled across Twelfth Street and continued north through the First Ward. After a few moments Alison released my hand and folded hers in her lap. She frowned as she asked, "Why were you so excited when Mrs. Tumulty told you the name of that jockey?"

"Because his name is Sparrow, and the only jockey named Sparrow I know is Sparrow Simpson, and he's riding the favorite, Mustafa, in the American Derby tomorrow. And something tells me the other jockey's name might not have been Ernie or Eddie, like she thought. It might have been Early.

"And Early Fetzer is the jockey who'll be riding Home Free in the same race — the horse that's owned by that esteemed sportsman Mr. Paul Vannatta."

11

Derby Day

Boz was awake when we arrived at the Huron Street apartment. He was sitting up in bed, playing cutthroat euchre with two competent-looking bruisers from the *Tribune*'s circulation department. As we entered the bedroom he gestured to us to maintain silence, and deliberately placed the jack of hearts on top of the jack of diamonds and queen of clubs which lay on the coverlet before him.

"Gentlemen," he said with great self-satisfaction, "as I believe I've explained to you before, the right bower invariably overtrumps the left bower. It may not seem fair, but there it is. Unless I'm mistaken, your joint indebtedness is now eight dollars. You may pay me now, before my sister runs you out of the room." He extended his hand and waited while the palm was covered with wadded bills and change. "A pleasure, as always," he said in dismissal, tucking the money under his pillow. "Raise some more wherewithal and I'll be delighted to accommodate you again."

When the two grumbling bodyguards had left the room he turned to us. "A bit late for a social call, but welcome for all that. Sit down and unburden yourselves. Having yourselves a night on the town, are you? I like that gown, sis."

"Boz, there are things you should know about," Alison began crisply. She remained standing by the bed during her report, like a grammar school student reciting her lessons. I sat down in one of the chairs vacated by the bodyguards and only spoke when called upon.

Boz's expression grew increasingly grave as Alison described our conversation with Bridey Tumulty, and when she told him about the cab waiting for her when she left the saloon he threw back his head and groaned. "Oh, my God, Allie — Allie, you little fool, if anything happened to you I'd never forgive myself!" He leaned forward and seized her by the arm. "Promise me — you hear? — promise me you'll forget this business! Promise me you'll stop asking questions and stay at Hull-House where you belong!"

"Don't you think it's a little late for that, Boz?" Alison asked. "Here are the three of us — you flat on your back from a bogus accident, Paddy barely a step ahead of a gang of ice-pick-waving hoodlums, and I almost lured into a cab for God knows what sinister ends. Don't you think it's a little late for staying out of trouble and keeping our noses clean?" She paused, but before he could reply, she continued with asperity: "And what do you mean about if anything happens, you'll never forgive yourself? I hope you're not flattering yourself that *you* got *me* involved in this business? If you'll remember, it was *I* who came to *you* about the three women we were helping who disappeared. And you, Paddy," she went on in a slightly softer voice, "remember that it was *I* who suggested to *you* that we continue our inquiries by tracking down Bridey Tumulty on the levee. So don't you think, Boz, that it's a little vainglorious of you to talk about 'never forgiving *yourself*'?"

"Wait a minute," I said. "We're making an assumption here. We're assuming that everything that's happened is connected, that Velma's disappearance and the disappearances of Alison's women, and Boz's accident and my trouble with the Quincys, and the police not wanting to get involved, and this stuff tonight at the Boots and Saddles, we're assuming it's all part of a pattern. But what if it's not?"

"That's right!" Boz slapped his hand on the coverlet. "Why in the world would there be any connection between this collector, whoever he is, and Paul Vannatta and a couple of jockeys?

Or with your friend, Velma, Paddy? To tell you the truth, old chum, I've never been happy with your attempts to shoehorn your departed Delilah into Alison's pack of practicing and reformed professionals. It seems more likely that the prospect of seeing you again was simply more than she could bear."

"Then why did the Quincys warn me off in my hotel room? I hadn't asked any questions about anybody but Velma."

"Yes, and why should they have tried to run you down on the street?" Alison demanded of her brother. "After all, you *hadn't* been asking questions about Velma, and Paddy *had*. So there must be a connection!"

"No, that's not logical," Boz argued. "It's enough that two reporters are known to be digging into stories that might result in bad publicity for the Exposition — for Chicago's sacred cow, from which all manna flows. The stories don't have to be connected at all; the point is, they might do damage. That would be enough to send the word down to the Quincys telling them to discourage any further activity on our part."

"What about tonight, at the Boots and Saddles?" Alison asked. "The man in the cab? Did the powers that be send the word down to him, too? Was he also supposed to discourage any further activity on our part?"

Boz attempted a leer. "He was probably there to avail himself of the handsomest female he could find, and you most amply filled the bill." He shrugged and continued seriously, "Or maybe he *was* the collector. Stranger things have happened. But if he was, I'll tell you one thing — his presence there had nothing to do with your vanishing Velma, Paddy. Your Velma has been a red herring from the start of this business."

"Why didn't you say so the first time I told you about her?" I retorted. "You agreed it was a totally mystifying experience, as I recall!"

"I was just trying to protect that fragile Italo-Irish self-esteem of yours. Actually I didn't think it was mystifying at all. A lady walked out on you. Accept it. Time is a great healer."

Alison said, in a deceptively cool voice, "And what is your advice on the other disappearances? Should we trust to Time there, too?"

"To tell you the truth, I think we should." Boz licked his lips uneasily. "I'm not overjoyed to say it, but I think it's the better part of valor at present. Look, sis," he continued earnestly, reaching out to take her hand in his, "I'm flat on my back here in bed. Moretti will be leaving town right after the derby. There either is or is not a mass murderer at work in Chicago. If there is not, then there is no problem at all, and we might as well have a drink and make up limericks. If there is, you'll be facing him alone, without either your right or left bower for protection." As Alison stiffened, he hurried on: "Oh, I know you don't need protection, but humor me. Aside from the two of us, you can't think of anybody in the city who'd raise a hand to help you create a stink and embarrass the Exposition. Your friend Darrow was right about that. And, Alison, I don't like that business in front of the saloon tonight."

"I'm not crazy about it myself. That's why I think something should be done about it!"

Boz rolled his eyes helplessly toward me. "You tell her, Moretti."

"He's right about you being alone in this. The derby's tomorrow, and I'll be on a train for New York the next morning. Boz'll be playing euchre in this bed for a week. And there's nobody else to help. Like he says," I finished unhappily, "it's the better part of valor, and all."

Her eyes snapped scornfully at the two of us. "And we'll assure the collector of an uninterrupted supply of women to murder all summer long. That's fine! Make sure you put in a bill to the city fathers for your services!"

We wrangled over the same ground for half an hour without changing our basic positions.

Finally Alison stamped from the bedroom and slammed the door behind her. I looked at Boz and raised my eyebrows. He shrugged.

"Well, it's late, and I have a full day's work ahead of me tomorrow," I said. "Which reminds me. How the devil am I to get past the guards at Washington Park? They've got orders to have me drawn and quartered if I pollute their sacred grounds again."

"Aha," said Boz, raising one finger. "Fortunately for you, I recently attended a costume party, in the not inappropriate garb of a pirate. If memory serves, you'll find it, complete with eye patch and villainous black mustache, in the bottom drawer of that chiffonier."

"The one where you keep your whiskey and dirty underwear?"

"The very one."

I dug out the crepe hair mustache, the eye patch, and bottle of spirit gum. I eyed the adhesive uncertainly, remembering a previous attempt at disguise that had ended disastrously when a small child had stripped a rabbi's beard from my guilty features. "Are you sure this stuff will work?" I asked.

"You could glue a cow to the ceiling with it," he assured me.

"Maybe I'll use what's left over for that." I put the items in my pocket. "Then I'll be saying good night to you, Bosley, and thanks for your assistance." We shook hands. "I'll stop in and see you again before I leave town."

"You do that, Paddy."

I started for the door and then paused. "You really think Velma walked out on me, and it had nothing to do with this other business?" I asked.

"Absolutely. Think about it with proper modesty and you'll agree."

"You could be right." I left the bedroom, closing the door behind me. Alison was standing in front of a window overlooking the street. I cleared my throat and said, "I hope you'll bear your brother's words in mind, Alison. It could be very dangerous for you to keep digging into these disappearances alone."

She didn't turn her head toward me. "Thank you," she said icily. "Please don't bother yourself about it."

I took a step toward her, and simultaneously she moved to one side until she was behind the seven-foot plaster of paris Priapus who dominated the room. "Yes? Was there something else?" she asked.

I halted. The prospect of playing ring-around-a-rosy with a young lady under such circumstances was more than I was prepared to handle. "If I don't see you before I go back to New York, it's been nice knowing you."

"Good-bye, Mr. Moretti," she said, still with her back to me. "Please close the street door on your way out."

The next day I arrived at the track half an hour before the first race, and had to wait in line at the entrance gate. There was a carnival atmosphere; ladies in their best dresses, faces aglow with excitement and fans fluttering like the wings of imprisoned birds; gentlemen bent under the weight of picnic hampers and red-faced with exertion; less respectable elements strutting their finery as though on the Easter parade, ladies of the evening curtsying to bull-necked toughs, and madams shepherding their charges with slaps and pinches and clucks of admonition. A band was playing marches lustily by the winner's circle, bookmakers were shouting their odds, and hucksters and candy butchers joined their voices to the cheerful cacophony.

I passed the eye of a policeman at the gate and entered the grounds. Immediately I spied a fellow sports reporter, Iggy Grodnitz, of the *Inter-Ocean*. He saw me at the same moment. I let my gaze slide over him without a sign of recognition, and started to walk past.

"Hello, Paddy. What happened to your

eye?" he demanded.

I glanced at him and assumed an expression of surprise. "I beg your pardon," I said in a creditable British accent.

"Somebody hit you with a bottle? You oughta stay out of places like that. How long you been wearing the soup strainer?"

Since the British accent seemed ineffective, I tried an Italian. "I'm sorry, I no understand." I tried to push by him, but he seized my arm.

"I get it. You're on the dodge. Who's after you, Moretti? A jealous husband? Your bookmaker? The law?" He leaned close and lowered his voice to a hoarse whisper. "You can tell me. Professional courtesy. A band of brothers." He had been eating onions.

My shoulders slumped. "It didn't even slow you up for a minute, Ignace?"

"Maybe about two seconds. But then, I've had a chance to study your phiz as few others have. Such as when you're bluffing out a busted straight and are forewarned of doom. People who don't know you as well, maybe they won't tumble." He put a chummy arm around my slumped shoulders. "What's the story, Paddy? Who are you hiding from?"

"You don't want to know, Ignace. If I could tell you about it, I would. But for now, just forget you saw me. Please?"

"Prevailing rates?" Iggy asked quickly, his close-set eyes glinting.

"Prevailing rates," I sighed.

"Jack Callahan's, right after the last race. I'll begin working up a thirst now." He took his arm off my shoulders and turned his attention back to the track, and I walked quickly away into the stands.

Grodnitz's quick identification had shaken my confidence, and during the first two races I found myself lurking behind pillars and shielding my face with my hands. Then gradually my nervousness subsided, and I was able to mingle with the crowd again. I was careful to stay in the rear of the stands, however, and kept my pencil and notebook in my pocket.

The American Derby was the fifth race. By the end of the third race the excitement of the crowd had become a palpable thing, pulsing like music through the grandstand, slowly approaching a crescendo. The fourth race was almost an interruption, as though the febrile crowd begrudged two minutes of concentration on anything except the derby, and when it was over the spectators breathed a collective sigh and began a vast babble of anticipation.

I was caught up in the increasing tension. My blood coursed faster, I breathed more deeply, and a sense of bravado swept through me. I felt I was approaching a climax of some kind. *It was a fluke that Iggy recognized me,* I thought. *It won't happen again, especially with everybody watching the big race.* Pressing my mustache firmly against my upper lip, I started down the aisle toward the boxes, pushing through a sluggish sea of compressed bodies.

I had just reached the cross aisle dividing the front and rear tiers of boxes when the paddock parade began, and half the spectators at the track simultaneously decided to view the contenders. I was swept along with them between the boxes with my feet barely touching the ground. Powerless to resist the pressure of the crowd, I felt the sudden flush of fear that accompanies the realization of one's complete ineffectuality.

At that moment I saw the policeman who had presided over my expulsion from the track the day before. He was standing close by his pillar to resist the crush of humanity around him, his jaw thrust out belligerently and his snub-nosed Irish features in profile to me. I tried to bend my knees sufficiently to conceal myself behind the intervening bodies, but before I succeeded his face had turned in my direction. I saw his eyes widen as they met my single unpatched orb.

God preserve us, he's even quicker than Iggy was!

He pushed away from his pillar like a swimmer entering a raging flood, and then my knees were bent enough to conceal him from view. Waddling furiously, I propelled myself forward, not daring to look in his direction.

From the corner of my eye I saw Anton Birkmann's box. Its occupants were the same as they had been when I visited it before — bald-headed Mr. Birkmann, his white burnside whiskers a-tremble as he turned his head from side to side and peered shortsightedly at the scene around him; the unruffled matinee-idol visage of his associate, Schacter, expressing a combination of interest and condescension as he leaned close to the woman beside him; and the woman herself, Birkmann's secretary Miss Verlac, sitting erect in her seat, lips parted and eyes bright, her cheeks flushed with excitement.

In a moment I was carried past them. Intent on keeping as much distance between myself and the policeman as possible, I angled to the right, and a few moments later found myself behind Paul Vannatta's box, where I had been during the "veiled lady" fiasco. Although the occupants all had their backs to me, I felt extremely uneasy being there, and pushed my way forward through the crowd with redoubled effort.

Just then the bugle signaled the end of the paddock parade, and summoned the horses to the starting gate. Immediately the crowd in the aisle lost all interest in moving toward the paddock, and everyone stopped where he was and turned toward the track. I was pressed against the bar at the back of Vannatta's box, completely immobilized, in exactly the same position I had occupied twenty-four hours before.

It was there I was destined to watch the American Derby.

Vannatta and his wife, heavily veiled, were sitting side by side at the left of the box. Razor Rapello sat beside Vannatta; he was peeling an apple with a pocketknife. Next to Razor was the Loogan, talking to one of the women in the next box. The other occupants of the adjoining box were four more women and their host, the colorful alderman of the First Ward, Bathhouse John Coughlin, resplendent in a mauve jacket, canary waistcoat, forest-green trousers, and dove-gray spats. Couglin was eating a chicken leg from a picnic hamper, and for a moment I had an almost unbearable feeling of déjà vu.

Unable to move, and feeling as conspicuous as a pig in a church pew, I studied the horses as they took their positions at the starting gate. Mustafa dominated the field. He was a magnificent gray stallion with a deep chest and a Roman nose, and the way he reared and curvetted indicated an arrogant or impatient nature. His jockey, Sparrow Simpson, seemed to be cursing as he struggled to keep the reins drawn tight.

The second favorite, Home Free, was smaller and built on less dramatic lines. He was a chestnut with a white blaze and three white stockings, and he carried his head low and placed his hooves daintily, as though he were walking down a path of stepping-stones. The rider on his back was known to me by sight, although I had never spoken to him. He was Early Fetzer.

Of the other six horses on the track, only one commanded my attention, a black gelding with a modest bearing and clean lines, deep-chested for his height, which I judged at fourteen hands. His jockey's colors were green and buff, and his number was 7, which identified him as the third favorite, Glenlivet.

As the handlers struggled to align the horses the band struck up "Columbia, the Gem of the Ocean." The crowd began to sing lustily. Mustafa balked at the gate, and the song ended in a fusillade of snare drums and cymbals before the big gray could be maneuvered into position. There was a moment of absolute stillness, and then a vast roar, and the race began.

Mustafa and Home Free were second and fourth from the rail, respectively. Glenlivet was eighth, on the outside. The horses were bunched together entering the first turn, but by the time they reached the backstretch the two favorites were leading the rest of the field by eight or ten lengths. They were almost neck and neck, with the gray stallion slightly ahead.

Suddenly the roar of the crowd turned to a great gasp of astonishment.

The two horses seemed to have collided. Mustafa, the nearer, lost his equilibrium momentarily. His head dropped and his rider lurched forward over his neck. In the moment it took for Mustafa and Sparrow Simpson to regain their balance, Home Free surged forward to claim the lead by a nose. Then Simpson struck at Early Fetzer with his whip. Fetzer pulled his head down between his shoulders and used his own whip on Home Free's rump. The two horses pounded along the backstretch with the smaller chestnut leading the gray stallion by inches, as Simpson continued to belabor his rival across the neck and shoulders.

Everyone in the stands was on his feet,

screaming — except the occupants of the box in front of me. Then, as the two leading horses entered the far turn, Paul Vannatta rose gracefully, pausing a moment to shake out the creases in his trousers, and offered his hand to his veiled consort. She acknowledged his courtesy with a nod and stood beside him. Neither Razor nor the Loogan left their seats. Razor carved a slice of apple and carried it to his mouth on his knife blade, and the Loogan sat stolidly and stared straight ahead.

Moving into the clubhouse turn, Home Free and his rider, no longer blocked by the big gray stallion and his jockey, came into clear view. As if he had been waiting for this moment, Fetzer turned in his saddle and slashed his whip across Sparrow Simpson's face. The crowd gasped in shocked surprise. Fetzer took a second swipe at Simpson, and Simpson seized the whip end and jerked it toward him, almost pulling Fetzer from the saddle. For a moment the two men tugged at the whip, and then Simpson drew close enough to Fetzer to clutch the fullness of his shirt.

As the two horses pounded neck and neck toward the finish line, their jockeys wrestled and pummeled each other with their fists like two schoolboys rolling in the playground dust, and the crowd roared its mingled outrage and encouragement.

Mustafa and Home Free crossed the finish line still neck and neck. A quick glance down the track showed me that the clean-lined black gelding called Glenlivet was leading the remaining horses by a comfortable margin. A moment later he passed the judges' booth in third place.

The stands were a bedlam. Everyone seemed to be shouting "Foul," and demanding the disqualification of one of the horses, but there was no agreement on which one should be disqualified. A stentorian voice in my right ear bellowed, "Robber! Kick him out! Kick Simpson out!" while a piercing tenor on my left screamed, "Home Free fouled Mustafa first, I seen it! It was Fetzer's fault!" Just beyond him two disputants shouted curses at one another until the larger silenced the smaller with a poke in the eye. Two struggling bodies behind me pressed me against the box railing and knocked the wind out of me. As I hung draped over the rail gasping for breath, Paul Vannatta, only two or three feet ahead, pulled a small bunch of papers from his pocket and handed them to Razor. They were betting markers. Razor thrust them into his side pocket as he rose from his chair and turned to face me.

Wait a minute, I thought as I gasped for air.

Vannatta handed him those tickets like they were winners. But you don't cash in tickets on disqualified horses.

Razor's eyes passed across my face without interest. Then a moment later they flashed back, narrowed and wary. "Mister Vannatta —," he said hoarsely.

"Yes? What?" Vannatta glanced at him, and then half turned to follow his gaze. When he saw me his eyes widened slightly and his face froze.

I drew a deep breath. "Those markers you just gave him, Vannatta — they wouldn't be on Glenlivet, would they? On Glenlivet to *win*, I mean!" I had to shout to make myself heard over the crowd.

As he recognized me, Vannatta's hand moved toward his wife's arm in a protective gesture. His face paled and his lips pressed together in a bloodless line. "You!" he said almost inaudibly. "Come here — I want to talk to you."

Responding to a belated sense of caution, I pushed backward against the struggling bodies behind me. It was no use; my best effort failed to move my belly an inch from the rail.

"Get him in here!" Vannatta snapped. Razor's hand grasped my wrist instantly, and a moment later the slower-moving Loogan had my other arm in a paralyzing grip and was dragging me forward into the box. I sailed over the bar and crashed to my knees on the concrete floor. The Loogan's huge hand closed on the nape of my neck and squeezed. I looked up into Vannatta's merciless face.

"A mustache, an eye patch, you think that makes you invisible? I know you. What is it you want to say to me?"

"Let me up! Tell your gorilla to let go of my neck!" The Loogan responded by tightening his grip until I felt my head was about to pop off like a cork from a champagne bottle. "Stop it!" I squealed. The pressure eased slightly. I tried to lower my head, but the Loogan prevented it by jamming his other hand under my chin.

Vannatta's wife stood close beside him, her face invisible behind her heavy veil. She said, in a husky, slightly muffled voice, "He's the one?"

"Yes, he's the one," Vannatta answered. "Moretti, his name is. A cheap reporter, a man who's been barred from the track. He wants to tell us something. Go ahead, Moretti. What did you say about Glenlivet?"

"Let me up! Let me up and I'll tell you!"

The Loogan's fingers tightened again on my neck. Vannatta leaned closer to me. "Tell me first, then we'll see." His voice was as smooth and unyielding as polished steel.

"I asked you if those markers were on Glen-livet. What's wrong with that? There's no law that says you have to bet on your own horse. I wish I had been smart enough to bet on him! Let me up before my head comes off!"

Vannatta regarded me for a few moments. Around us the crowd continued to bellow its frustrated impatience. In the next box the flamboyant figure of the alderman of the First Ward towered over the covey of twittering women that surrounded him. Bathhouse John Coughlin was shaking his fist at the judges' stand and shouting words that were inaudible at a distance of fifteen feet. *If I can't hear him, he surely won't be able to hear me,* I thought.

"Stand him up," Vannatta ordered. The Loogan jerked me to my feet, without removing his hand from its paralyzing hold. Razor stood close by my side, one hand inside his coat. Vannatta toyed with the knot of his tie with well-manicured fingers. "Moretti, you've already made trouble for me, and I think you'd like to make more. Well, I won't have it. You've been barred from the track, and you have no business here, and I'm going to ask my associates to escort you to the gate. You have no one to blame but yourself." His eyes flicked to Razor and then to the

Loogan. "Gentlemen, if you please."

"Oh, no, you don't! I'm going nowhere with those hoodlums! If you want me kicked out, call a cop!" I tried to twist out of the Loogan's grip, but his iron fingers tightened remorselessly, and spinning black stars swam across my vision. I gasped in pain and stood motionless.

"Take him the back way — it's shorter," Vannatta said. Razor nodded and withdrew his hand from beneath his coat far enough to show his hand curled around the butt of a small pistol. When he saw that I had seen it, he slid it back under his plaid lapel. "Let's go," he said. "Follow right behind me, Moretti. And don't try nothing smart if you know what's good for you." He ducked beneath the box rail and pushed his way into the jammed aisle. The Loogan directed me with his thumb and forefinger to follow.

The back way is shorter, I thought as I doubled up and followed Razor under the iron bar. *Indeed it is. It's the shortest way to the grave I know. Maybe if I can get a few people between me and Razor . . .* But my attempt to hang back was an immediate failure. The Loogan's fingers tightened like pincers, and Razor paused until I was touching him before continuing his swiveling movement through the crowd.

For five minutes, helpless as a babe, I was

ignominiously frog-marched along the clamorous aisle by my captors, without a single opportunity to escape, or even to call for help. My spirits were so low it seemed impossible that they could sink lower, but they plunged sickeningly when Razor reached a narrow flight of stairs leading beneath the stands, and unhesitatingly led the way down. My instinctive resistance brought me nothing but the tightening of the vise at the back of my skull, and fireworks exploded behind my eyes as I stumbled down the stairs.

Suddenly the roar of the crowd was muted, and the air felt cool and dank. We were in an area underneath the sloping floor of the stands, a wedge-shaped space perhaps fifty feet wide and thirty feet deep, backed by a wall of poured concrete. On the uneven ground around us I could make out old newspapers, empty bottles, a woman's high-heeled shoe, a broken picnic basket. A stack of lumber half concealed by a tarpaulin stood against the rear wall.

Razor continued to lead the way toward the rear. I stumbled behind him, my mind numb with apprehension. How many seconds did I have left in my life? Thirty? Ten? Five? *You've got to do something, Moretti — but what?*

"I hope you're not planning anything drastic, boys, because I've got to tell you —"

"Shut up." Razor turned to face me, and his hand reappeared from inside his coat. "Put him down here," he ordered. The Loogan's hand propelled me forward, and my knees hit the dirt. I raised my head and focused my eyes on the muzzle of the revolver six inches from my forehead. "So long, Moretti," Razor said. His trigger finger tightened and the hammer drew back.

My past life didn't pass before my eyes. Instead, I saw a highlight from my life-to-be, a life I was destined never to know. It concerned me and a slender but well-endowed young woman, totally unclothed and totally unabashed. "Paddy," Alison breathed, "I've dreamed of you like this. Come to me!" *Oh, Lord,* I groaned, *why are you deviling me with this now?*

The hammer was back at full cock, and the pistol barrel was implacably steady. I set my mind to more appropriate thoughts. *Hail Mary, full of grace . . .*

"Razor, if you pull that trigger, you're a dead man." The voice came from behind me, from the stairway to the grandstand. It was a voice I had heard before, businesslike, impatient, sardonic. Afraid to turn my head, I stared into the blind eye of the pistol. "Arbuckle, is that you?" I cried in a quavering voice.

"That's the best guess you've made since you got to Chicago," the detective answered. "Razor, lower that pistol real careful and drop it on the ground. You, Loogan, just stand where you are. And Moretti, kindly get out of the line of fire before you get hurt."

I obliged. Arbuckle and two uniformed policemen were standing at the foot of the stairway. All three had service revolvers in their hands. Razor read the odds accurately and tossed his weapon to the ground. "Okay, copper, it's your play," he sneered.

"I thought it was," Arbuckle agreed mildly. "Take 'em to the paddy wagon, boys; I want them at Eleventh Street when I get there. Come on, Moretti. Let's you and me go back upstairs. There's some other people I want to invite to our party."

12

Return of the Hi-Lows

Arbuckle, with a cough and a deferential glance at his immediate superior, Deputy Inspector Tim McGaughey, turned to face the other occupants of the room. "We've got us a problem here, or I should say a couple of problems, but if you ladies and gentlemen will cooperate with us, we should be able to straighten things out in a jiffy, and most of you will be free to leave."

"What do you mean, 'most of us,' Detective?" growled Anton Birkmann. "We know who the guilty parties are. We know who deserves to be behind bars. So do you. I want to know what business you have dragging the rest of us in here anyway?"

There were sounds of agreement from around the room. Arbuckle threw another glance at his superior, and Deputy Inspector McGaughey smiled reassuringly. He was a heavy-set man with smooth round cheeks, small eyes, and a large, loose mouth. Although well tailored and well barbered, he had hands the size of a day laborer's. "I can assure you, Mr. Birkmann, we feel your presence is necessary for the cause of Justice to be done," he said in a melodious voice. "I know this is an imposition on you and your friends, but Detective Arbuckle and I ask for your patience." Birkmann grunted in unwilling acquiescence, and McGaughey's nod signalled Arbuckle to proceed.

It was two hours after the disastrous running of the American Derby, an hour and a half after both Mustafa and Home Free had been disqualified, and Glenlivet had been declared the winner, at twelve to one odds. In that brief time, Arbuckle had organized a meeting in McGaughey's spacious office that included Anton Birkmann, his associate John Schacter, and his secretary, Miss Carla Verlac; Paul Vannatta and his veiled wife; Razor and the Loogan (both under the close supervision of armed uniformed policemen); the jockeys Sparrow Simpson and Early Fetzer, making up in belligerency what they lacked in physical stature; the steward of Washington Park, Colonial Whitley Wallop, who glared at everyone else in the room from red-rimmed basset eyes; and — suffering from bruised knees, a headache, and a severe sense of disorientation — me.

Arbuckle began again, "Like I said, we've got

us a couple of problems here. One of them is the race, and what happened out there today. The other one is what led up to all this. The first one includes swindling and attempted murder, and the other one is an honest-to-God murder that really happened."

"*A* murder, Arbuckle?" I interrupted. "Just one?"

"Hush up, Moretti. When I want something from you I'll ask for it." He interlaced his fingers in front of his chest and popped his knuckles. "Let's take the swindle first, eh, Vannatta? Do you want to tell them, or shall I?"

Vannatta shrugged his superbly tailored shoulders. "Suit yourself. You just better know where you're going." He placed his hand on top of his wife's, and gazed at Arbuckle with cold defiance.

"All right. Vannatta needed money. I don't know why, or how much, but we'll find out. He needed money, more than he could get from betting on his own horse, which would only be paying five to one if it won, which it probably wouldn't. Want to tell us what you needed it for, Vannatta?"

"You're talking," Vannatta said.

"So I am. The favorite horse in the race was Mr. Birkmann's Mustafa, at eight to three. Terrible odds, not nearly good enough to get you out of your hole, eh, Vannatta? But the third favorite, Glenlivet — ah, that was something else, wasn't it? If Glenlivet won, he'd pay twenty dollars for a two-dollar bet. You could get healthy on that real fast!"

Disregarding the detective's orders, I interrupted: "That's what he did, Arbuckle! He had a wad of markers on Glenlivet that would choke a horse — I saw him give them to Razor to collect."

"I know, Moretti — we found them in his pocket when we brought him in. Now, if you don't mind — Vannatta saw how he could make a bundle if the two favorite horses lost, and I don't suppose it would have been any problem to make sure Home Free came in out of the money —"

"Hey, wait a minute! Are you saying I'd throw a race?" Early Fetzer demanded. Sparrow Simpson made a rude noise with his lips.

"Hell, Fetzer, you'd throw a Decoration Day parade if you could figure a way to make a buck on it," Arbuckle said. "You weren't the problem. Sparrow Simpson was the problem — Sparrow and Mustafa, who figured to win no matter whether you pulled Home Free or not. Somebody had to fix Sparrow, or the swindle wouldn't work."

"Balls," Simpson grated. "Nobody fixes Sparrow."

"That's the truth, Arbuckle," I cried injudiciously. "Everybody in the racing business knows that Simpson will kill his horse, or himself, or anybody else, to win! They say he's too mean to throw a race!"

Arbuckle glared at me. "Moretti, I'm warning you, button it up!" He paused and looked around the room. "That happens to be true. You found it out when you tried to get to Simpson, didn't you, Vannatta?" When Vannatta didn't answer, Arbuckle went on thoughtfully, "Who was it you tried to work through? Not Mr. Birkmann — no amount of money could make him agree to let Mustafa lose."

"By God, I should hope not!" Birkmann burst out, his muttonchop whiskers vibrating in outrage.

"But his associate, Mr. Schacter? That might be a different story. What about it, Schacter? Did Vannatta open negotiations with you, try to use you to make a deal with the Sparrow? You might as well tell us now — it's all going to come out in the wash anyway."

Schacter licked his lips. "Certainly not! This is outrageous!"

Arbuckle shrugged. "Maybe I'm wrong. We'll

find out for sure when we check the book-makers. If you've got heavy money down on Glenlivet, we'll find out — even if it's laid off out of town. Then we'll know, won't we?" Schacter opened his mouth to reply and thought better of it. He turned to Miss Verlac and gave her what was intended to be a confident smile. She moved six inches away from him.

Sparrow leaned forward, his sullen face compressed into a frown of concentration. "Hey, you could be right! That guy come sniffing around a couple weeks ago. He says what a shame it is that the odds on Mustafa and Home Free in the derby are so short. He says the only way a horseplayer can make a buck is if a plater like Glenlivet was to win."

"And what did you say, Sparrow?" Arbuckle asked.

"I tell him that would never happen! I tell him me and Mustafa can take a nag like Glenlivet six days a week and twice on Sunday! I says, 'If you don't want to see Mustafa win, what are you sucking around here for?' I says, 'Get lost!'"

Arbuckle nodded. "In other words, you let him know there was no way you could be bought. Which meant that Vannatta and his associate" — he gave an ironical little bow to

291

Schacter — "whoever he was, had to find another way to get the job done.

"Which brings us to the meat and potatoes." He turned to Colonel Whitley Wallop, who was resting his dewlapped head on one liver-spotted hand. "Are you following me so far, Colonel?"

"Of course! Certainly! Shocking business! What meat and potatoes?"

Deputy Inpector McGaughey, who looked almost as confused as the steward, interposed: "I don't blame you, Colonel Wallop — it's an amazing story Arbuckle has for you, and one that only trained officers like ourselves could have unraveled."

Glaring like an outraged bald eagle, Anton Birkmann growled, "Get on with it, man!"

"Vannatta realized he couldn't bribe Simpson to throw the race in Glenlivet's favor, so he did the next best thing — he worked out a plan to use Simpson's foul temper to get the two favorites disqualified during the race. That meant Glenlivet would win by default. It wasn't an absolute certainty, of course — there was an off chance some long shot might pick up all the marbles — but nothing in racing is ever absolutely certain, is it? Anyway, it was good enough for Vannatta.

"And Vannatta had something good to work

with — something we're indebted to Moretti, here, for bringing to our attention." Arbuckle tried popping his knuckles again, but the result was disappointing. He turned toward Sparrow Simpson and asked, "Have you seen your girl Velma lately, Sparrow?"

"Huh?" Simpson's frown of concentration deepened. "Velma? That bitch? Hell, no! When she starts giving the eye to this skunk" — he gestured toward Early Fetzer — "it's the end of the line where Sparrow Simpson is concerned! What do you want to know about her for?"

"That was Tuesday night, at the Boots and Saddles?" Simpson nodded. "And you haven't seen her since then?" Simpson nodded again. Arbuckle clapped his hands together and said, "Excuse me a second, folks. I have to arrange for a piece of medical testimony." He crossed the room and opened the door to the corridor. A uniformed officer was leaning on the jamb outside. "Find Doc Menifee and get him down here right away," he ordered.

"Yes, sir." The policeman disappeared from view and Arbuckle, closing the hall door, returned to the center of the room. Before he began speaking again, he exchanged a look with Deputy Inspector McGaughey. McGaughey's eyes flickered toward a second door that stood slightly ajar in the wall opposite the door to the corridor. His eyebrows rose slightly, and Arbuckle responded with an almost imperceptible shrug. Then he turned back to the rest of us.

"We're talking about Sparrow's girl Velma — or maybe I should say Fetzer's girl Velma, or even Paddy Moretti's girl Velma. Moretti certainly had an interest in her, anyway — that's why he came to police headquarters to report when he found her missing from her hotel."

"I wasn't aware my interest was shared by the authorities," I said.

"Perhaps it wasn't, right at first." His gaze rested on me a moment, mockingly. "But later on —" He left the thought unfinished. "Velma said some interesting things to Moretti on the train from New York last Tuesday, things he later told me. Remember, Moretti?"

All eyes turned to me. Vannatta regarded me with cold rage, Birkmann with suspicious disapproval, Schacter with apprehension; Early Fetzer sneered and Sparrow Simpson glowered jealously; Colonel Wallop and Deputy Inspector McGaughey looked equally at sea; Razor's cruel face was expressionless, and the Loogan seemed bored; Miss Verlac's lovely features expressed a distaste for the whole scene, while behind her heavy veil Mrs. Vannatta's emotions could only be guessed at.

I said, "I guess what you mean is her interest in Vannatta and in the American Derby. I remember she asked me if I knew who Vannatta was, and when I said I did, she said, 'Ain't it a small world, though.'"

"You got the impression she knew him personally?"

"I couldn't say. But she certainly knew something about him."

Arbuckle nodded encouragingly. "And what about jockeys? Didn't you tell me she made some comments about jockeys?"

"She made a joke about them being fast every which way. Then she looked tired for a moment and said something like, 'You'd think I would have learned by now. It's not as if I didn't have the chance, but it doesn't seem to take.'"

"But she didn't mention Sparrow Simpson by name?" Arbuckle asked. "She didn't say anything about coming to Chicago to see him?" I shook my head.

"I didn't know she was coming," Sparrow said. "She told me she wanted it to be a surprise. Some damn surprise — half an hour after we get to the saloon she's giving the glad eye to this bastard Fetzer!"

"Watch your language! There are ladies present, Simpson!" snapped Deputy Inspector McGaughey. Arbuckle raised his eyebrows dubiously, but made no comment. Instead, he continued to question Simpson.

"So Velma didn't waste any time making a play for Early?"

"She hadn't hardly sat down and ordered a drink before they was winking and whispering and laughing at each other. Why the hell did she ride out from New York to visit me, if she was fixing to give a come-on to the first asshole she sees?"

McGaughey rumbled warningly, but Arbuckle ignored the epithet. "Almost seems like they *wanted* to get a rise out of you, Sparrow. Almost looks like Velma and Fetzer were *trying* to get that famous temper of yours stirred up. Almost looks like they *wanted* plenty of bad blood between you and Early by the time you were riding against each other in the derby."

Simpson shook his head. "Hey, wait a minute. Why would Velma — I don't get it!"

Arbuckle abandoned his Socratic approach. "Because Vannatta's plan was to use you to get both Mustafa and Home Free disqualified. You had to be so furious with Fetzer that when he fouled you during the race you would forget your common sense and foul him back, so obviously that the judges would have no choice but to kick you both out and give the race to Glenlivet."

It took a moment for Arbuckle's explanation to sink in. When it did, Sparrow Simpson gave a yelp of rage, pivoted in his chair, and struck Early Fetzer in the face. Fetzer's chair went over backward, and Simpson followed his enemy to the floor, kneeling on his chest and raining blows down on his head and body. "Get him off me!" Fetzer yelled. "Stinking sonofabitch!" Simpson cried.

The two policemen guarding Razor and the Loogan moved toward the struggling jockeys. As they did so Razor turned to look at Vannatta, and Vannatta nodded. Razor leaped from his seat and dashed toward the hall door, the Loogan close behind.

"Stop those men!" Deputy Inspector McGaughey shouted.

Razor had to pass me on his way to the door. I scooted down in my chair and extended my legs just in time to interpose them between Razor's flying feet. He dove forward on his face, and a second later the Loogan piled on top of him. I left my chair and sat on top of the Loogan until one of the policemen relieved me and herded the two thugs back to their seats. Meanwhile the other policeman had succeeded in separating Sparrow Simpson and Early Fetzer. Fetzer dabbed ineffectually at his bloody nose, and Simpson continued to pound one fist into the other palm, as if that pointless violence were better than no violence at all.

Vannatta stood beside his wife, his hand protectively on her elbow, as he had since the disturbance had begun. His expression was impassive.

Arbuckle raised his hands to ask for quiet. "Please, if everybody will sit down again, we'll get on with it. We're almost finished." Razor and the Loogan, now both handcuffed, were soon back in their chairs, as were the two jockeys. Vannatta seated his wife and resumed his place beside her. Colonel Wallop, who hadn't left his seat, exchanged a look of affronted incomprehension with Anton Birkmann. Schacter and Miss Verlac sat stiffly on their bench, six inches apart.

Before Arbuckle could continue, however, the door to the corridor opened and Dr. Menifee, the police medical examiner, burst in, followed by the policeman who had been sent to find him. The doctor had evidently been disturbed in the midst of his labors, for he was in his shirtsleeves, with cuffs turned back and rubber gloves on his hands. His face was bright red, either from exertion or anger. He shook off the restraining hand of the officer and shouted, "By God, Arbuckle, I want an explanation! What right have you got to drag me from my work without so much as a by your leave? . . . And me in the middle of a piece of work you couldn't begin to understand if I explained it to you for an hour! Damned high-handed arrogance — I won't have it, do you hear?"

Arbuckle raised his hands pacifically. "I'm sorry, Doctor, forgive me. But we need some information from you directly. It's something that won't wait, I'm afraid."

Menifee crossed his arms and stood glaring at the detective. "All right, then, if it can't be helped — Well, what is it, man? Spit it out! Don't keep me waiting here all day!"

Arbuckle stepped quickly to the door which stood ajar, across from the hallway door. He said something in a voice that was inaudible to the rest of us in the room, and seemed to listen to an equally inaudible reply. Then he turned back to Dr. Menifee. "All I want to ask you, Doctor, is where you planted Velma LeSeure? If you don't tell us, we'll have to dig up every body that's been buried in potter's field since last Tuesday night."

Menifee stood as if carved from stone. Except for the sharp intake of breath in a half-dozen throats, there was absolute silence in the room. The first person to speak was Deputy Inspector McGaughey. "Now, wait a minute, Arbuckle — I didn't give you permission to accuse one of our own people —"

"But you didn't tell me I couldn't, did you?" Arbuckle pushed open the door behind him, revealing the seated figure of a woman. The shining black bombazine of her dress strained over the bulging flesh it encompassed, her small hands were folded in the valley between her massive thighs, and her tiny patent leather shoes, neatly crossed, peeped from under the hem of her skirt. The smoked glasses that hid her eyes were as opaque as the blindfold of Justice.

"This woman is Bridey Tumulty," Arbuckle announced. "She was at the Boots and Saddles saloon on Tuesday night, the night when Velma LeSeure stirred up some bad blood between Sparrow Simpson and Early Fetzer. As you can see, she is blind, and as you know, blind people generally have an excellent memory for voices. Now tell us, Mrs. Tumulty, do you recognize any of the voices you've been listening to for the last few minutes?"

"Sure I do." She raised her chin and pushed out her little pink mouth decisively. "Them two jockeys, like you said. They're the ones that was fighting over the twist. And that New York reporter, he came in a couple of days later, asking questions."

Arbuckle nodded encouragingly. "That's fine, but let's stick to Tuesday night, the last time

Velma LeSeure was seen alive. Are there any other people here that you remember hearing at the Boots and Saddles Tuesday night?"

Bridey Tumulty had a sense of the dramatic that would have stood her in good stead if she had chosen the theater for a career. She sat as motionless as a Buddha for an interminable five seconds. Then abruptly, with perfect confidence, she leveled a small, jeweled finger at Dr. Menifee. "Him, the doctor. He was there." Her finger flipped through a ninety-degree arc until it pointed unerringly at Paul Vannatta. "And him, Vannatta. He was there, too."

Menifee exploded. "What? What the devil is this? Who is this fat trull, Arbuckle? Was this why you pulled me away from my work? You must be out of your mind!"

Arbuckle ignored the interruption. "You sound very sure, Mrs. Tumulty. How can you be so positive it was these two men you heard? I mean, you hear two voices for a few minutes, one time in your life —"

"One time, hell! I've heard them a thousand times! They're the Heidenreit brothers! They set me up in New York, fixed the cops, paid off Tammany Hall, kept the girls in line — you think I'd ever forget them?" She bobbed forward in her chair in an ironical sit-down curtsey. "Hello, Hugo," she said, facing Dr. Menifee.

"You're a sure-enough sawbones now. All that practice on the girls paid off, huh?" She turned her blind face toward Vannatta. "And you, Louis — are you still the handsomest stud in the Tenderloin? Cock of the walk — you could have had any of us you wanted. But it had to be Dutch Wilma, didn't it?"

Menifee's color had ebbed away, and now he was as pale as chalk. His heavy features had lost their decisiveness; the square jaw hung slack, and the fleshy cheeks were grooved. He opened his mouth to speak, but Vannatta anticipated him.

"I have no idea what your man here thinks he's doing, McGaughey, but I promise you that if it goes any further both of you will regret it. There are laws to protect innocent citizens even in Chicago."

"There were in New York, too, but that never cut no ice with the Hi-Lows," Bridey Tumulty answered. "Hell, Arbuckle, there's no point in arguing about it. I've got a hunch they're both wearing gloves. Am I right? Make 'em take 'em off, and look between the second and third fingers of their right hands. Then tell me which of us is lying!"

Menifee crossed his arms, his rubber-gloved hands pressed under his armpits, and took a step backward into the grip of the policeman behind him. Vannatta stared coolly at McGaughey and Arbuckle, glanced toward the two uniformed officers standing behind Razor and the Loogan, and shrugged. Deliberately he began to draw off his gloves. Tossing them on the floor in front of him, he held up his right hand with the first two fingers and the second two fingers forming a vee. "Look and be damned," he said.

In the web of skin where the second and third fingers met was a small blue circle. Inscribed within the circle, separated by an X, were the letters H and L.

"Thank you," Arbuckle said. "Now, I ask you again, Dr. Menifee, or Heidenreit, if you prefer, where did you bury Velma LeSeure?"

Menifee made a whimpering noise. With his hands tucked under his armpits he looked as though he were wearing an invisible straitjacket.

"Come on, Doctor, we don't think you did it," Arbuckle said. "We know you were only brought there to dispose of the body. Tell the truth and nothing too bad will happen to you. Maybe you'll even draw a suspended sentence. But lie to me, and by God I'll see you with a rope around your neck!"

"I — I — It wasn't my idea! None of it was my idea!"

"We know that. Where did you bury her?"

303

Menifee's mouth opened and closed as he tried to shape words that would save him, words that wouldn't come. Then he withdrew one rubber-gloved hand from under his arm and wiped his mouth with it. "Where you said — in the potter's field we use for unclaimed bodies. I'll show you the place."

Vannatta released his breath in a long hiss. "You fool," he said softly, "you miserable gutless fool."

"I filled out the death certificate myself. I said she died of the plague. That explained why we had to get her underground immediately, in case anybody ever asked."

"And what *did* she die of, Doctor?" Arbuckle paused for an answer, and when it didn't come, went on: "Come on, we'll find out soon enough, when we dig up her body."

Menifee turned to look at his brother before he answered. His expression was both a reproach and a plea for forgiveness. "She was stabbed to death," he said hoarsely.

Deputy Inspector McGaughey suddenly remembered he was the senior police officer present. "You men, on your toes!" he snapped at the uniformed officers. "This is a case of murder we're dealing with!" He trotted to the hall door and flung it open. "Hey, you two, get in here! There's a couple of mugs I want you to put the bracelets on!"

Five minutes later the group in McGaughey's office had thinned out considerably. The Heidenreit brothers, alias Vannatta and Menifee, had been marched off in handcuffs, followed by the two thugs Razor and the Loogan. Sparrow Simpson and Early Fetzer still sat in their chairs, but an armed policeman stood close behind Fetzer. Mrs. Vannatta had left, acknowledging McGaughey's awkward expression of sympathy with a silent nod. Schacter was still with us, nervously crossing, uncrossing, and recrossing his legs, between a glacial Miss Verlac, sitting as far from him as the bench allowed, and the grim Anton Birkmann, crouching in his chair like a predator about to leap. Colonel Wallop mopped his face with a soggy linen handkerchief. Bridey Tumulty was now sitting in the largest chair in the room, which barely accommodated her bulk. Beau, her gaunt protector, stood behind her; his face resembled a gargoyle's both in color and feature, and his hand clutched the back of her chair like a claw. McGaughey was sitting behind his desk smoking a cigar with evident satisfaction, and Arbuckle rested one buttock on the edge of the desk as though enjoying an indulgence from a higher authority.

Colonel Wallop said, "I suppose all this business will have to come out, damn it all. I mean, I guess there isn't any way to keep it quiet, is there?"

" 'Keep it quiet'!" exploded Anton Birkmann. "Mustafa was cheated out of his rightful victory by these criminal wretches, and I stand to lose a good fifty thousand dollars! 'Keep it quiet'? I'm going to see it's shouted from the housetops! Goddammit, I want Mustafa declared the winner and I want Home Free disqualified and I want Fetzer barred from Washington Park and every other track in the country, and if I don't get it I'll raise a stink like nobody's smelled before in the history of American racing!"

Colonel Wallop's face folded into furrows of bassetlike melancholy. " 'Fraid you'd take it like that. Can't say I blame you, but it's going to be a dreadful hooraw. Black eye for the sport of kings."

"It'll be a hell of a lot worse if you try to keep a lid on it," Birkmann promised.

"Gentlemen, if you don't mind, we have a murder to straighten out," McGaughey said, slapping his desktop for emphasis. "Maybe you better dot the I's and cross the T's for them, Arbuckle."

Nodding, Arbuckle turned to Bridey Tumulty. "All right, Bridey, let's go over what you heard that night, sitting behind your screen.

First it was Velma LaSeure stirring up trouble between Sparrow and Early Fetzer —"

"Yeah, only then I didn't know it was her. I didn't place her voice till later." The blind woman picked up the narrative. "She really done a job on Sparrow. When he left he was fit to be tied. They practically had to throw him out. Then Louis Heidenreit — Vannatta — joined Velma and Fetzer at their table. I recognized his voice right off. He told Fetzer to take a walk."

"That's the truth!" Fetzer interjected. "He told me to leave, and I left, and that's all I know about it, I swear to God! I never seen Velma again after that! Whatever happened to her, you can't pin nothing on me!"

Sparrow swore and reached Fetzer's face with a straight jab before the policeman standing behind him could intervene. Fetzer's nose began to bleed again.

"Nothing but conspiracy to defraud," Arbuckle said cheerfully. "Go on, Bridey."

"Louis and Velma must have sat talking for half an hour. I couldn't hear much of what they were saying because their voices were low and the joint was getting noisy. Then Velma starts to get a snootful. I hear her saying, 'I ain't settling for no lousy two hundred bucks. I know what's happening, and I want a piece of it.' I can hear Louis's voice trying to reason with her, only it's too low to make out the words. Velma keeps on like that, getting louder and meaner. 'You thought you could get away with dumping me for that bitch,' she says. 'Well, nobody pushes Velma around. I showed you then, and by God, I'll show you now.'

"Louis tells her to shut up, but it's too late, she's got the bit in her teeth and she's running with it. 'I bet you've got fifty grand laid out, at ten to one,' she yells. 'Well, I'm going to get my piece, by God, or I'll blow the whistle on the whole shooting match. And if you don't think I will, then ask that wife of yours!' "

As I listened to the blind madam's account, there was a sudden taste of brass in my mouth. In my mind I saw Velma as I remembered her on the train, full-breasted and slim-waisted, with red-gold hair and slanted eyes and a heavy, self-indulgent mouth, a woman to be wary of and a woman to tempt a man from his wariness. I remembered the rising excitement I had felt when I sensed that she might be available. *Oh, Velma, I wonder what we missed, the two of us,* I thought, and then added, *and I'm lucky never to have found out.* I wondered if even then I had had a presentiment of the recklessness and the cruelty in her.

"Then Louis started to soft-soap her and

quiet her down," Bridey went on, "and about five minutes later I heard them leave their table. Velma sounded real drunk. That was the last I heard of her."

"Damn near the last anybody heard of her," Arbuckle said. "Okay, what then?"

"Louis came back in, it must have been two, two and a half hours later. There was somebody with him — could have been the one they call Razor, but I'm not sure. They didn't say much. I get the idea they were waiting for somebody. And in about ten minutes he comes in. It's Hugo. When I heard his voice I about dropped my teeth. Both the Heidenreits, here in Chicago! So I started to listen real good.

"Hugo says, 'What the devil do you mean getting me down to this pigsty in the middle of the night?' Louis says something I can't hear, and Hugo says, 'What disposal problem? What are you talking about?' Then Louis talks for a minute, real low, and then Hugo says, 'I won't do it! You got no right to ask me!' Then Louis talks some more, and every so often Hugo says, 'No!' or 'Please!' Finally Hugo gives in. He sounds like he's about ready to bawl. He says, 'All right, let's get on with it, for God's sake! Take me to her.' And I hear them getting up from their table, and that's the end of it."

"That's right," Arbuckle said soberly. "Velma

rocked the boat and bought herself a one-way ticket to potter's field, and that should have been the end of it. Would have been except for a buttinsky reporter." His eyes glinted at me briefly before he turned to Deputy Inspector McGaughey. "That about does it, wouldn't you say, Inspector? I've got some questions to ask Early Fetzer downstairs, but I think we can let the rest of these folks go, if you have no objection."

"By all means." McGaughey turned to Anton Birkmann and said deferentially, "Thank you for coming in, Mr. Birkmann. You, too, Colonel Wallop. If we can do anything to help you straighten out your problem at the track, let us know."

Birkmann got to his feet, his gaze fixed balefully on Schacter, who avoided his eyes. "Just tell me what you find out from the bookmakers about people who bet heavy on Glenlivet. That's all I need from you."

McGaughey nodded his assent. Miss Verlac rose from the bench and took Birkmann's arm, and he placed his liver-spotted hand over hers possessively. They walked from the room together, Miss Verlac's hip brushing against his side at every step. At McGaughey's stern glance Schacter shuffled after them, a considerably different man from the fashion plate who had entered the room less than an hour before. Sparrow Simpson, thwarted in reaching Fetzer's nose with a sudden jab by a vigilant and quick-moving policeman, left the room in search of someone else on whom to vent his indignation. Fetzer disappeared, presumably headed for a windowless room in the bowels of police headquarters. Bridey Tumulty followed on the arm of the skeletal Beau, moving with glacial irresistibility. Finally only I was left. McGaughey and Arbuckle looked at me inquiringly.

I said, "There are just one or two little questions I still have, if you don't mind. For instance, what about all the other women who've disappeared in Chicago?"

Arbuckle's fingers grasped my elbow. "We don't want to take up any more of the inspector's time, Moretti. Let's you and me move over to my desk and continue this conversation."

McGaughey cleared his throat. "Perhaps that would be best. Appreciate the help you've given us, Moretti. Always a wise thing for a reporter to stay on the good side of the police. Know you'll remember that."

I assured him I would. Arbuckle steered me out of the big office and into the bustling corridor outside. We went down a flight of stairs, through a set of double doors, and into the large open area where Arbuckle's desk was crowded between many others. He gestured to the scratched oak chair where I had sat twice before. "Sit down, if you think you'll be here long enough." He dropped into the chair across from me and folded his arms behind his head. "You said you had one or two questions?" he asked politely.

"One or two. For God's sake, Arbuckle, you don't intend to stop it here? You're not going to pretend this is all there was to it, are you? What about all the rest of it?"

He raised his eyebrows uncomprehendingly. "The rest of it? What 'rest of it' do you mean?"

"The other disappearing women! The Quincy Gang with an ice pick pointed at my throat! The beer wagon that ran down Boz Markey! The man in the carriage who tried to pick up Alison — or maybe I didn't tell you about that —"

"Moretti, you're not thinking clearly," Arbuckle said with a sigh.

"— and what about my room at the Tuscany Hotel? Who got me kicked out of there? Who got to my editor back in New York, for heaven's sake? Vannatta? Come on, Arbuckle!"

"Moretti, shut up!"

"Who sicked Johnnie Dee and Louis Rabshaw on me? Not you, I hope. I mean, not you *personally*. I'd find that very depressing, after the fine relationship the two of us have built up!"

"Now that's enough." Arbuckle's voice was still low and even, but his eyes were narrowed and lips were taut. "You're a fool, Moretti, and I don't owe you a damn thing. But listen to me, and possibly, just possibly, you may be allowed to come back to Chicago again sometime before you pack it up for good."

I decided it was time to accept his suggestion. I sat down in the empty chair and closed my mouth. He studied me for a moment as if deciding how best to complete an irritating chore.

"The reason I'm telling you this is because you've been a very small amount of help in solving a case, and to a very slight extent I'm grateful to you. When you came to me with your story about your friend Velma, mentioning her interest in Paul Vannatta, I thought it was worth a telegram to New York. They didn't have anything on her under the name of LeSeure, but they had quite a bit on Wilma Verhulst. She graduated from being a hooker to playing house with a certain Louis Heidenreit, the head of the old Hi-Low Gang. She was queen bee for a year or two, until Heidenreit dumped her for another chippie. This was just about the time the Hi-Lows were losing their fix with Tammany, and the business started going downhill. Right in the middle of everything else, somebody threw a bottle of vitriol on Heidenreit's new baby doll. Nobody ever found out who was responsible, and as soon as the woman could leave the hospital, she and Louis Heidenreit and his brother Hugo all disappeared.

"So I did a little checking on Paul Vannatta," Arbuckle continued. "As far as I could find out, there's no record of him living in Illinois before about eight years ago, when he bought himself a farm out in the Fox River Valley and started raising horses. That would have been just a few months after Louis Heidenreit disappeared from New York. So it was something to think about."

"Indeed it was. I wish you'd told me. I might have been able to help you."

"I didn't need your help, Moretti. I found Bridey Tumulty and brought her down here to finger the Heidenreits myself." His voice remained polite enough, but the corner of his mouth curled down slightly as he added, "In Chicago we like our detectives to do their own detecting."

"It's the natural order of things, and I couldn't agree more. And how did you happen to smell a rat with Doctor Menifee?"

"I never did, exactly. It was more like a combination of things, but I wasn't sure until Bridey pointed him out in McGaughey's office just now.

First, it was the way he blew up at you when you wanted to do a newspaper story about him. Not many people get so upset over publicity, particularly such good publicity. And then I happened to think, who in Cook County would have the easiest job disposing of dead bodies? Legally, right out in full view, any time he wanted?"

"The police medical examiner?"

"The police medical examiner. It was just a thought. I don't know how I happened to think of it." Arbuckle allowed himself the tiniest trace of self-satisfaction. "And then there were those damned gloves of his. I realized I'd never seen him without a pair of gloves on, either rubber gloves when he was here at headquarters, or cotton gloves when he was off duty. Were they covering up something? And finally, there was the telegram from New York. It mentioned that Louis Heidenreit's brother Hugo had been in charge of the women in the Hi-Low whorehouses — that it was him who kept them healthy. Just as if he had been a doctor. It was something he was good at — something he enjoyed doing."

"Still and all, it's not so much to go on," I said ingratiatingly.

"I told you, I didn't go on it — all I did was set it up for Bridey to make the identification if she could." He sat up straight and laid his palms flat on his desk. "So. Now you know all of it, and you can write a decent story about the great criminal attempt to fix the American Derby. But you better get it off to your editor fast. If I know Deputy Inspector McGaughey, he's giving a statement to the press right now."

"About Velma," I said. "Vannatta brought her here to make bad feeling between Sparrow and Fetzer — he must have known she had been Sparrow's ladyfriend." Arbuckle nodded. "Then Velma decided to cut herself in for a larger share. That was why Vannatta had her killed?"

"Maybe. But I think she signed her death warrant when she dropped that hint about Vannatta's wife. I think Vannatta realized for the first time who had thrown the vitriol." He grinned at me. "That Velma was a pippin. You sure have an eye for the winners, Moretti."

"We all have our off days," I said.

"Well, don't brood about it. Go write your big story and send it off to New York. Remember to spell Deputy Inspector McGaughey's name right. Good luck. I trust our paths won't cross again."

His expression indicated that our conversation was over, but I ignored the message. "Tell me something, Arbuckle. After the fair's over, and after the tourists go home, and after Chicago's sunk as deep in the Depression as the rest of the country — do you think somebody will start looking for the collector then?"

Arbuckle's brow furrowed in irritation. "What? What do you mean? What collector?"

"That's what the whores call him, Bridey says. The collector. They say he collects women, or rather, he collects the parts of them he wants to save. Their scalps — or whatever. Then gets rid of the rest. Truly, a nasty kind of business, Arbuckle. So I was just asking — when, if ever, do you think somebody will start looking for the fellow?"

Arbuckle stared at me for half a minute without speaking. Then he said quietly, "There is no problem with missing women. There is no collector. There is no reason for an investigation. Those are the facts as they exist today, and I'm goddamned sick and tired of telling them to you. Now get out of here, Moretti. Get out right now, before you make me mad."

I got.

13

House of Horror

Oblivious to the glares of waiters and busboys, I sat in a cheap restaurant on Van Buren Street for the better part of two hours, drinking coffee and writing my dispatch to *The Spirit of the Times*. Even restricted to its racing elements it was a remarkable story, and I gave full attention to its dramatic aspects — the brawling between the two jockeys during the race, the disbelief and indignation of the crowd, the disqualification of the two front-running horses and the apparent certification of Glenlivet as the winner at twelve to one odds, and the subsequent denouement at police headquarters, featuring the arrest of the Heidenreits and their henchmen. The murder of Velma LeSeure took a secondary place to the race-fixing plot, and I omitted the fact that Hugo Heidenreit had functioned as Chicago's police medical examiner.

All right, Hochmuth, I thought as I walked across the street to the Western Union office, *you niggardly spalpeen, let's see you find some-thing to carp at in this story.* I jumped out of the way of a clanging streetcar and added ruefully, *As if you needed an invitation.*

I headed north, stopping in one saloon for a glass of beer, then continuing for two or three blocks and stopping in another. My work in Chicago was finished, I would be on a train heading back to New York the following day, and I had every right to relax and unwind, I told myself. I had helped solve a crime and had scored a beat on my competitors. Why wasn't I in a festive mood?

Because disappearing women still weren't news in Chicago?

As I crossed the Chicago River the sun had set and the sky to the west was striped with lavender and magenta and robin's-egg blue. A breeze from the lake carried a welcome smell of cool fresh water, and the clamor of the city was muted for a moment. I paused and leaned on the railing, looking down at moving water below. *It's not good enough,* I thought. *It's not right. But what in the world is a man to do about it?*

A few minutes later I entered Boz Markey's building and ascended the odorous stairway to the second floor. My knock was answered by a burly roughneck with a face that looked as if it had been hewn from hardwood with an ax. He scowled at me suspiciously as I identified myself and asked to see Boz.

"It's all right, Cappy, he's on our side," called a familiar voice from the bedroom. The circulation gorilla stepped back to allow me inside, and I crossed the living room, skirting the sofa and the priapic construction behind it.

Boz lay on his bed propped up with pillows, his slippered feet crossed and his left arm supported in a sling. He was wearing a blue brocaded dressing gown with frayed cuffs and food stains on the lapels, over polka-dotted yellow and red pajamas. An empty straight-backed chair stood next to the bed, and two hands of cutthroat euchre were laid out on the mattress. His upraised right hand saluted me.

"Ah, the Moretti, looking only slightly the worse for wear. Get yourself a drink out of the drawer. Did you bring Alison back here with you?"

I unearthed the bottle from under a dirty shirt, uncorked it, and swallowed an ounce or two. "I have to tell you, your pirate's disguise wasn't worth a damn. I could have been leading a parade in my birthday suit and I wouldn't have attracted more attention." I replaced the bottle and closed the drawer. "But aside from a few hair-raising moments, it's been an edifying afternoon."

"Oh? I haven't heard about the derby. Mustafa won, I suppose?"

"Oh, yes, but not without a certain amount of unpleasantness."

"Mustafa — *won?*" he repeated slowly.

"That's right. In perhaps the dirtiest race ever run at Washington Park, or anywhere else, for that matter. But fortunately your little chum here was able to show how it was a frame-up to get both front-runners disqualified — with a bit of help from the police, I must admit. Also to clear up the mystery of my missing ladyfriend, Velma." I dropped my flippant tone. "She was murdered, Boz. And not by the collector — you were right about that."

White-faced, Boz asked hoarsely, "By whom, Paddy?"

"By Vannatta, or by the man who works for him. It doesn't matter, Vannatta ordered it. She was in on the scheme to get Mustafa and Home Free disqualified, and tried to chisel a larger share for herself. I think there was something else besides — something that happened back in New York a while ago. Anyway, you can read it all in the *Tribune* tomorrow." I stretched and yawned. "Why did you ask if I brought Alison back with me? When would I have seen her?"

Boz licked his lips. He was staring straight ahead, wide-eyed, and seemed not to have heard my question. I repeated it. He turned to face me. "Why, after the race, at the station. That's where you wanted her to go, wasn't it? That's what the note said."

A cold worm of dread uncoiled in my stomach. "What note?"

"The note your man brought two hours ago." His eyes suddenly widened even more. "It was from you — it was signed! And the man said you were at the police station — that you needed Alison's testimony."

"I didn't send any note, Boz."

"Oh, my God!" he whispered.

I sat down on the chair and gripped his right forearm. "The man — what did he look like? What did he say, exactly? How was he dressed? Tell me anything you can remember about him — anything!"

"He was — he sounded like a gentleman, I'd say, well spoken, polite — Paddy, you don't think — Paddy, you're not joking, are you? Oh, of course not!" His mouth began to form into a grin. "You bastard! I should have known —"

"I'm not joking, Boz! Listen, I didn't send any note! That's the truth! Now think! What else can you remember about the man?"

He shook his head slowly from side to side.

"I don't know. I never saw him. He had a deep voice, I remember that. He sounded as if he would have made a good preacher. But that's about it. Paddy" — his voice wavered uncertainly — "was he the collector?"

"Tell me about when he came!"

Boz closed his eyes, and his head fell back against the pillow. "I was napping here, and Alison was reading, I think, in the other room. The knock on the door waked me. I heard Cappy open the door. The man said something to him, and then Alison told Cappy to let him in. I could hear them talking. Alison said, 'You've a message from Mr. Moretti?' and the man said, 'Yes,' and I guess he handed it to her. Then she said, 'Where is he?' and the man said, 'At police headquarters. He wants you to come as soon as you can, ma'am. He said you'd know what it's about.'

"Then I gave a call, and Alison came into the bedroom. She said, 'It's Paddy — he must be on to something! He wants me to come to the police station. He sent me a note.'"

"Have you got that note?" I interrupted.

Boz shook his head. "No, but I can tell you what it said." He concentrated for a moment and then recited, " 'This will introduce a friend, Mr. Henry Maxwell. I hope you will accompany him and meet me at the police station. Rest assured, he is worthy of your trust.' And it was signed 'P. Moretti.' "

" 'P. Moretti,' " I snorted. "I never signed my name 'P. Moretti' in my life. My God, Boz!"

"Well, anyway, that was the way it was signed."

"And she took the note with her when she left?"

He nodded. "I've never seen your signature, Paddy. How was I to know?"

" 'P. Moretti,' " I repeated incredulously. "And how was it addressed? To Miss A. Markey?"

"Just to Miss Markey — not even an initial. And the street address of the building here."

I remembered that the name Markey, with no first name or initials, was on the mailbox downstairs. "He must have followed her home and gotten her last name off the mailbox. Maybe last night, after that bungled attempt to get her into his cab." I slapped my forehead. "And I never even thought to look back over my shoulder!"

"What are we going to do, Paddy?" Boz's voice was unsteady, and his face was as lumpy and gray as putty.

I closed my eyes to think. Something stirred restlessly in the back of my mind. "Tell me

324

again what the note said."

"'This will introduce a friend, Mr. Henry Maxwell. I hope you will accompany him and meet me at the police station. Rest assured —'"

"'Rest assured, he is worthy of your trust,'" I said. "'Rest assured, he is worthy of your trust —' Boz, I've heard that somewhere before! Heard it, or read it, somewhere in the last two or three days! I know I have! But, oh God," I groaned, "where?"

Boz stared at me. "You mean, you think —," he began, and then fell silent, not daring to finish the sentence.

"Yes! If I can just remember, maybe — maybe just possibly — let me think a minute!" With my eyes squeezed shut and my fists so tightly clenched the nails cut into the palms, I began to review in my mind every event since my arrival in Chicago. Like a magic lantern show, I projected scene after scene — the station, the Palmer House, the streetcar, the Tuscany Hotel, the White City, Little Egypt and the Streets of Cairo, Washington Park, Boz's apartment and Billy Boyle's saloon, police headquarters, H. H. Holmes's pharmacy on Sixty-third Street —

Wait a minute. Wait a minute!

I saw again a neat cardboard sign in a

clean plate-glass window:

QUALITY DRUGS

Prescriptions Filled
Rest assured — We are worthy of your trust

H. H. HOLMES, PROP.

I remembered the careful hand lettering, with thicks and thins and serifs on each letter. I remembered the texture of the pebble board, the clean razor-cut beveled sides and ninety-degree corners. Suddenly I had a feeling of absolute conviction.

"Boz, I've got it! A pharmacist on the South Side named Holmes — he wanted to rent me a room, and then changed his mind when he found out I'd mentioned it to the police! He's got that sentence on the sign in his window. His voice is straight off the Chautauqua circuit, he's crazy about Little Egypt, and he's built himself a castle across from his shop!" I jumped out of the chair and started for the door.

"Paddy, wait!"

"Wait, hell! It may be too late already!"

"I'm coming with you!" He struggled from the bed, kicked off his slippers, and shrugged his good arm out of the robe's sleeve. "God-dammit, help me! Please!"

I tried to reason with him, but even as I was speaking he had pulled on a pair of trousers over his pajama bottoms. "I'm coming, too!" he repeated. "I've got to! Help me!"

Cappy came into the room to see what was happening, and between the two of us we managed to dress him in a shirt and trousers, shoes and socks. His left arm was still supported in its sling. As I tugged him toward the door, he cried, "Wait!" and turned to his dresser drawer. For a moment I thought he was digging out his whiskey, and opened my mouth to remonstrate. Then he turned back to me, and I saw he was holding a revolver. "In case," he said as he tucked it carefully between his splinted left arm and the sling.

We hurried down the stairs and onto the street, where Cappy headed one way and I the other in search of a cab. I had reached Michigan Avenue in an unsuccessful quest when I heard a clatter and a shout behind me, and wheeled to face a *Chicago Tribune* circulation wagon braking to a halt. Cappy and another equally unprepossessing bruiser shared the driver's seat, and Boz leaned out of the back. "Get in here! Hurry!" he called. I vaulted over the tailgate into the dark interior. Boz was sitting on a stack of newspapers, and another circulation department thug was squatting beside him. "Where to?" Boz demanded.

I told him Sixty-third and Wallace. He relayed the information to Cappy, and added, "Get there the fastest way you can!" I heard Cappy's shout and the crack of a whip, and the horse in the shafts leaped forward in a canter. We swept around the corner into Michigan Avenue at full speed.

Circulation wagons are intended to deliver newspapers to both near and outlying neighborhoods in the least possible time. Often a difference in delivery time of five minutes between two competing "extras" will result in a sellout for the winner and an almost total loss for the loser. Therefore they are not built for comfort nor driven for comfort. The horses are strong and fast and well cared for; the drivers are reckless of their own safety and contemptuous of the safety of others; and the wagons themselves are built light and strong and almost springless. As we headed south on Michigan, I don't believe there was a carriage or buggy in Chicago that could have kept up with us.

It was a minute or two before Boz and I could accustom ourselves to the bouncing and lurching and sudden shrieks of the brakes sufficiently to talk. I picked up a newspaper from one of the stacks and peered at it in the dim light. It was slugged "Extra!" and its four-deck headline read:

SCANDAL CLOUDS AMERICAN DERBY:
Two Favorites Disqualified
as Jockeys Battle
Mystery Woman Murdered in Plot –
Suspicion Points to Well-known Owner
Glenlivet Declared Derby Winner,
Pays 12 to 1!

"Congratulations. That's a very fast paper you work for," I said.

Boz shook his head impatiently. "Do you think we'll get there in time? What if it's not the right place? What if he's not the collector at all? What if you've dreamed the whole thing up? If anything happens to Alison –"

I tossed the paper to the floor. "It's going to be all right. I'm the seventh son of a seventh son, and I know. Get hold of yourself, Boz."

He stared out into the street. "It's my fault," he said tonelessly. "It's a judgment on me. If I hadn't needed the money so badly – if the goddamned market hadn't crashed –"

I stared at him blankly. "What are you talking about?"

The wagon swerved suddenly, and I had to steady myself against the wagon side to keep from sliding off my seat. Boz swayed toward me, but made no move to keep his balance. Surprisingly, he didn't fall. He continued in his flat voice, "Alison would be safe now, except for me. It's a judgment. I have no one to blame but myself. God help me, God help me if anything happens to her."

The Twelfth Street station appeared on the right, its lighted windows glowing against the darkening eastern sky, and immediately receded into the distance. Beyond Boz, the circulation bruiser squatted like a troll beneath a bridge. I felt a sudden queasy sensation, as if I had eaten a surfeit of greasy food.

"You were surprised when I told you that Mustafa won," I said. "You pretended to expect it, but when I said it was true, you could hardly believe me." I paused; when he didn't speak, I went on unwillingly, "You expected Mustafa to lose. Didn't you, Boz? You *expected* Mustafa to lose. Will you tell me why?"

He turned to look at me, his eyes squinted in pain. "Because it was my idea — it was all my idea! Don't you understand? I figured it out! I had heard that Vannatta needed money, and when my stocks took a dive on Wall Street, I went to him with it. All I asked was that he would let me know when the fix was in, so I could put up five thousand on Glenlivet for myself. Five thousand! That was all my broker had managed to save for me! But that five thousand would have been worth sixty thousand now!" His face contorted in an expression that was half vengeful, half contrite. "Except for you and your snooping, Paddy, old friend! I tried to tell you the Velma business was a red herring, but you had to keep digging, didn't you? And now — oh, God, it's a judgment!" He bowed his head and covered his eyes with his right hand.

"Boz, listen to me! It doesn't make any difference whose idea it was! Vannatta ordered the killing, you didn't! You can't blame yourself for that. And anyway, you were right — the whole Velma business *was* a red herring, it had nothing to do with the collector and the disappearing women! It's not your fault about Alison!"

He groaned and rolled his head from side to side. The bruiser squatting beside him glanced at us uncomprehendingly, then resumed his blank gaze out of the back of the wagon. I put my hand on his shoulder. "Boz, get a grip on yourself. Even if the business with the horses *was* your idea, you have no responsibility for

Velma's death. She was killed on Tuesday night, and I didn't even see you till Wednesday! If you'd told me the whole thing then, it wouldn't have helped to save her!"

He didn't answer. I sighed and sat swaying on my pile of extras, steadying myself with one hand and staring into the street that unreeled behind us. The pounding of the horse's hooves and the creak and clatter of the wagon blended into a pulsing monotone, and the passing lights flared and receded with almost hypnotic effect. I saw a street sign for Twenty-third Street, and then another for Thirty-first, and then one for Thirty-ninth.

"Boz," I said, "who tried to run over you with the beer wagon?"

"Vannatta's people," he replied without interest.

Yes, I thought, that made sense. When the Quincy Gang came after me in Streeterville, it was because I had disobeyed instructions and returned to the Palmer House in search of information about Velma. It hadn't been on orders of the Chicago Establishment, because the Chicago Establishment couldn't have known at that time that Boz and Alison and I planned to search for the truth about the collector. Therefore it must have been because Vannatta was covering his trail.

"Vannatta hired the Quincys to get us both," I said. "When he learned that I had visited you on Wednesday night, what could he think? That somehow I had found out a connection existed between Velma's disappearance and the plan to fix the derby. No wonder he wanted both of us out of the way."

Boz didn't answer.

The wagon pounded on. Forty-seventh Street flashed by. Fifty-third. The hoofbeats were noticeably slower now, and the rhythm was slightly irregular. "They're killing that horse," I said. "I hope he lives to get us there."

To the east the sky was lightening, but dawn was six hours away. It was the White City, luminescent as decaying wood in a marsh, ministering to its customers, the spenders who had brought their checkbooks to Chicago for an interlude of edification and entertainment, the sports who were keeping the Depression at bay, the sharpers who sheared the sheep as a civic duty.

But for all of that, I thought, *we'll never see the likes of it again.*

At Sixty-third Street we lurched around the corner and headed west. I could hear the voice of the driver cursing, and the crack of his whip. The horse had slowed to a trot, and his wheezing breath was audible inside the wagon. We crossed La Salle Street, then Wentworth. I shook Boz's arm. "We're almost there. Look, let's split up — I'll check out the store and you and the others take the house." Boz nodded. His right hand was hidden in the sling supporting his broken arm.

As we entered the intersection of Sixty-third and Wallace I jumped over the tailgate and hit the street running. The windows of the drugstore were dark, and the door was locked. I pounded on it, waited a moment, and pounded again. There was no response. I stepped back, raised my foot, kicked out the glass panel, and unlocked the door.

"Alison!" I called. The silence was stuffy, oppressive, as if my voice had been blotted up by strange-smelling chemicals.

Enough light entered the shop through the plate-glass window to show me the front room was empty. I made my way cautiously to the rear. The laboratory was pitch-black. "Alison!" I called again. "Alison, are you here?" There was no answer. I took out a box of matches and struck one, which hissed and flared and stank of sulfur. In the flickering yellow light the deal table appeared, and the threadbare armchair, and the sink in the corner. Next to the apothecary scales on the table was a small cardboard box, half open. I peered into the pools of shadow that lapped the floor beneath the table and the sink, and called, "Alison!" a third time, with no hope of an answer.

The match went out, and I lit another. The silence was tangible, a weightless yet smothering presence. Even though I was sure there was nothing living in the shop, I felt a sudden spasm of fear. I put out a hand to steady myself, and it came down on the small cardboard box.

Something made me pick it up and raise the lid, and in the last second before my second match spluttered out, I recognized the thing that was inside it.

Mother of God, it's been cut out of her! Cut out, and dried, and put in a box!

I stood in the blackness, my senses reeling. In my stunned horror I was unable to realize that this ghastly memento, this hellish trophy, was many months old. For an interminable second I believed it must be — Alison. I swayed, and almost fell.

Then my faculties returned, and with a shudder I flung the box away and began to run toward the front of the shop. What I had only suspected before was now confirmed, most horribly; there wasn't a moment to lose. I lurched into a counter, heard glass and crockery smash, felt liquid splash my hand and face, breathed a cloud of powder that burned in my throat. I felt my way along the counter edge until I rounded a corner and could see the light that entered the shop from the streetlight outside, silvering the edges of the broken glass on the floor. I ran through the open door.

Across the street Holmes's mansion seemed unreal, like an illustration from a book of Gothic tales. It loomed, lightless, over its bare and littered yard, its gingerbread decoration sinister, its pretentious tower threatening.

The *Tribune* circulation wagon stood empty by the curb. The horse in the shafts hung his head in exhaustion. The front door of the mansion was open. I ran toward it. "Boz!" I shouted. "Is she there?"

From inside the mansion came a woman's scream.

Springing through the door, I found myself in a small entry hall. It was in darkness, but thirty feet down a corridor that led to the rear of the house a bar of yellow lamplight lay across the floor. It came through the open door of a lighted room. I dashed through it, then stopped, frozen, on the threshold.

Immediately inside the room, with their backs to me, stood my four companions. The three circulation toughs, shoulders hulking and arms hanging impotently at their sides, formed a corporal's guard behind Boz, who was a foot or two farther into the room. The pistol was in Boz's right hand, and its barrel pointed at an angle toward the floor.

Across the room, seated on the edge of a canopied bed, was the pharmacist H. H. Holmes. He was in his shirtsleeves, his cuffs were turned back, and his collar and tie had been removed. Alison was beside him. She was fully dressed, although her shirtwaist had been torn open to reveal the undergarment beneath. Her hands were out of sight behind her. One of Holmes's hands grasped her hair, and the other held a clasp knife with a four-inch blade against her throat. The steel edge pressed a quarter of an inch into the flesh.

Holmes was smiling, and his smile broadened when he recognized me. "You, too, eh, Moretti? That explains it, then. Although I must say you're a bit more acute than I gave you credit for."

I said through stiff lips, "Put the knife down, Holmes."

"Oh, I think not. Not with that gentleman there pointing a pistol at me. That wouldn't be wise at all. No, I think a better idea would be for you, sir" — he nodded to Boz — "to drop your revolver on the floor and kick it gently over to me." He waited a moment, then drew the knife blade an inch across Alison's neck. Immediately a thin red line appeared. "Now, please," he said firmly.

"You filthy —," Boz cried in a strangled voice.

Alison's eyes were wide, but her expression was more careful than frightened.

"Boz," she said in an even voice, "I think you better do what he says."

The pistol wavered in Boz's fingers. "You think I'll let — Goddammit, I won't! I'll —"

The knife in Holmes's hand moved, and the red line extended across another inch. Alison gasped, and a moment later Boz's revolver thudded to the floor.

"Much better," Holmes said approvingly. "Now if you'll push it over here with your foot —" The pistol scooted across the floor, and Holmes leaned down and scooped it up with the effortless grace of a star shortshop. "Excellent! You have no idea how it improves one's mood to equalize the odds a bit." Slipping the gun into his waistband, he grasped Alison's hair again and drew her with him until they were both standing. "And now, if you'll excuse us —"

I took a step forward. "Oh, no, Holmes. You're not going out of here, not with her you're not!"

Holmes gave an affected sigh. "Moretti, I really should have rented you that room after all. If you people don't move back and let me walk out that door with your little friend here, I'll cut her throat this instant. Is that what you want? If it is, tell me, and I won't waste any more time." Again the knife blade moved, and again the red line advanced across the creamy throat. Holmes hesitated a moment, his clever eyes flickering from one of us to the next. "Very wise," he said. "Where there's life, there's hope." He took a step toward the door, and Boz took a step backward and to his own right.

The two wagoneers turned to Cappy for instruction, and he cried to Boz, "Whaddya want us to do?" His brutal features were almost childlike with indecision.

"Nothing. Do as he says. Move out of the way." Boz took another step to his right rear. Cappy moved back in the same direction, and the other two toughs moved backward toward the opposite wall, leaving Holmes an aisle to the hallway door.

I stood where I was. "Hold on a minute, Holmes. Don't you see, you're in a no-win situation. Kill the girl and you're dead. Even if you start shooting, you'll only get one or two of us before the rest of us get you."

"Do you want to be the one I get?"

Holmes asked mockingly.

"Listen! We're not going to let you walk away! We're going to stay with you, right behind you. You can't get away from us. We know that no matter what you threaten to do to Alison, you can't kill her, because you'd be signing your own death warrant if you did! We know it, and you know we know it, and we know you know we know it. So it won't work, Holmes. Let her go, and I give you my word we'll wait fifteen minutes before we leave this house!"

His grin widened. "You're a born liar, Moretti. No wonder you're a reporter."

"All right, then. How's this?" I could feel the sweat from my armpits running down my arms. Alison, completely motionless, stared at me through wide, apparently unfrightened, eyes. Her head was drawn back and her chin elevated, so that her smooth throat was stretched to its fullest length. Blood trickled in two thin crimson ribbons down to her collar. I drew a deep breath. "Take me instead, and I guarantee nobody will follow you. Isn't that right, Boz? If he leaves Alison, you'll stay here and give him his fifteen-minute head start? You won't try to follow us?" Boz stared at me and nodded. "And you'll keep Cappy and the others here too?" He nodded again. "Do it, Holmes!" I cried. "It's your only chance to get out of this with a whole skin! Use your brain, man! Is it worth your life to cut up another girl?"

Holmes's eyes narrowed, and he seemed to ease the pressure of his blade against Alison's throat. He thought for a moment, then shook his head. "Afraid not, old man. They could still follow me, no matter what they promise. Then all I could do would be to kill you, and that would definitely be second best." He took a step toward me, pushing Alison in front of him, and then hesitated. "But you've given me an idea, Moretti, you surely have." His eyes crinkled and his grin widened. "I'm going to take *both* of you, thank you very much!" He released Alison's hair and whipped the pistol from his waistband, thrusting it into my face. "An interesting problem in logistics, Moretti. With only one hostage, as you pointed out, it's an all-or-nothing situation — I can't enforce my demands without robbing myself of my insurance. But with *two* hostages, the situation is quite different, isn't it?"

My eyes met Boz's. "Quite different," I agreed.

"Yes — because now if they try to follow us, I'll simply kill *you*, and I'll still have this charming young lady in, ah, mint condition, so to speak. Oh, *very* good." His eyes glittered with delight at his own cleverness. He pushed

Alison forward and covered us both with the pistol, then glanced at Boz. "You understand? You and your muscular friends don't leave this room for fifteen minutes. If you do, you'll stumble over Moretti, here, on the front sidewalk. But if you do what you're told, I'll release them both in a reasonable time. I give you my word." He could barely keep the giggle out of his voice.

Boz's eyes flickered to mine, and I nodded slightly. "All right," Boz said. "I promise. What else can I do?"

"Very well. Through the door, children. The girl first, then you, Moretti. Turn right, move very slowly, and head for the front door. I'll be right behind you. That thing you feel between your shoulder blades is my gun." I stepped behind Alison, facing the hallway door. "Now!" his voice snapped, and the pistol barrel ground into my spine. I moved a step forward, bumping into Alison, and she stepped into the doorway. We each took a second deliberate step, and Alison began to turn to the right, as Holmes had ordered.

If there was to be a moment, this was it.

I raised my hands and shoved her forward and to the left and dove after her into the dark hallway. The pistol roared, and something slammed along my right side, and Alison cried out as she struck the floor, and I crashed down on top of her, her elbow digging into my stomach and her shoulder catching me under the chin. We landed on the edge of the light-spill from the open door, and I grabbed her and rolled into the darkness before Holmes's second shot blasted through the echo of the first.

He stood silhouetted in the lamplight, crouched and peering into the darkness, the pistol weaving like a hunting snake. Alison drew a gasping breath and I instantly covered her mouth with my hand. He was so close, and so clearly revealed in the light, it was hard to realize that we were invisible to him, and that our only safety lay in stillness and silence.

"Moretti," he called softly. "I know you're there. Don't be foolish, now."

I could feel Alison's body trembling against me, and my face was buried in her hair, which was fine and dry and smelled of castile soap. The moment we lay there, pressed together, was as brief as a half-dozen heartbeats and as endless as a night of love.

Then Boz moved. I saw him appear in the doorway behind Holmes, his good arm raised and hooked to encircle Holmes's neck. But before he could tighten his grip, Holmes spun around and fired again. Boz staggered backward, colliding with Cappy, who was directly behind him, and for an instant they were both motionless. Then with a shout Cappy pushed past Boz, and the two wagoneers appeared beside him.

"Oh, hell," Holmes said, and fired again. The pistol shot blended with a crash of glass, and the light in the room went out.

In the sudden blackness, all sense of direction was lost. Everyone cried out, bodies thudded against other bodies, shoes pounded on the floor. Alison's voice came from a few inches away: "Boz, are you all right? Boz, where are you?" Cappy roared, "Where'd he go? Get that guy!" I cried, "Light a match, somebody!"

And in a few moments a match flared. In its uncertain light we stared at Boz Markey, sprawled on his back on the floor with his splinted arm across his chest and a widening stain darkening the shirt beneath it. And at the wall panel which stood open like a closet door, revealing a spiral staircase that led to the basement below.

H. H. Holmes was gone.

14

A Perhaps Unsatisfactory Ending

It was two hours before the immediate necessities had been taken care of — Boz given first aid for a serious but by no means fatal wound just below his rib cage and taken off to the hospital in an ambulance; me having a nasty groove in my side disinfected and bandaged; Alison making a statement and following Boz to the hospital to keep vigil; Cappy and his two associates also making statements before returning to their duties in the circulation wagon; a squad of uniformed policemen and plainclothes detectives combing every inch of the mansion and grounds and the pharmacy across the street — and Detective Arbuckle was able to turn his attention back to me.

"So, Moretti. You had to make a liar out of me, didn't you?"

"As though you haven't been a true believer the whole time," I said ingratiatingly. "I understood the pressures you were working under. You never fooled me for a minute."

His lips thinned. "Shut up. I'm going to tell you what happened here tonight, Moretti. A local druggist named Holmes apparently went off his rocker and kidnapped a social worker. In an attempt to rescue her, two passersby, newspaper employees named Markey and Moretti, received minor wounds. The social worker was released unharmed and the druggist escaped." He crossed his arms and regarded me coldly.

"End of story?" I asked.

"End of story," he said.

"The hell it is!" I cried. Before I could say anything more, a police officer entered the bedroom and coughed deferentially.

"Yes, what is it?" Arbuckle snapped.

"Some things I think you ought to see, sir. In the basement."

"All right." Arbuckle stood up. "Come on, Moretti. I haven't finished with you yet." We followed the policeman to the rear of the house and down the basement stairs. The basement was lit by half a dozen ceiling bulbs as well as a number of bull's-eye lanterns. We walked through two rooms crowded with suitcases, trunks, portmanteaus, hatboxes, purses, umbrellas, ladies' overshoes, and stacks of folded coats and dresses. In the first room Arbuckle stopped and stared. "Is this what you meant, Officer?"

"No, sir. It's on ahead."

We continued on through the second room and into a brilliantly lit chamber that resembled the operating room of a hospital. A surgical table sat in the center. Beneath it in the floor was a drain. A panel in the wall was open, and beyond it was the circular staircase leading to the room above.

"This is it, then," Arbuckle said.

"No, sir," the officer repeated apologetically. "Still on ahead."

We continued past a table upon which various surgical instruments were neatly arranged in rows. There was a spotless white porcelain sink in the corner, and above it on the wall was a rack of knives and saws.

The next room was at the front of the house. In the light of a lantern on the floor we could see that it was unfinished, with dirt walls at both sides interrupted by irregular areas of concrete.

The policeman led us to the wall on the left, where another officer, stripped to his undershirt, stood with a sledgehammer in his hands. There were chunks of broken concrete around his feet. The air was heavy, and smelled of dirt and lime and something else.

"Here," said our guide, and pointed into a hollow recess in the wall.

347

Arbuckle leaned forward. "Merciful Jesus," he said in an awed voice.

The recess, four feet square by two or two and a half feet deep, was entirely filled with bones. There were long thigh bones, delicate finger and toe bones, curving ribs and pelvises, intricately formed vertebrae, grinning skulls, all mottled with dirt and shreds of desiccated flesh and skin.

"I figure there must be four or five different bodies in there. Maybe more." The officer swallowed. "You want us to pull them out?"

Arbuckle continued to stare into the recess without answering. Then he shook himself like a spaniel coming out of the water. "No," he said quietly. "Leave them there for the sawbones to play with. You men break out all the other concrete patches down here. Let me know when you're finished."

We went back upstairs, Arbuckle leading the way in silence. We continued along the hall and out onto the front porch, where we each filled our lungs with the night air of Chicago. Arbuckle sat on the steps and waved me down beside him. His shoulders slumped, and when he spoke his voice was tired.

"There were a dozen of those concrete patches down there. Say five bodies to each hole. What does that make? Sixty bodies?

348

More? How about in the backyard? How about in the walls upstairs? Take a guess, Moretti. We can have a pool."

"I wouldn't want to guess," I answered.

We sat in silence, watching the activity in the pharmacy across the street, as policemen moved back and forth in front of the lighted window.

"There's a woman," I said. "She worked with him in the store. Name of Minnie Williams."

"We'll pick her up if she comes back." He sighed. "Where do you think he went, Moretti?"

"I have no idea. You're going to put out an alarm for him, aren't you?"

"Of course." He turned to look at me and added tonelessly, "But that's not what you're asking, is it?"

"No, I guess it isn't."

"You want to know if we're going to tell all the papers about this, so they can put it right on page one all over the country. Make a seven-day's wonder out of it. 'Come to Chicago and get yourself cemented in a wall.'"

"The question had occurred to me."

Arbuckle's face expressed so much disgust I involuntarily drew away from him. "I'm happy to tell you the decision is not mine to make. But if I was making book on it, I would predict that the first public announcement of Holmes's antics will be on October Thirty-first — the day after the Exposition closes. How do you like them apples, Moretti?"

I answered carefully, because I sensed that Arbuckle was at this moment nobody to take chances with: "It's not a question of me liking them or not liking them. It's a question of whether you can keep the lid on it for two more months."

His lip curled. "Do you think you'll blow the whistle — on that rag you work for in New York?"

"No, sir. It's not our kind of story — and anyway, some of the powers that be from Chicago have already reached our office. No, sir, it won't be me, or anybody on *The Spirit of the Times.* But your own papers here — once one of them thinks it's likely to be scooped by its competition on a story as big as this, it'll be Katie Bar the Door."

Arbuckle shook his head. "No, it won't. They all know that nobody's going to get scooped. No paper will break the story until they all do. You may not know it, Moretti, but we're *organized* in Chicago."

"I'm finding it out, Mr. Arbuckle."

He was silent a moment, and when he spoke again, the anger in his voice — whether it had been against me or against himself — was gone: "Meanwhile, we'll be quietly running one of the greatest manhunts in history. If Holmes stays in town, we'll get him, even without any publicity. If he leaves, every other police department in the country will be looking for him on the First of November. Don't worry — Mr. Holmes is a gone gosling. He'll hang. You can bet your life on it."

I thought. *It's not my life you're betting, Arbuckle* — but I didn't say it. Instead, I said, "If you're finished with me for the night, I'd like to be getting back to my hotel."

He nodded and pulled himself to his feet. "All right, Moretti. Drop in at headquarters tomorrow, in case I think of anything more to ask you."

"Yes, sir," I said. He nodded in dismissal and reentered the house. I heard his slow footsteps as he moved along the hall toward the basement stairs.

The next evening I paid a farewell visit to Huron Street. Boz and Alison were in the bedroom playing Double Canfield on a large square board balanced on the edge of the bed. Boz waved off the circulation bruiser who had let me into the apartment. "If you think you're going to get a drink here, you're sadly mistaken,

Moretti. This is the new, abstemious Markey you're dealing with now."

"Please!" I protested. "I come merely to inquire about your health. Have they taken care of that perforation of yours?"

Alison took my hand in both of hers. "Oh, Paddy, it's such good news! First, the bullet wound isn't really serious at all. It didn't hit any important organs, and the doctor says two weeks of bed rest should be all it takes to put Bosley back on his feet. But that's not the big news!"

"It's not?"

"No! It's what he told you when you came in! He's stopped drinking! My brother has agreed to take the pledge!"

I glanced from her radiant face to Boz's impassive one; the only expression of emotion he showed was a whiteness of his flared nostrils. "Why – why, that's grand!" I said. "Of course you're thrilled! As the Good Book says, 'There shall be more joy in Heaven over one sinner that repenteth,' and so forth! Words fail me, Boz!"

The whiteness spread from Boz's nostrils to his compressed lips. "Thank you, Paddy. It's gratifying to have your support. Alison, I wonder if you might excuse us for a moment? I have something of a private nature to share with our friend."

"Why, certainly! I'll just wait in the living room." She gave both of us an affectionate smile as she left, closing the door behind her.

I glanced inquiringly at Boz. "In the drawer under the dirty laundry?"

He shook his head. "No. You won't believe me, but what she says is true. I'm on the wagon. For the indefinite future. Even perhaps, God help me, for good."

I stared. "You're right. I don't believe you."

"Nevertheless, it's the Gospel. I'm serious. I don't know whether I have the strength of character to carry it off, but I intend to try." His face was determined, and its paleness was now uniform over all his features. "I owe it to Alison."

"Oh, hell, Boz, we had that all out in the cab! The business with Vannatta had nothing to do with the disappearing women! You had nothing to do with Velma's death! You have absolutely no reason to blame yourself!"

He shook his head stubbornly. "I think you know better than that, Paddy. Certainly I do. What I did was criminal. If nothing else, I was an accessory before the fact." When I tried to interrupt, he silenced me with a gesture. "Listen to me. One reason I'm giving up the booze is an act of atonement for putting my sister in mortal jeopardy. The other reason is more practical. My days as an independently wealthy dilettante in the journalistic profession are ended, Moretti. My last five thousand dollars was riding on Glenlivet to win. From now on, my weekly paycheck is the be-all and end-all, and any time I find myself unemployed, I don't eat! Under these conditions, my wisest course is to abjure the grape and establish myself as an exemplar of teetotal dependability. From now on, no tyrannical employer will be able to use my social indulgences as a weapon against me, for I intend to be as dry as Carrie Nation."

Although his tone was mock-heroic, his expression was serious. I regarded him for a moment in silence, and then extended my hand. "Congratulations on your good intentions. I hope you carry them out. I have the greatest respect for virtue in other people."

"Thank you." We shook hands. After a moment of awkward silence, I cleared my throat and started to make my farewells. He interrupted diffidently. "Paddy, if you don't mind, would you dig that bottle out from under the laundry there? No, I don't want any. Just stick it in your hip pocket and take it out of here. I'm a person of tremendous willpower, but I don't want to test it under any more pressure than is absolutely unavoidable."

Alison was sitting on the sofa in the living room, leafing the pages of an illustrated magazine. She gave me a welcoming smile, and then turned to the circulation department slugger sitting across the room. "Oh, Horace, would you run over to the store now? A loaf of bread, half a pound of cold cuts, a pound of cheddar cheese, and a large onion, remember." The slugger put down his newspaper, said, "Yes'm, Miss Alison," and left the apartment. Alison turned back to me and patted the sofa cushion by her side. "Sit down, Paddy. Isn't it wonderful about Bosley? And we're so grateful to you! If it hadn't been for you, heaven knows what might have happened!" She touched her fingers to the narrow scab that made a horizontal brown line on her throat. "I'm so glad it's all over! Now, as soon as everybody reads about that Holmes person in the newspapers —" She hesitated, and a slight frown crossed her features. "I would have thought there would have been extras on the street by now, Paddy. The public should be alerted as soon as possible."

"Ahh, Alison," I said, "I don't think there are going to be any extras. Not for the next few days, I mean to say."

Her frown deepened. "I don't understand. No extras? How can that be?"

"Well, it's a matter of police procedure. As I

understand, they think it would be better strategy to let the force do its job without panicking the whole city. They think they'll get him faster that way —"

"They're not going to warn anyone that there's a mass murderer at work?" she asked in disbelief. "When they know for a fact he's killed dozens and dozens of women, and is free right this minute to kill more?"

"Every policeman and detective in town is looking for him, Alison. They'll find him soon. They're bound to."

"And what if they don't? What if he leaves town? Don't the women in other cities deserve to be protected, too?"

"Of course they do. And they will be. Every railroad station is being watched, and I'm sure the Chicago police have already alerted all the major cities in the country — confidentially, of course. It's the best way, Alison. Or, if it's not, it's the way things are going to be. The decision's been made."

She stared at me, head back and chin raised. "And you agree with it?"

"There's nothing I can do about it. There's nothing anybody can do about it."

"So Mr. Darrow was right. And Mr. Sullivan. 'The Whited Sepulcher.' Nothing must interfere. The tourists must keep coming to

Chicago and spending their money, even if some of them never make it back home alive!"

I put my hands on her shoulders. In less than an hour my train would be departing for New York, and I very strongly disliked the idea of leaving Alison Markey harboring a low opinion of me. I squeezed her arms gently. "It's not our doing, Alison, and if it was up to me I'd put the whole story on the streets in a minute, and so would Boz. But maybe it's for the best this way. Who's to say for sure? What if there was a panic, and innocent men were lynched? Or had their houses burned down, and started another Chicago fire? Or who knows what? Because the police *will* get him, you can be sure of that. And it won't be too long, either."

She gazed at me from under level brows. "I won't accept it. I shall do everything I can to get the story told. I would never respect myself again if I didn't."

"And so you should, for that's the kind of person you are! And who would want you any other way?"

"It's corrupt! It's a perversion of the purpose of a Free Press, and I'll fight it with all my strength!"

"Of course you will!"

"It would be a blot on the history of Chicago forever!"

"It surely would."

"Somehow I'll find a way to spread the truth, I swear I will!"

"I haven't the shadow of a doubt."

She sighed. "You don't think there's anything to be done, do you?"

"To tell you the honest truth, I don't. But if there's anybody in the world who could prove me wrong, I believe it's you. All I ask is that you be careful, and don't visit any more of those terrible deadfalls than you need to, and stay out of carriages with strange men. Will you do that for me?"

She regarded me gravely. "I'll try," she said.

We sat awkwardly in silence for a few moments. There didn't seem to be anything more to say, and the realization was painful. I cleared my throat: "Well, I'm afraid I'd better be getting along —"

"Yes, you do have a train to catch, don't you?"

"I'm afraid so." I rose to my feet carefully, remaining in a crouch until I was out from under the Damoclean digit. Alison rose with me, turning her slender body to face mine. She extended her hand.

"You must know how grateful I am to you,

Paddy," she said quietly. "I owe you my life. It's a debt I can never repay."

I took her hand. "There's only one payment I'd ever ask." My throat was suddenly dry, and my heart was pounding like a drum. I dropped her hand and pulled her toward me, and felt her arms encircle my neck.

From the bedroom Boz's voice called, "For God's sake, kiss her, Moretti!"

No advice has ever been more superfluous.

Author's Note

The man who used the name of H. H. Holmes (his birth name was the somewhat less elegant Herman W. Mudgett) murdered God knows how many women in Chicago in 1893 – the figure has been estimated at anywhere from one to three hundred, which establishes him as this country's premier mass murderer. Women were disappearing in wholesale numbers, but no mention of it appeared in the Chicago press until well after the Fair had closed. I can't prove that a lid was put on the story for economic reasons, but I can offer a documented historical parallel:

In 1933, during the Chicago Century of Progress World's Fair, there was an outbreak of amoebic dysentery. Dr. Herman Bundesen, the health commissioner, traced two cases to the Congress Hotel, and on August 16, 1933, discovered fifteen clinical cases among the food-handling staff. No story appeared in the

Chicago press. In October Bundesen submitted a report to the American Public Health Association convention in Indianapolis, and the *Indianapolis Times* scooped the country with the news — but no Chicago newspaper touched the story. On October 19, Bundesen made a new investigation and found a hundred and eighteen additional infections among hotel workers. He then sent out sixteen thousand questionnaires to persons who had been guests at the Congress, and by November 8 had received thirty-five replies indicating infections. Only then did any reference to the facts appear in a Chicago newspaper, and the story that ran claimed the situation "is entirely under control, and there is no need for any alarm whatsoever." *The Fair was to close in three days.*

Gives one to think, doesn't it?

The American Derby was, in its time, as important as the Kentucky Derby, but my description of the 1893 running is completely imaginary. The actual race that year featured an English horse named Strathmore, who was brought to the track by his owner, the Duke of Beaufort, with much whoopdeedoo, and then finished dead last.

Streeterville continued to affront the

financial morality of the Chicago business community until 1918. By that time it had grown to a hundred and eighty acres of the most valuable real estate in the world, a small army of lawyers had been enriched for life, and Cap Streeter had declared it to be the District of Lake Michigan, subject to the laws of neither Chicago nor Illinois. But once again might made right, and deputies followed a court order to raze Streeter's home and remove him. Two years later he was dead.

Other Chicago characters who figure in this story – Bathhouse John Coughlin, Eugene Field, Finley Peter Dunne, Clarence Darrow, Louis Sullivan – are drawn as accurately as I could draw them. The period was so rich in colorful personalities the problem was not who to include but who to exclude. For readers desiring to make the acquaintance of such fascinating individuals as John Peter Altgeld, the Haymarket martyrs, Eugene V. Debs, Jane Addams, Hinky Dink Kenna, Theodore Dreiser, and Frank Lloyd Wright (to name only a few eminent Chicagoans of the period), I recommend the following books: *Altgeld's America*, by Ray Ginger; *Lords of the Levee* and *Chicago: A Pictorial History*, by Herman Kogan and Lloyd Wendt; *Gem of the Prairie*, by Herbert Asbury; *Twenty Years at Hull-House,* by Jane Addams; *The Autobiography of an Idea,* by Louis Sullivan; and Dreiser's novels *Sister Carrie, The Financier,* and *The Titan.*

J.S.

THORNDIKE PRESS HOPES you have enjoyed this Large Print book. All our Large Print titles are designed for the easiest reading, and all our books are made to last. Other Thorndike Press Large Print books are available at your library, through selected bookstores, or directly from the publisher. For more information about current and upcoming titles, please call us, toll free, at 1-800-223-6121, or mail your name and address to:

THORNDIKE PRESS
P. O. BOX 159
THORNDIKE, MAINE 04986

There is no obligation, of course.